ANDROMACHE
AND OTHER PLAYS

JEAN RACINE was born in 1639 at La Ferté Milon, sixty miles east of Paris. Orphaned at an early age, he was educated at the Little Schools of Port Royal and the pro-Jansenist College of Beauvais. He soon reacted against his austere mentors and by 1660 he had begun to write for the theatre and had been introduced to the court of Louis XIV. In 1677, when he had ten plays to his credit and was high in favour with both the court and the public, he abandoned the theatre, which was regarded as far from respectable by the Church, and joined the Establishment as Royal Historiographer. It was only after a silence of twelve years that he wrote his last two plays (both on religious subjects), *Esther* and *Athaliah*. He died in 1699.

•

JOHN CAIRNCROSS was educated at Glasgow University, at the Sorbonne, and at Trinity College, Cambridge. After a period in the British Civil Service, he settled in Rome, where he still spends much of his time. He later worked for the United Nations in Bangkok, and was for a time Head of the Department of Romance Languages, Western Reserve University, Cleveland. John Cairncross has also translated Racine's *Iphigenia*, *Phaedra* and *Athaliah* and six of Corneille's plays in two volumes, *Polyeuctus/The Liar/ Nicomedes* and *The Cid/Cinna/The Theatrical Illusion*, for the Penguin Classics. He is also the author of *Molière bourgeois et libertin*, *New Light on Molière* and *After Polygamy was Made a Sin*.

Jean Racine

ANDROMACHE · BRITANNICUS
BERENICE

Translated and Introduced by
JOHN CAIRNCROSS

PENGUIN BOOKS

Penguin Books Ltd, Harmondsworth, Middlesex, England
Viking Penguin Inc., 40 West 23rd Street, New York, New York 10010, U.S.A.
Penguin Books Australia Ltd, Ringwood, Victoria, Australia
Penguin Books Canada Ltd, 2801 John Street, Markham, Ontario, Canada L3R 1B4
Penguin Books (N.Z.) Ltd, 182-190 Wairau Road, Auckland 10, New Zealand

—

This translation first published 1967
Reprinted 1971, 1974, 1976, 1978, 1981, 1982, 1985, 1987

—

Made and printed in Great Britain by
Richard Clay Ltd, Bungay, Suffolk
Set in Monotype Garamond

CONTENTS

Translator's Foreword 7

Jean Racine 9

Note on the Term 'Romanesque' 26

List of Racine's Plays 27

Bibliography 28

ANDROMACHE

Introduction 31

Racine's Dedication and Prefaces 37

The Play 47

BRITANNICUS

Introduction 115

Racine's Dedication and Prefaces 127

The Play 139

BERENICE

Introduction 213

Racine's Dedication and Preface 221

The Play 227

TRANSLATOR'S FOREWORD

RACINE, it is often said, is untranslatable. But it was no desire to disprove this proposition that prompted me to render, first the French dramatist's *Phaedra*, and later his *Iphigenia* and *Athaliah*, into English. It was rather that, to borrow the words of the queen who gives the last play its name:

> What I have done . . . I had to do. (467)

And in this I was no doubt impelled by the same motive as so many other translators who, having derived exquisite pleasure from some foreign poet after their own heart, find an English version forming – almost despite themselves - in their inner ear.

Yet it would be wrong to imagine that Racine can be rendered without considerable effort. For the would-be translator is faced from the outset with three formidable obstacles.

First of all, there is no alternative, in my view, to the adoption of blank verse of ten syllables as the medium for the English version, while the French poet has twelve (the Alexandrine). The translator has therefore to condense Racine by a sixth and to strip his version of every syllable that is not utterly essential, or else abandon literal transposition and devise a concise formula which gives the gist of Racine's line. Occasionally I have had to sacrifice a word, or even several words, which seemed less vital to the sense than the rest. But, fortunately, there is almost always some margin for reduction – in the form of somewhat decorative adjectives (such as 'noble', 'just', 'dear') in formal titles ('My princess', 'My lord', and so on), or in names.

The second problem is the need for accuracy. Racine is as precise as he is concise – and he is clear. But this is not to say that he is simple for the modern reader. For one thing, he is a seventeenth-century poet, and the usage of that age, it is almost superfluous to observe, differs markedly and often treacherously from modern custom.

7

But, obviously, the stiffest barrier in translating Racine is that of his subtle, taut, and exquisite verse. No other French poet, with the exception of one of his metrical disciples (Baudelaire), has such an impeccable ear, or such a capacity of evoking music from the most unpromising material. One can hardly hope to do justice to Racine unless one is bilingual, or practically so. For he yields his secrets to the Anglo-Saxon reader far less readily than, say, Dante or Goethe, owing in part to the weakness of the tonic accent in French, and above all to the difference of the conventions governing his poetry and ours.

*

The B.B.C., as readers of the Foreword to my first volume of Racine will remember, were not particularly helpful when I submitted my version of *Phaedra*. It is all the more pleasant to thank them now for their kind permission to print my translation of *Andromache* which was specially commissioned by them.

Rome, 1966   JOHN CAIRNCROSS

JEAN RACINE

RACINE, quoting Aristotle, calls Euripides, whom he admired so much, 'the most tragic of all poets'. And the words can be applied with equal felicity to Racine himself. Yet, by origin and upbringing, he seemed an unlikely candidate for the tragic muse.

He was born in 1639 at the small depressing township of La Ferté Milon, which, though only some sixty miles east of Paris, was regarded as buried in the depth of the provinces. He was orphaned at a tender age, and had to be brought up on charity. His relatives belonged to the Puritanical Catholic sect known as Jansenists, and for them, as for all strict church-men in France of the time, the stage and all its works were of the devil. Nevertheless, it was to the Jansenists that Racine owed his initiation to literature. The Little Schools of Port Royal (the famous abbey which was the spiritual centre of the sect) provided an education famous for its soundness and thoroughness. In particular, it included an excellent grounding in Greek – a most unusual practice at the time. After he left these masters in 1653, Racine spent two years at the college of Beauvais, which was entirely under Jansenist influence.

But Racine was not long in reacting against his austere mentors. By 1660, his vocation for the theatre revealed itself, and he was hard at work on a play (of which nothing is known but the title). The following year he was hobnobbing in Paris with the notorious freethinker and epicurean La Fontaine (who was later to compose his celebrated *Fables*). The young man in his own words was 'running with the wolves'.

Port Royal not only gave Racine the schooling that he was to turn to account in his plays; it also introduced him to the aristocratic circles that were to give him his entrée to the Court of the young Louis XIV. The duc de Luynes, formerly a Jansenist sympathizer, had appointed to his service a cousin of Racine's who had risen to the dignity of chief steward.

But de Luynes, for personal reasons, turned his back on the Jansenists, who were never popular at Court, and rallied to Louis' support. The duke, soon smiled on by the king, smoothed the path of the ambitious and gifted young poet. How well he profited from the opportunity may be seen from the select list of names of the patrons to whom he dedicated his plays. *The Thebaid,* his first work (1664), bears the name of the duc de Saint Aignan (the organizer of Louis' colourful Court fêtes). The duke is followed by the king himself, Henrietta of England (the king's sister-in-law), the duc de Chevreuse (the duc de Luynes' son) and lastly the great Colbert, who was the main instrument of Louis' policy and was in effect the Minister for Culture. Gratifications, honours and applause all came Racine's way in a steady stream. But this success was due at least as much to his ability and tact as a courtier as to his literary genius. By 1677, he had ten plays to his credit (see list on p. 27) and was basking in the king's favour. He had achieved the rare feat of winning the approval of the general public and the esteem of the Court and learned circles.

It was at this point that Racine was reconciled with religion and abandoned the theatre. The information on the reasons for the change is scanty and controversial, for the poet's sons took good care to destroy any material that might present their father in an unedifying light. In particular, practically the whole of Racine's correspondence for the period from *The Thebaid* to *Phaedra* (1664 to 1677) has gone astray. There is a hint in a contemporary ditty that he was supplanted in his mistress's affections just before his conversion. But we know almost nothing of the poet's feelings at that time. The guilt-laden atmosphere and terrible sensuality of *Phaedra,* however, point to a crisis. It is not impossible that his disappointment in love is linked with the return of his religious convictions.

Outwardly, Racine's 'conversion' differed little from what would now be termed 'settling down', and in no way implied a flight from the world; it was in line with the general trend towards sobriety and orthodoxy observable at Court. Racine abjured the stage and actresses. He made a marriage in which, according to his son Louis, 'love had no part', but which brought him considerable material advantages. In the same year, thanks to the support of the sister of Madame de Maintenon (the king's mistress), he was appointed, jointly with Boileau, to the coveted post of royal historiographer. This honour marked a substantial move up the social ladder, and made the commoner Racine the envy of many an aristocrat.

After a silence of twelve years, at the request of Madame de Maintenon, he composed *Esther* (1689) for the young ladies of a boarding school run by her at Saint-Cyr. The work was a tremendous success, and he was encouraged to write another work on the Old Testament subject of Athaliah (1691). Ironically, the play was attacked by those bigots who would not tolerate the stage in any form whatever. And Racine, discouraged, let his pen drop for good, except for a few lesser works. In 1699 he died, high in the royal favour and deep in piety.

Racine was a writer of the *avant-garde*. His plays are of a ruthlessness, an extremism, an amorality, which, in his own day, shocked the conservatives, upset the average theatre-goers and appealed to the radicals. Louis XIV, in particular, was an enthusiastic admirer. If Racine carried the day against the entrenched opposition of the supporters of his great rival, Corneille (then, it is true, long past his prime), his success was in large measure due to the firm backing of the king. The link between the two men was by no means accidental. Louis and Racine, each in different ways, made a sharp break with the hitherto prevailing ethos of the feudal aristocracy that may conveniently be referred to as baroque. On assuming personal charge of affairs in 1661 (three years before the performance of Racine's first play), Louis set out to bring the nobility, and indeed all the other privileged and unproductive sections of the nation, under the control of a strong central administration. The emphasis was laid on the expansion of trade and industry, by state intervention if need be; and religious intolerance was not allowed to stand in the way of the achievement of these aims.

Before the young king took over, the nobility had dominated France, and their outlook had shaped French literature. For the baroque writers, the king was merely the first of the feudal lords. He was their equal, not their ruler. Any attempt to exercise the supreme power was regarded as tyranny, and was usually represented as being directed to base or selfish ends.

Racine's plays, on the contrary, reflect the attitude to statecraft visible in Louis' radical new policies. The dramatist shows his kings as usually all-powerful, and surrounds them with an aura of majesty. A monarch is great and respected only if he rules firmly and effectively. If Athaliah, the Old Testament queen, can boast that her reign has been glorious, it is because she

> . . . fell upon her startled enemies,
> And never let the crucial moment pass.   (873–4)

Decisiveness and ruthlessness, rather than generosity, are prerequisites of stable rule. The interests of the state, which are broadly equated with those of the throne, must take absolute precedence over the rights or claims of the individual. The origin of this attitude is clear. It derives straight from Machiavelli, the great Florentine thinker of the Renaissance, who was, generally speaking, the delight of the freethinkers and anathema to the Church. For him, as for Racine, statecraft was a science, not a moral philosophy, and its laws could be defied only at the risk of downfall or death. This is the theory preached by such 'realists' as Acomat, the Grand Vizier in *Bajazet*, or Ulysses in *Iphigenia*. The former reminds Bajazet that the Turkish sultans regarded

> The interest of the state [as] their only law

while the latter,

> . . . jealous of the honour of our [i.e. Greek] arms,

is quite prepared to press for Iphigenia to be sacrificed if that is the price of victory.

In *Iphigenia*, it is true, the 'realists' are defeated, but only at the last moment and with the aid of a good deal of luck. The play in any case is exceptional. It was written at a time (1674) when the force of Louis' drive to alter the social structure was weakening. The wars in which he was entangled compelled him to suspend his reforms and to lean more and more heavily on the nobility who captained his armies. The baroque ideas, naturally enough, staged a comeback.

In respects other than statecraft, Racine's divergence from the baroque is equally clear. The plays, while observing the proprieties, are by no means moral, for the good are not rewarded, and crime is not punished. Providence does not watch over the hero. The baroque drama, on the contrary, usually saw to it that the characters received their deserts, and concluded with a vote of thanks to the powers that had steered the plot to a happy ending. Racine's readiness to break with this convention may not seem very daring nowadays. It was a bold move in the 1660s.

The point is made with great force and brilliance by Butler in his *Classicisme et baroque dans l'œuvre de Racine* (p. 290). Racine's 'impatience at the outdated truths of the baroque, the passion with which [he] strips it of its masks and trappings, his anti-Corneille manifestoes, this is the form that the love of truth takes in his case. There is in Racine a sort of intellectual Puritanism – or Jansenism – which, in the same way as moral Puritanism, distrusts everything that can cause us too much pleasure and regards *a priori* as suspect any proposition that flatters or suits us. . . . The fine gallantry, the noble fictions and the becoming poses that have taken the place of the battle between man and woman, these he casts aside. He is unwearying in his efforts to undermine the idea of a paternal and reassuring providence, placed like a stage setting in front of the dread forces which govern the universe and the state of man. All the hallowed prejudices of the baroque, all its comforting illusions, all the themes of its resounding eloquence appear in his plays, only to be brilliantly disposed of.'

But Louis and the enlightened minority around him were not dismayed by this revolutionary approach to literature. It was, after all, in this decade that the king supported Molière against the bigots, and finally (in 1669) authorized the public performance of the violently anti-clerical comedy of *Tartuffe*.

If the modern reader (especially outside France) is no longer struck by the savage realism of Racine's psychology, the reason is to be sought partly in the prevailing proprieties which banned crudity of language and physical action, but even more in the survival of certain baroque elements. The constant insistence on title – Princess, my Lord, my Lady – the preoccupation with rank, with certain caste conventions and with theatrical declamatory gestures: they can all be met with at some point in the plays. And they strike the reader who is not steeped in French classical tragedy as pompous and stilted.

Yet they occur mainly in the later *Iphigenia* and *Phaedra*, written when the power of the nobility had revived, and with it the feudal ways of thought that had for a time been relegated to the background. *Iphigenia*, in particular, is borne along on a flood tide of martial enthusiasm. And the fiery warrior Achilles defies the overlord Agamemnon as a feudal lord might have challenged a 'tyrannical' sovereign. Iphigenia herself shows an absolute submission to her father's will, even when he is sending her to death. His grief at her fate is equalled only by his concern that his daughter shall prove worthy of her breeding and her birth when the priest's knife strikes home. Morality, as in the baroque writers, tends to be equated with social origin.

In *Phaedra*, the same tendency is noticeable, although it is completely subordinated to the Jansenist anguish that suffuses the play. Thus, in his *Preface*, Racine expresses the view that 'calumny was somewhat too low and foul to be put in the mouth of a princess whose sentiments were otherwise so noble and virtuous. This baseness seemed to me more appropriate to a nurse, who might well have more slave-like inclinations . . .' It has rightly been pointed out that Phaedra might tremble on the verge of incest and adultery, but could never be guilty of an affair with a stableboy.

Yet, whether in these or in the earlier plays, the baroque traits in Racine are always tempered by a restraint, an ease and naturalness of tone, that sets them apart from the declamatory and grandiose style of the earlier dramatists. We are already in the modern world, with its sobriety, its understatement, its realization that the cruel complexities of life are not to be disposed of by eloquence, theatrical gestures and emotional clichés.

Louis' support and the new climate of tolerance created by his policies not only made it possible for Racine's amoralism to find its audience, but also provided an opening for the poet's tragic vision to assert itself in an age that had been brought up on a diet of tragi-comedies – that is, plays on elevated subjects but with a happy ending. As Butler has observed (op. cit., p. 210), there is a profound incompatibility between baroque and tragedy. For the baroque writers, the powers that governed the world were just, and it was sacrilege to complain. Animated by this conviction, Corneille had succeeded in making almost a tragi-comedy out of the sombre stuff of the legend of Oedipus. Racine lived and moved in another climate. In his plays, passion, circumstance and the gods combine to send the main protagonists to their downfall. Even in *Berenice*, where the young Emperor Titus and the foreign queen who gives her name to the play are passionately in love with each other, the two ultimately feel obliged to part, condemned to a lifetime of despair. 'A mad play', it was termed, understandably enough, by that ardent admirer of Corneille, Madame de Sévigné.

But why did Racine have to compose tragedies in a highly untragic age? Neither Louis' policies nor Racine's personal situation provided the slightest grounds for such pessimism. Nor is it enough to assert that Racine preferred to write tragedies. The explanation lies elsewhere. The passage from Butler quoted above on Racine's love of the truth gives us a clue. It is defined as 'a form of . . . intellectual Jansenism', and, Butler goes on (pp. 290–1), it usually appears as a concern to present things in their worst light, as a strange determination to close every way of escape.

And this is not all. The only other tragic writer of roughly the same period is Pascal. And Pascal, it will be remembered, was a Jansenist, though an unorthodox one. Can it be just a coincidence that Racine, too, was brought up as a Jansenist, even though he soon fell out with his masters? A closer look at the dogmas of this sect reveals its close connexions with the world of tragedy. The Jansenists regarded man as fundamentally corrupt, whereas the baroque writers, basically optimists, took a positive view of humanity, or, more exactly, regarded the nobility (which was the only section of society that counted) as not only socially but morally noble. If God's grace was lacking, the desire for virtue and the human will were but a weak bulwark against the lures of the flesh and the world. The Jansenists may have denied that they believed in predestination. But they were obsessed with the concept, and their whole outlook inevitably drove them close to a position in which men and women were damned or saved from all eternity. Nevertheless, somewhat inconsistently, every believer was expected to conform to the most severe moral standards, and, in the view of the extremists, to retire altogether from an utterly wicked world.

The Jansenists disliked Louis' policies, and even more his love of pleasure, women and fêtes, including theatrical performances; and their dislike was heartily reciprocated. But the sect was even more bitterly at odds with the optimism of the feudal outlook. It was not therefore necessary for the anti-baroque Racine to jettison everything that he had learned at Port Royal in order to achieve greatness in tragedy. On the contrary, the theory that man had small chance of salvation if unaided by divine grace was admirably suited to that art form.

It has been objected that the poet had lost his faith before he started to compose his plays and indeed, since Jansenism was so fiercely opposed to the stage, could not have become Racine without doing so. But there is surely no lack of men in any age who have been brought up in a severe faith, have drifted away from it but retained its imprint, and in some cases (as in that of Racine himself) have eventually returned to the fold. It is quite possible, therefore, that Racine never really discarded certain habits of thought absorbed at an early impressionable age and not basically inconsistent with his new ideas.

Naturally, it is pointless to look for a systematic exposition of the dramatist's attitude to his former faith in his plays. A work of art is not a religious tract. In any case, he was to a great extent debarred, either by his new, presumably sceptical beliefs, or by the contemporary conventions, from dealing with Christian dogma openly and critically.

In such circumstances, the obvious vehicle for the treatment of the tragic issues of life was Greek mythology, and the obvious models were the ancient Greek playwrights – Sophocles and Euripides. By a fortunate chance, Racine had enjoyed a thorough grounding in these masters' language. It is hardly surprising, therefore, that his first play, *The Thebaid*, deals with a Greek subject – the trials of the children of Oedipus. Racine's work, as Butler has shown (op. cit., pp. 215–16), goes far beyond his sources (Greek or French) in its grim horror. The two sons of Oedipus (already punished for his involuntary incest) hate each other even in their mother's womb – a detail, like most other particularly appalling touches in Racine, invented by the author himself. This hatred, 'the outward sign of divine malediction' (Butler), drives them to war against each other and finally to kill each other. Even Oedipus' innocent daughter, and indeed her fiancé as well, are caught up in the general contagion, and they too expire before the final curtain. Small wonder that Jocasta (Oedipus' widow) declaims against the gods who have decreed this massacre:

> This is the justice of the mighty gods:
> They lead us to the edge of the abyss;
> They make us sin, but do not pardon us.

This conception of the viciously and arbitrarily cruel gods (working, however, against a chosen family), and of the revolt on the part of their victims, is new in French literature. But it can easily be traced back to Jansenism, even if it betrays a note of hostility towards the poet's erstwhile faith. The central theme is that the cruel gods incline men to crime, and then make them pay for it. Moreover, the sins of the fathers are visited on the children and even on their fiancés. The latter doctrine (minus the fiancés) clearly stems from the Old Testament, although misfortunes run in certain families in the Greek legend too. As to the central idea of the play, Racine, while retaining the Jansenist idea of man's inherent weakness, has omitted divine grace as a remedial feature, and made God directly responsible for human sinfulness, whereas, for the believers, it was the fruit of 'man's first disobedience' in the garden of Eden. The cruel gods are pilloried. Yet they are to reappear, with the doctrines underlying *The Thebaid*, in *Phaedra*, written when Racine was groping his way back to his religion, and even in *Athaliah*, when he had been practising his faith devoutly for fourteen years.

In the plays immediately following *The Thebaid*, fate becomes anonymous and is ensconced in the hearts of men. But it is none the less vindictive. If we omit *Alexander*, the weakest of his plays, we come to *Andromache*, the work in which the real Racine emerges. The tragedy unfolds within a triangle of absolute political power, irresistible passion and another absolute – death. In this terrifying scheme of things, there is no respite from the hounds of destiny, no margin for compromise, no way out of the fatal labyrinth in which the predestined victims of the tragedy are trapped.

Yet in *Andromache*, the first of his great tragedies, Racine hesitated to apply his grim formula in full. In his later works, the disaster was to derive from the initial situation with rigorous precision. In *Andromache*, the poet is not quite so merciless. Orestes loves Hermione, who loves Pyrrhus, who loves Andromache, who loves her dead Hector. But Andromache is prepared to compromise. To save her infant son, the widow devises 'an innocent trick' whereby she will marry Pyrrhus, but kill herself after leaving the altar. As it turns out, this stratagem does not save the situation. It touches off a murder: Orestes kills Pyrrhus and goes mad as a result. Later, Racine was to rule out any suggestion of 'transigence' in his main characters. Everything was devised solely to give a further turn of the screw to the instruments of catastrophe.

But the tragic outcome is already ensured by the basic ingredients of his formula. The kings and queens are all-powerful. And they are usually savage, ruthless or imprudent. Roxana has but to say one word to send Bajazet to a horrible death at the hands of the deaf-mutes. Nero can casually issue instructions for the poisoning of Britannicus, in the certainty that he will be obeyed. And Theseus, even better equipped, can call on the services of the sea-god Neptune to rid the world of his son Hippolytus.

The evils of absolute power are compounded by absolute love. For the baroque writers, passion was noble and ennobling. The knight was obliged to conform to his lady's will and to perform great deeds in order to win her favour. Pyrrhus (and the same could be said of most of Racine's characters) 'had not read our [highly romantic] novels. He was violent by nature.' Thus Racine, in the Preface to *Andromache*. Pyrrhus in fact is prepared to blackmail the woman he loves into marrying him on pain of seeing her son surrendered to the Greeks, and almost certainly put to death. Mithridates has no hesitation in stooping to deceit in order to extract from his fiancée, Monime, the secret of her love for Xiphares, Mithridates' son. The gentle Atalide naïvely admits to Bajazet that she would at times prefer to see him dead than married to another. And Roxana, having discovered that Bajazet does not love *her*, but Atalide, revels in the thought of confronting him with the dead body of his sweetheart.

Love is at bottom represented as more akin to hate than to devotion or affection. 'Can I not know whether I love or hate?' asks Hermione in *Andromache*; and most of the characters in love swing violently and irresolutely between these two poles, largely because passion in Racine is almost always unreciprocated. But, even when (as in *Berenice*) there is no emotional obstacle, outside forces come between the lovers.

There are, it is true, a few couples that escape the final holo-
caust – Achilles and Iphigenia, Xiphares and Monime.
Hippolytus and Aricia are less fortunate. And it is certainly
not true that Racine could conceive only of a blindly sensual
and possessive type of love. Yet he does seem to have been at
ease only when his lovers are unhappy, inhibited or placed
under the shadow of death. Hippolytus and Aricia, who lack
some of these qualifications, are for most of the time colourless
and precious. The poet's gifts called for more sombre stuff.

For him, the vanity of love and its darker sides are matched
by an insistence on its intensity which at times reaches almost
religious fervour. When Roxana pleads with Bajazet

On you my joy, my happiness depends, (556)

the line raises strange echoes of Tartuffe's pseudo-religious
courtship:

On you my suffering or my bliss depends.

And one is reminded of Madame de Sévigné's quip that,
after his conversion, 'Racine loved God as he loved his
mistresses' – and hence, one assumes, that, before he was
touched by grace, he had loved his mistresses with religious
devotion. Not for nothing did Boileau define his friend's
character as 'mocking, uneasy, jealous, and voluptuous'. Is
it being too fanciful to suggest that Racine, an orphan from
his earliest years, and endowed with a quivering sensitiveness,
brought to love a particular intensity, sharpened by the trans-
fer of a lost religious faith to earthly objects? Whatever the
truth of the matter, Venus is usually in Racine, 'the goddess of
love and death', to use his own words.

But circumstance, too, makes its contribution to the final
disaster. It may be a compromising letter found in Atalide's
bosom when she faints (*Bajazet*), the unexpected return of
Theseus after a false report of his death (*Phaedra*), or (in
Iphigenia) the failure of the mission undertaken by Arcas, sent
out by Agamemnon to warn the king's daughter to return
home, since death awaits her at the Greek army's camp in
Aulis. Whatever the means chosen, all roads lead to death.

The dice are weighted against humanity from the start. The only difference between this new type of fate and the gods of *The Thebaid* is that there is no equation between crime and punishment. Indeed, one can say that the innocent or guileless fall most readily. And when Narcissus, Nero's crafty adviser, is done to death in *Britannicus*, we can be sure that the episode is added merely to satisfy the conventional need for retribution.

In *Iphigenia* (1674), Racine turned to Euripides and Greek mythology for inspiration, and the gods return. They are just as cruel as in *The Thebaid*, though not, this time, the avengers of crime. On the contrary, King Agamemnon emphasizes that he does not know why the gods are angry. (Yet there was a simple explanation in the Greek original.) All that is clear is that Diana, by an oracle, demands the blood of a human sacrifice if she is to allow the winds to carry the Greek fleet to Troy. And in fact a victim is sacrificed (though not the one thought to be designated by the oracle), and the winds blow immediately. The outcome is not tragic, though it might easily have been so. Racine was beginning a new cycle, and, as in the case of *Andromache* which began the previous series, the first play in it shows signs of hesitation.

With *Phaedra* (1677), on the contrary, he takes the decisive step. This time, the play is profoundly and utterly tragic. And it is the gods who drive the action forward. Venus makes Hippolytus inspire a guilty passion in the heroine's heart, and again, as in *Iphigenia*, no reason is given for the goddess's hatred. Thus, the gods incline men to sin – just as in *The Thebaid*. And, just as in that play, they punish the sinner. Only, in *Phaedra*, punishment does not consist in death, but in dishonour, and above all in the torments of the afterworld, where the heroine's own ancestor, Minos, will sit in judgement on her. From being the final curtain in the tragedy, death has become a factor in a moral drama. The whole play is pivoted on the fierce struggle raging in Phaedra's soul. However, her heroic resistance to temptation, her obsession with guilt (new in Racine) avail her nothing. She is defeated by the combined forces of Venus and a malicious fate which weights the scales against her even more heartlessly than in the earlier plays. No wonder she was defined by an eminent Jansenist theologian as 'one of the just to whom grace was not vouch-safed'. The play is a perfect demonstration of the Jansenist doctrine that the human will, unaided, can never stand up to temptation. But, if grace is absent (as it had been hitherto in Racine), there is no trace of revolt (as in *The Thebaid*). The poet was moving towards Jansenism, not away from it.

After his conversion, the picture naturally changes. The Jansenist God is no longer concealed behind the Greek façade. In *Athaliah* (1691), the 'cruel Jewish God' tracks down the old pagan queen, just as Venus had encompassed Phaedra's downfall. But, as against this, Jehovah not only strikes down his enemies, he also raises up those whom he has chosen as his instruments. Even the chosen ones, however, are corrupt – just as much as the 'wicked' pagans. The abso-lute corruption of mankind is only equalled by the unwavering fanaticism of Jehoiada, the high priest of Jehovah – a faith which we can be fairly certain was not dissimilar from Racine's own. Only in one respect does the play fall short of being the perfect exemplar of Jansenism. And this weakness is due precisely to Racine's excess of devotion. The miracles through which God weakens Athaliah are very palpably such, whereas Jansenist doctrine demanded that they should appear natural to the sceptic, and their supernatural origin be clear only to the orthodox. From this point of view, *Phaedra* is much more in line with the pure doctrine. For there the spectator has no difficulty in believing that the heroine's in-fatuation has been caused by the physical splendour of the young ephebus, Hippolytus, and not necessarily only by divine intervention.

Such, then, is the curve of Racine's plays, which follows closely that of his waning and waxing faith. This evaluation would seem to follow four main phases. First, in *The Thebaid*, the attitude is one of conscious revolt. Then come the middle plays, where religion is dormant. Thirdly, in *Phaedra*, it awakens. And in *Athaliah*, after his conversion, it is full-blooded and explicit.

It should be clear, therefore, that there is no dichotomy, as is so often alleged, between Racine the man and Racine the writer. The fallacy goes back to an essay of Giraudoux.* That piece of analysis is magnificent, but it is not serious criticism. In part, too, the view rests on the curious romantic belief that a work of art must be either a personal declaration of faith or a purely technical construction. For, it is argued, Racine is such a conscious, consummate craftsman, he subordinates his personal feelings so completely to the exigencies of play writing, that it is pointless to look for the man in his work. On the contrary, the spirit that informs his tragedies and that makes them so different from those of his contemporaries tallies exactly with what little is known of his outlook and character. His close association with Louis and Colbert and with their anti-feudal policy, his intellectual ruthlessness, his Jansenist-inspired pessimism, and, it would seem, his conception of love – all these are common to both the plays and the poet. If we go further, we can add a cruelty towards his characters amounting almost to sadism. This may be linked with his pessimism, an overwrought sensitiveness, especially to criticism, a savageness towards his enemies in his epigrams and in his Prefaces, and a brilliance both as a courtier and as a business man who knew the value of money. All these suggest a character that would be able to construct a technically perfect but poetically intense tragedy in which all the main aspects of life were searchingly examined and in which, perhaps with a certain detached pleasure, the author scanned the depths of human passion, frailty and folly.

The technical mastery of Racine's work is so palpable that it is almost superfluous to describe it. Supreme economy of means is combined with extreme care in their selection, and the details are put together in such a way that every move can be seen to have been prepared and rendered plausible. Suspense is rapidly built up to an almost unbearable degree, and simultaneously a moving depth of tragedy is achieved.

Much has been made of the proprieties as a deadening factor in Racine's work. And it is true that no one screams or

* *Racine* by Jean Giraudoux, Paris 1930.

gesticulates in these plays. Action is only described, and
nothing is allowed to ruffle the surface of formal politeness.
For a modern audience, used to naturalist excesses and 'frankness', such restraint is unsettling. Yet it is an integral part of
the fabric, and not merely a pointless convention imposed on
Racine by the age. His tragedies are played out at Court,
where dissimulation is essential, not only for success but also
for survival. Given the dangers which can arise from a situation where the king wields absolute power, one revelation
(such as that A loves B) is enough to launch a disastrous series
of catastrophes. Not for nothing do the words 'stratagem',
'conceal', 'hide', 'declare', 'reveal', 'break silence', 'burst
out' crop up at every turn of his plays. Agrippina's plan (in
Britannicus) to recover the control of her errant son, Nero,
might well serve as a motto of the playwright's works:

> Bare, if we can, the secrets of his soul. (127)

Given this framework, it is inevitable that the force driving
most of the plays forward should be the disclosure of firmly
held secrets.

In the same way, language is often used to allow the truth
to be guessed at rather than to express it directly. There is a
constant tension between the hidden feelings of the characters and their spoken words. In such circumstances, it is
natural that irony should be a frequent weapon in Racine's
armoury. Thus, in *Iphigenia*, when the heroine asks her father
whether the whole family is to be at the forthcoming sacrifice,
he replies to his daughter (who is, though she does not realize
it, to be the person sacrificed):

> ... Yes. You will be there. (578)

Nor is the secret of Racine's craftsmanship to be sought in
the famous unities of time, place and subject. His great rule
was, as he said himself, 'to please'. No doubt the concen-
tration of the action into the space of one day (the daylight,
that is, and not twenty-four hours) contributes powerfully to
the sense of urgency that drives the action headlong down the
slope to death. The place always has its significance. For

example, it is a camp in the war play, *Iphigenia*, and the harem of the Sultan in *Bajazet*. But the real tragedy is performed in the hearts of the protagonists. When Giraudoux tells us that the characters are all piled on top of one another in the same house and therefore get on each other's nerves, that the same sounds echo in their dreams and that their linen goes to the same laundry, he is talking nonsense. For there are no sleeping apartments or arrangements, no laundries in Racine – in fact none of the ordinary activities such as letter writing or settling bills which might distract the characters from the only business in hand, which is how to go to disaster as rapidly as possible in the five acts allowed them.

The picture of Racine would not be complete without a word, however inadequate, on his incredible mastery of language. His style is simple, but concentrated, direct and vigorous. In his Greek plays, where he draws skilfully on the rich storehouse of ancient mythology and legend, it is superbly evocative. But there are lines which, across three centuries, would still pass unnoticed in an everyday conversation:

My daughter? And who says she's coming here? (*Iphigenia*, 179

or:

    And who asked you to mind my family? (*Iphigenia*, 1349)

The secret of the greatness of Racine as a poet, as of all great art, is probably that the style reflects the power, subtlety, and insight that form the strands of his work. Only a genius could produce tragedies that reach into the deepest corners of the human heart with such an incredibly restricted and simple vocabulary, such constant restraint, such an absence of facile effects.

Such, then, is Racine. This outline gives only the general picture of the man and his achievement. To appreciate to the full his richness and variety, the reader must turn to the more detailed analysis prefaced to each of the plays in this volume.

NOTE ON THE TERM 'ROMANESQUE'

'ROMANESQUE' (literally 'romance-like') is a term employed in France for a type of literature current up to the seventeenth century and after, whereas *romantique* is associated only with the Romantic school of the nineteenth. Romanesque literature specialized in fanciful and complicated tales, dealing mostly with chivalry, martial prowess and courtly love.

RACINE'S PLAYS

The Thebaid	1664
Alexander	1665
Andromache	1667
The Litigants	1668
Britannicus	1669
Berenice	1670
Bajazet	1672
Mithridates	1673
Iphigenia	1674
Phaedra	1677
Esther	1689
Athaliah	1691

BIBLIOGRAPHY

The following books on Racine (all in French and all published in Paris) may be useful:

Bénichou, Paul: *Morales du Grand Siècle* (including an essay on Racine), Gallimard, 1948.
Butler, Philip: *Classicisme et baroque dans l'œuvre de Racine*, Nizet, 1959.
Dubech, Lucien: *Jean Racine Politique*, Grasset, 1926.
Goldmann, Lucien: *Le Dieu caché*, Gallimard, 1955.
Maulnier, Thierry: *Racine*, Gallimard, 1935.
Picard, Raymond: *La Carrière de Jean Racine*, Gallimard, 1956.
Picard, Raymond: *Corpus Racinianum*, Belles Lettres, 1956.

The best edition is that of the Pléiade – by Picard – in two volumes (Gallimard, 1952). The Prefaces to the plays are brilliant.

As this volume was going to press, I was permitted to read the proofs of an excellent edition by Butler of *Britannicus* (Cambridge University Press).

The best studies known in English are Geoffrey Brereton's *Racine: A Critical Biography*, Cassell, 1951; and John C. Lapp's *Aspects of Racine*, University of Toronto Press and Oxford University Press, 1955, which is a particularly penetrating analysis of the French dramatist's structure and symbolism.

ANDROMACHE

A Tragedy

INTRODUCTION TO *ANDROMACHE*

WITH *Andromache* Racine swept Paris. From being the relatively successful author of two minor tragedies – *The Thebaid* and *Alexander* – he became overnight a writer of note, and this when he was a young man only twenty-seven years old. His triumph recalls that of Corneille's *The Cid* some thirty years earlier, and for much the same reasons.

Andromache is above all the work of a young man, with all the fire and power so often to be met with in the first masterpieces of great writers. There is an ease, a power, an almost insolent confidence in the richness of invention, the poetry and vigour of the language and the perfection of craftsmanship which, in their total effect, give the play an overwhelming, irresistible reality. It is perhaps the most compelling of all Racine's tragedies.

Yet, if we can detach ourselves from the sheer artistry of the tragedy, we will realize that, at the time, *Andromache* was also something of a revolution in its approach to the subjects with which it deals. For one thing, the plays of the time, steeped in baroque or aristocratic habits of mind, were highly involved in their plot and structure. Racine's work, on the contrary, is admirably simple, and the action flows inevitably from the initial premises which are few in number and consist of the passions of the cast and the situation in which they find themselves. There are none of the divine interventions, false oracles, mistaken identities or *coups de théâtre* so popular among the playwrights of the age.

In fact, the pattern of *Andromache* has often been reduced to a mathematical formula. A loves B who loves C who loves D, and in each case the love is unrequited. But if D accepts C's addresses, B lends a kindlier ear to A, who then, to please B, murders C. If we put a face to each of these letters, we see that Orestes, the son of Agamemnon, loves Hermione, his cousin, the daughter of Menelaus and Helen of Troy, who, in her turn, has been lingering on for a year at the court of King Pyrrhus (son of Achilles) waiting for him to keep his pledged word and marry her. But Pyrrhus has fallen in love with Andromache, widow of Hector of Troy, and she is irrevocably bound to him, dead though he be. Moreover, her love is fed by her young son, Astyanax, the living image of his father.

Orestes, though realizing that his love for Hermione is hopeless, accepts an assignment from the Greeks to summon Pyrrhus to give back Astyanax, for the child had been saved only by a trick. Pyrrhus, when approached, refuses. But Andromache, instead of proving more disposed to accept his proffers, remains obdurate. Thereupon Pyrrhus tells Orestes that he has changed his mind. He will hand over Astyanax and marry Hermione. But Andromache, when faced with the threat of what is in effect her son's death, recoils, and, after consulting her husband at his tomb, decides to practise an 'innocent trick' (1097). She will marry Pyrrhus, but immediately after kill herself in order to keep her virtue unsoiled. Hermione, on learning the news, summons Orestes and orders him to murder Pyrrhus, and thereby win her hand. Orestes, after fighting with his scruples, obeys, but, when he comes back to claim his reward, he is disowned. 'Who told you to murder Pyrrhus?' the demented creature shouts at him in all sincerity. Orestes, already under the most hideous strain, goes mad, and Hermione commits suicide over Pyrrhus' dead body.

Secondly, passion is all-powerful. It comes before *la gloire*, fame, reputation and power, which usually prevail in Cornelian tragedy. Love is an absolute, sweeping reason and all other opposition aside. Moreover, there is nothing chivalrous about it. It is simply the desire to possess the beloved, and, since love is always unreturned in the play (let alone satisfied in the physical sense, which would be ruled out by the proprieties), the explosive potential is unlimited. When thwarted, love turns to hate. Regardless of whether the sign is positive or negative, it is an obsession, as is superbly brought out in Hermione's wild cry:

I'll strike out blindly in a frenzied rage.
All, even Orestes, will be Pyrrhus for
My hand.   (1489–91)

If the Greek gods of *The Thebaid* have disappeared, the
forces of love take their place as an equally cruel and sar-
donic force of destiny. But it is a destiny in which retribution
and moral values play no part. Yet these values had been
decisive in baroque tragedy. The contrast between the two
approaches is lucidly defined by Butler in his *Classicisme et
baroque dans l'œuvre de Racine* (pp. 146–7):

The murder which Orestes finally brings himself to commit is the
unforgivable sin, an out-and-out felony which excludes him for
ever from the community of his peers . . . Pyrrhus succumbs alone
and disarmed, treacherously attacked and overwhelmed by sheer
numbers. And the murder committed by Orestes and his *bravi* is a
trifling act of violence compared with the constant outrage of
Pyrrhus, both by his person and his acts, upon ways of acting and
feeling universally demanded of a gentleman and of the tragic hero
who is the elevated and sublimated form thereof. [Orestes at least
feels some scruples.] Pyrrhus, thrice foresworn, towards Hermione,
Andromache and the Greeks, has no regrets. Indeed, Racine, had
he deliberately sought to ridicule the chivalrous ideal in fairness in
combat, faithfulness to the sworn word, the sacred character of
woman and mother, the protection of the weak and the oppressed,
could hardly have done better.
The same is true of the women. Hermione, despite her pride, has
been throwing herself at a man who despises her, for a year.
Andromache, queen and widow, of royal blood, guardian of
'Hector's blood', refuses a crown on his behalf:

My lord, such grandeur touches me no more.   (333)

The sceptre for which the baroque heroines are ready to sacrifice
their love and life is rejected by Andromache with a weary gesture.

She says 'No' to ambition and glory considered by the
baroque age

as a social and moral imperative independent of personal prefer-
ences, as a duty to oneself first of all and to one's race and one's
'blood', to one's peers.

This whole process of undermining the heroic morality is powerfully aided by the skilful interweaving of flashbacks which portray the 'glorious' war of Troy as a pitiable and cruel enterprise in which thousands are butchered, including Hector's old father and the innocent Polyxenes (1333–9). However, it was inevitable that the prevailing values should make themselves felt in the play. And, as Butler observes:

Andromache . . . has its baroque aspects and moments. Orestes and Pyrrhus ask nothing better than to perish heroically for the lady of their thoughts in the grand baroque style or like the knights of the courtly epoch. Pyrrhus is ready to play his part unflinchingly as the protector of the widow and the orphan (282–8) . .
When Hermione asks him to avenge her, Orestes can imagine no other solution than a challenge, a declaration of war on the 'rebel' which will be 'by rightful conquest' (1157–63). . . . An adventure undertaken for their mistress and at her request, unfolded before her eyes, is the constant theme of the aristocratic literature of the seventeenth century and well before that age. ... . The obstinate pursuit by Pyrrhus and Orestes of Andromache and Hermione and their no less obstinate refusal correspond to the typical situation of the relations between man and woman according to the baroque convention. . . . Women shelter behind their duty, their *gloire*, or their modesty which forbid them to make a complete avowal of their feelings. Hermione takes refuge behind the orders of Menelaus [her father]. . . . And did she not become enamoured of the glory and the great reputation of Pyrrhus (464–9)? It was for Achilles' son and the victor of Troy that her imagination was inflamed.

In the same way, it is significant that, in the earlier version of the *dénouement*, Andromache, after Pyrrhus's death, accords him the love which she refused him in his lifetime:

Pyrrhus seems to have taken Hector's place.

And so [notes Butler] it was really her *gloire* and not her hatred which prevented her, as Hector's widow, from giving herself to Achilles' son. Her fidelity and even her hate were primarily a duty demanded by honour.

This ending, he observes, 'was more in line with the literary and psychological convention' of the time, and 'reveals the inner tension of his art, caught between opposing pressures'.

Similarly, there is no retribution in the tragedy, as there usually was in the similar works of the period. Yet the public instinctively expected the customary indications. And in fact, can it not be said, asks the same critic,

that Pyrrhus leaves the stage with the curses of the outraged Hermione and her appeal to the 'righteous gods' ringing in his ears? Is not Orestes' madness a natural consequence of the inexpiable crime to which he stoops, despite his inner revulsion as a prince and a gentleman? Lastly, Andromache, in whom passion is not essentially different in nature from love in the other characters, seems to reap the reward of an at least apparent disinterestedness (op. cit., pp. 223–4).

Once the contemporary climate has been outlined, the play may be safely left to speak for itself. Descriptive comment is superfluous. The action does indeed open on a 'fateful morning' just as a crisis is imminent, and the spectator is propelled forward at breathless speed to the catastrophic ending in an atmosphere of doom heightened by matchless verse and charged with the intensity of history and legend. If there is a work which can initiate those unfamiliar with Racine to his world and compel the admiration of those who are allergic to him, it is this.

RACINE'S DEDICATION TO
ANDROMACHE

To Madame*

MADAME,

It is not without good grounds that I place your illustrious name at the head of this work. And with what other name could I dazzle my readers' eyes than the one with which my spectators have been so happily dazzled? It was known that YOUR ROYAL HIGHNESS had deigned to take a hand in the shaping of my tragedy. It was known that you had lent me some of your insight so as to add fresh ornaments to it. It was known, to conclude, that you had honoured it with some tears at my very first reading of it to you. Forgive me, MADAME, if I dare to boast of this auspicious beginning of its destiny. It offers me most glorious consolation for the harshness of those who would not let themselves be moved by it. I readily allow them to condemn Andromache as much as they please, provided I am allowed to appeal against all their hair-splitting to YOUR ROYAL HIGHNESS'S heart.

But, MADAME, it is not only with your heart that you judge the quality of a work. It is with an intelligence which cannot be led astray by any deluding appearances. Is it possible to stage a story which you do not master as much as we? Can we spring a plot on you all the complications of which you do not grasp? And can we conceive noble and delicate feelings which are not infinitely beneath the nobility and delicacy of your own thoughts?

It is known, MADAME, and YOUR ROYAL HIGHNESS cannot keep it secret, that in that lofty and glorious rank to which nature and fortune have been pleased to raise you, you do not disdain that obscure glory which we men of letters had regarded as our own preserve. And it seems as if you wished to outshine our sex as much by your knowledge and by your sound judgement as by all the excelling graces which attend on you. The Court regards you as the arbiter on

* 'Madame': the title reserved for the wife of the king's oldest brother.

everything that takes place in the world of taste. And we, whose job it is to please the public, have no longer any need to ask the learned whether we work according to the rules. The sovereign rule is to please YOUR ROYAL HIGHNESS.

This is no doubt the least of your excellent qualities. But, MADAME, *it is the only one of which I can speak with some knowledge. The others are far above me. I cannot speak of them without lowering them by the feebleness of my thoughts and without departing from the profound veneration with which I am*

MADAME,
  Your Royal Highness's
    Most humble, most obedient and most faithful servant

RACINE

RACINE'S PREFACES TO
ANDROMACHE
*

FIRST PREFACE

VIRGIL *writes in the third book of the* Aeneid (*Aeneas is speaking*):

> *Littoraque Epiri legimus, portuque subimus*
> *Chaonio, et celsam Buthroti ascendimus urbem. . . .*
> *Solemnes tum forte dapes, et tristia dona . . .*
> *Libabat cineri Andromache, Manesque vocabat*
> *Hectoreum ad tumulum, viridi quem cespite inanem,*
> *Et geminas, causam lacrymis, sacraverat aras. . . .*
> *Dejecit vultum, et demissa voce locuta est:*
> *'O felix una ante alias Priameia virgo,*
> *Hostilem ad tumulum, Trojae sub moenibus altis,*
> *Jussa mori, quae sortitus non pertulit ullos,*
> *Nec victoris heri tetigit captiva cubile!*
> *Nos, patria incensa, diversa per aequora vectae,*
> *Stirpis Achilleae fastus, juvenemque superbum,*
> *Servitio enixae tulimus, qui deinde secutus*
> *Ledaeam Hermionem, Lacedaemoniosque hymenaeos. . . .*
> *Ast illum, ereptae magno inflammatus amore*
> *Conjugis, et scelerum Furiis agitatus, Orestes*
> *Excipit incautum, patriasque obtruncat ad aras.'**

* These are verses 292–332. The translation is: 'We sailed along the coast of Epirus and entered the port of Chaonia, and we went up to the high city of Buthrotes. . . . It happened that this day Andromache was bearing to Hector's ashes her solemn libations and sad offerings; she was summoning his shades to the empty tomb on the green mound which she had consecrated with twin altars, a source of tears. . . . She lowered her eyes and said in a low voice: "Happy among all women the virgin daughter of Priam, singled out to die on an enemy's tomb, under the lofty walls of Troy! She did not suffer the injury of being chosen by lot; she did not enter, captive, the bed of a conqueror as her master! I, leaving behind my fatherland in flames, dragged over distant seas, I have given

39

Here, in a few lines, is the whole subject of this tragedy. Here is the scene, the action, the four main actors and even their characters. Except for that of Hermione, whose jealousy and outbursts are fairly clearly defined in Euripides' Andromache.

But really my characters are so famous in olden times that, however little one's knowledge of them may be, it will be obvious that I have depicted them as the ancient poets have handed them down to us. And so I have not felt authorized to change anything in their characters. The only liberty I have taken has been to tone down slightly the ferocity of Pyrrhus which Seneca in his Troades *and Virgil in the second book of the* Aeneid *have carried much farther than I felt I ought.*

And yet there have been people who have complained that he loses his temper with Andromache and that he wanted to marry that captive at any price. I confess that he is not resigned enough to his mistress's wish and that Celadon had a better knowledge of 'perfect love' than he. But what is one to do? Pyrrhus had not read our novels. He was naturally violent. And all heroes are not cut out to be Celadons.*

Whatever the truth, the public reaction has been too favourable for me to worry about the personal chagrin of two or three persons who would like all the heroes of ancient times to be reformed and turned into perfect heroes. I find it most amusing that these critics should want only men devoid of faults put on the stage. But I must beg them to remember that it is not for me *to change the rules of the stage. Horace recommends us to depict Achilles as fierce, inexorable, violent, just as he was in fact, and as his son is depicted. And Aristotle, far from asking us to provide perfect heroes, asks on the contrary that tragic characters (that is, those whose misfortunes constitute the catastrophe of the tragedy) should not be entirely good or entirely evil.*

---

birth in slavery; I have suffered from the haughtiness of Achilles' son, of this haughty young warrior, who, later marrying Hermione, allied himself with the Spartan race of Leda. . . ." But suddenly, in his ardent passion for the woman Pyrrhus had carried off, Orestes, pursued by the Furies of the crime, took him unawares and killed him near the altars of his [Pyrrhus'] fathers.'

* The hero of the *Astrée* by Honoré d'Urfé. Ironic term for the perfect lover.

He does not want them to be completely good, since the punishment of an upright man would arouse the indignation rather than the pity of the spectator; nor that he be a scoundrel, or excessively wicked, since nobody would feel pity for a scoundrel. They should therefore be not too good and not too bad, that is, their virtues should be capable of weakness, and they should fall into misfortune through some error which makes them pitied without making them detested.

SECOND PREFACE*

VIRGIL *writes in the third book of the* Aeneid (*Aeneas is speaking*):

> *Littoraque Epiri legimus, portuque subimus*
> *Chaonio, et celsam Buthroti ascendimus urbem . . .*
> *Solemnes tum forte dapes, et tristia dona . . .*
> *Libabat cineri Andromache, Manesque vocabat*
> *Hectoreum ad tumulum, viridi quem cespite inanem,*
> *Et geminas, causam lacrymis, sacraverat aras . . .*
> *Dejecit vultum, et demissa voce locuta est:*
> *'O felix una ante alias Priameia virgo,*
> *Hostilem ad tumulum, Trojae sub moenibus altis,*
> *Jussa mori, quae sortitus non pertulit ullos,*
> *Nec victoris heri tetigit captiva cubile!*
> *Nos, patria incensa, diversa per aequora vectae,*
> *Stirpis Achilleae fastus, juvenemque superbum,*
> *Servitio enixae tulimus, qui deinde secutus*
> *Ledaeam Hermionem, Lacedaemoniosque hymenaeos . . .*
> *Ast illum, ereptae magno inflammatus amore*
> *Conjugis, et scelerum Furiis agitatus, Orestes*
> *Excipit incautum, patriasque obtruncat ad aras.'†*

Here, in a few lines, is the whole subject of this tragedy. Here is the scene, the action, the four main actors, and even their characters. Except for that of Hermione, whose jealousy and outbursts are fairly clearly defined in Euripides' Andromache.‡

This is practically the only point which I have borrowed from that author. For, although my tragedy bears the same name as his, the subject is entirely different. In Euripides, Andromache fears for the life of Molossus, a son she had borne Pyrrhus and whom Hermione wishes to kill, together with the boy's mother. But in my play, Molossus does not come into the picture. Andromache has never had

---

* Taken from the edition of 1676.
† See First Preface, footnote, p. 39.
‡ So far as in the First Preface.

any other husband except Hector nor any other son except Astyanax. In taking this line, I felt I was conforming to the idea which we have nowadays of this princess. Most of those who have heard of Andromache hardly know of her otherwise than as Hector's widow and Astyanax's mother. It is not felt proper that she should love another husband or another son. And I doubt whether Andromache's tears would have made the impression they did on my spectators if they had been shed for another son than the one she had from Hector.

It is true that I have been forced to make Astyanax live a little longer than he did. But I write in a country where this liberty could hardly be taken amiss. For, quite apart from Ronsard, who chose this very Astyanax as the hero of his Franciade, *everyone knows that our kings of olden times are supposed to be descended from this son of Hector's, and that our ancient chronicles save this young prince's life after his country is laid waste, so as to make of him the founder of our monarchy.*

How much bolder was Euripides in his tragedy, Helena. *In it, he openly flouts the common belief of the whole of Greece. He supposes that Helen never set foot in Troy, and that, after that town was set on fire, Menelaus finds his wife in Egypt, from which she had never stirred. All this founded on an opinion which was accepted only among the Egyptians, as may be seen from Herodotus.*

I do not think I needed the example of Euripides to justify the slight liberty I have taken. For there is a considerable difference between destroying a fable at its base and changing some of the incidents in it, which in any case are altered by all those dealing with them. Thus, Achilles, according to most of the poets, can be wounded only in the heel, although Homer shows him wounded in the arm and does not think him invulnerable in any part of his body. Thus, Sophocles makes Jocasta die immediately after Oedipus has been recognized, which is quite the opposite of Euripides, who makes her live till the fight takes place between her two sons and they die. And it is in connexion with some complaints of this kind that an old commentator* of Sophocles observes so well 'that one must not amuse oneself quibbling with poets about the few changes they may have made in the story; but one must concentrate on the excellent use they have made of these changes and the ingenious way in which they have adapted the fable to their subject'.

* Apparently Camerarius, in a commentary on *Electra,* published 1603.

ANDROMACHE
A Tragedy

CAST

ANDROMACHE,* *Hector's widow, captive of Pyrrhus*
PYRRHUS, *Achilles' son, King of Epirus*
ORESTES, *Agamemnon's son*
HERMIONE, *Helen's daughter, betrothed to Pyrrhus*
PYLADES, *Orestes' friend*
CLEONE,† *Hermione's confidante*
CEPHISA, *Andromache's confidante*
PHOENIX, *mentor of Achilles, and subsequently of Pyrrhus*
ORESTES' RETINUE

*The scene is at Buthrotes, a town in Epirus, in a chamber
in Pyrrhus' palace*

* Pronounced An-drò-ma-che in four syllables. The final 'e' is sounded.
† Pronounced Cle-òn-e in three syllables. The final 'e' is sounded in
this case as well.

ANDROMACHE

ACT ONE

Scene One
ORESTES, PYLADES

ORESTES

Yes, since I find again so true a friend,   1
Fortune's about to take a different turn;
Her anger seems already to abate
Since she took pains to reunite us here.
Who would have thought on this unkindly shore   5
Orestes would at once meet Pylades;
And, when you had been lost for six long months,
At Pyrrhus' court you'd be restored to me?

PYLADES

I thank the heavens which always, so it seemed,
Barred my return to Hellas ever since   10
That fateful morning when the raging waves,
Just off Epirus, drove our ships apart.
How often have I, in this exile, known
Disquiet, and have wept for your mishaps,
Fearing new perils for you ceaselessly   15
Which my sad friendship could not share with you!
I dreaded above all that sombre mood
Which for so long I saw enshroud your soul:
I feared lest heaven's cruel helpfulness
Might offer you the death you always sought.   20
But you are safe, my lord: and, dare I say,
A happier fate to Epirus guides your steps;
Your splendid retinue does not denote
A poor unfortunate who's bent on death.

ORESTES

25 Alas! who can foretell my destiny?
Love for a cruel beauty brings me here;
But who knows what it holds in store for me,
And whether it will give me life or death?

PYLADES

What! Can your soul, deep in the toils of love,
30 Make it your being's only arbiter?
Forgetful of the torments you've endured,
How can you be its vassal once again?
Hermione in Sparta frowned on you.
Will she be kinder in Epirus now?
35 Ashamed of having wooed so long in vain,
You loathed her; well, no longer talked of her.
Sir, you deceived me.

ORESTES

I deceived myself.
Ah! Have some mercy on your wretched friend:
When have I hid from you my heart? You saw
40 The blossoming of love, my earliest sighs.
When Menelaus then gave his daughter's hand
To Pyrrhus who avenged his family,
You witnessed my despair, and ever since
I've dragged my sorrows over endless seas.
45 Against my will, in my sad plight, you chose
To follow everywhere Orestes led,
Halting my fits of frenzy constantly,
In short, saving me daily from myself.
But when, in all this turmoil, I recalled
50 Hermione on Pyrrhus lavishing
Her charms, you know that anger seized my heart.
I strove for vengeance by forgetting her.
I feigned, indeed believed, my victory sure;

41 *Menelaus:* Hermione's father. Her mother was Helen of Troy. See
line 245.

I took my triumph for a burst of hate.
Cursing her frowns, disparaging her charms,⁣   55
I dared her to disturb my peace of mind.
I thought to stifle thus my tenderness.
In this deceptive calm I came to Greece,
And found her kings assembled to debate
What seemed to them a serious danger. I   60
Plunged headlong in. I thought renown and war
Would occupy my mind with greater things;
That, as my senses' vigour was restored,
Love would completely vanish from my heart.
But, friend, admire the fate that hounded me   65
Into the snare I wanted to avoid.
Threats at King Pyrrhus fly from every side.
All Greece hums with a hubbub of complaint;
He is alleged, mindless of race and vow,
To bring up, at his court, the Grecians' foe –   70
Astyanax, Hector's young and hapless son,
Last of the princes buried under Troy.
They tell me that, to save the boy from death,
Andromache deceived Ulysses' guile.
In fact, another child, snatched from her arms,   75
Was substituted for her son and slain.
It's said my rival shuns Hermione,
Offering elsewhere his passion and his crown.
Her father doubts it, but seems deeply grieved,
Complains her marriage is too long delayed.   80
Midst the afflictions that beset her soul,
In mine there rises pleasure, half-confessed.
I triumph, yet delude myself at first
That my elation springs from vengeance, but
The ingrate soon reoccupied my heart.   85
I saw my passion's embers blaze again;
I felt my hatred was about to end;
Or rather felt that I adored her still.
And so I canvassed all the Greeks, and was
Named envoy to King Pyrrhus. I set out.
My mission was to wrest from him the boy

Whose mere survival frightens Hellas' states.
Happy if in my ardour, I could seize
Not Astyanax but my Hermione.
95 For do not hope my new-inflamèd love
Can by the greatest dangers be dismayed.
Since stubborn, long resistance is in vain,
I follow blindly my impelling fate.
I love, and come to win Hermione,
100 Carry her off or die before her eyes.
You know the king. What think you he will do?
Tell me, what happens in his court, his heart?
Does he still kneel to my Hermione?
Will he give back what he has stolen from me?

PYLADES

105 I would mislead you if I promised you
That he would ever place her in your hands.
Not that his conquest seems to flatter him;
Of Hector's widow he is openly
Enamoured. Yet, heartless Andromache
110 Only with hate so far repays his love.
And day by day he tries by every means
To woo his captive or to frighten her.
He hides her son from her, threatens his life,
Making her weep, but stops her tears at once.
115 And countless times Hermione has seen
Pyrrhus thus angered turn to her again,
And, bringing back to her his troubled heart,
Court her with sighs of fury, not of love.
Do not expect me then to answer for
120 A heart so little master of itself.
He may, sir, in this frenzied turmoil wed
The one he hates and spurn the one he loves.

ORESTES

But tell me how Hermione regards
Her charms neglected and her marriage stayed?

PYLADES

Hermione, at least to outward view,   125
Appears to scorn the king's inconstancy,
And thinks he will come back, and deem himself
Only too glad to make her heart relent.
But I was privileged to see her tears.
She weeps in secret for her charms disdained;   130
About to leave, yet always staying on,
Sometimes she calls Orestes to her aid.

ORESTES

Ah! If I thought so, Pylades, I'd rush
And throw myself. . . .

PYLADES

        Finish your embassy.
Sir, you await the King. Speak to him. Show   135
The whole of Greece leagued against Hector's son.
Their hate, far from securing them the boy,
Will make his mother dearer to the king.
Try to disjoin these two; you'll bind them fast.
Press your demands – so that they'll be refused.   140
He comes.

ORESTES

    Well, go. Prepare Hermione
To see a prince who comes for her alone.

Scene Two

PYRRHUS, ORESTES, PHOENIX

ORESTES

Before all Greece speaks to you by my voice,
Let me express my pleasure at their choice
Of envoy, and my happiness to see   145
Achilles' son, the conqueror of Troy.
Yes, we admire his exploits and your deeds;

Hector succumbed to him, and Troy to you;
And you have shown, by many a daring feat,
150 Only Achilles' son could take his place.
But he would not have done what Greece regrets
To see you do – rebuild a ruined Troy,
And, yielding to the dint of pity, save
The sole survivor of so long a war.
155 Have you forgot who Hector was, my lord?
Our prostrate peoples still remember him.
His very name makes all our widows pale.
The length and breadth of Greece, no family
But does not of this ill-starred son demand
160 A father or a husband Hector slew.
And who knows what one day the son may do?
Perhaps we'll see him fall upon our ports
Even as his father set our ships on fire,
And, torch in hand, follow them out to sea.
165 Dare I, my lord, express my inmost thoughts?
Beware lest, as reward for your concern,
This snake reared in your bosom one fine day
Chastise King Pyrrhus for preserving him.
In short, give satisfaction to the Greeks.
170 Ensure your vengeance and ensure your life.
Suppress a foe all the more dangerous since
He'll learn to fight the Greeks through fighting you.

PYRRHUS

On my behalf Greece shows undue alarm.
I thought that weightier matters were at stake,
175 My lord, and her ambassador's prestige
Made me expect more grandiose designs.
Who would believe in fact that this démarche
Was worthy of great Agamemnon's son?
That a whole people, crowned with victory,
180 Would stoop to plot only an infant's death?
And who demands this sacrifice of me?
Does Greece still hold some title to his life?
And may not I alone in Greece dispose

Of this my captive that was mine by lot?
Yes, prince, when near the reeking walls of Troy,   185
The blood-stained conquerors shared the spoils of war
By lot, as was agreed, I was assigned
Andromache, together with her son.
Ulysses drew woe-laden Hecuba.
Cassandra took the road to Argos with   190
Your father. Did I interfere with them,
Or tamper with the fruits of their exploits?
With a new Hector Troy will rise again,
You say. His son, if spared, will be my doom.
My lord, such prudence shows too much concern.   195
I cannot see troubles so far ahead.
I call to mind that town in former days,
Its soaring ramparts, heroes myriad,
Mistress of Asia, and I contemplate
The fate of Troy, its future destiny.   200
I see but towers covered with ashes and
A river stained with blood, deserted fields,
A boy in chains, and I can not conceive
That Troy laid low can ever seek revenge.
Ah! If the death of Hector's son were sworn,   205
Why did you wait until a year was by?
On Priam's breast he should have been dispatched,
Buried beneath the dying, under Troy.
Then, then, all things were just. Old men and boys
In vain upon their feebleness relied.   210
Victory and night, more cruel far than we,
Incited us to wanton, murderous blows.
And to the vanquished I was merciless.
But that my cruelty should outlive my wrath,
That I, despite the pity that I feel,   215
Should wallow calmly in an infant's blood,
No, sir. Let the Greeks find some other prey.
Let them pursue elsewhere Troy's poor remains.
My fierce hostility has run its course.
Epirus guards all that was saved by Troy.   220

199 *Asia:* Asia Minor.

ORESTES

My lord, you know too well by what deceit
A false Astyanax was led to death –
A death reserved for Hector's son alone.
It is not Troy, it's Hector we pursue.
225 The father's sins we visit on the son.
He's merited their wrath by seas of blood,
Which can by his blood only be assuaged.
And he can draw the Greeks even to this land.
Act now before they do.

PYRRHUS

         No, let them come,
230 And in Epirus seek another Troy.
Let them, with blinding hate, mingle the blood
Of conquered and of conquering generals.
This, after all, is not the only time
That Greece has ill repaid Achilles' deeds.
235 Hector himself once turned it to account.
His son might take advantage of it too.

ORESTES

So Greece in you finds a rebellious son.

PYRRHUS

And have I triumphed to depend on her?

ORESTES

Hermione, my lord, will hold you back,
240 Stepping between her father and yourself.

PYRRHUS

Hermione can still be dear to me.
I need not therefore be her father's slave.
And some day I shall find the means perhaps
To reconcile my glory with my love.

You may, however, see Queen Helen's child.   245
I know the ties of blood that bind you close.
And now, my lord, you may take leave of me,
And tell the Greeks of my refusal.

Scene Three

PYRRHUS, PHOENIX

PHOENIX

                                        So
You send him back to kneel to his beloved.

PYRRHUS

Yes, it is said he long has pined for her.   250

PHOENIX

But if his passion should revive, my lord?
If, bringing back his heart, he won her love?

PYRRHUS

Ah! Let them love, dear Phoenix. Let her leave!
Let them go back to Sparta each with each
Entranced. Our ports are open to them both.   255
What trouble she would spare me! What constraint!

PHOENIX

My lord. . . .

PYRRHUS

            Some other time I'll tell you all.
Andromache is coming.

245 *Helen's child*: Hermione, whose father, Menelaus, was Orestes' uncle.

ANDROMACHE

Scene Four
PYRRHUS, ANDROMACHE, CEPHISA

PYRRHUS
Dare I hope
That it was I that you were looking for?

ANDROMACHE
260 I'm on my way to where my son is kept,
Since once a day you let me visit him –
All I have left of Hector and of Troy.
I was about to weep a while with him.
I have not yet embraced the boy today.

PYRRHUS
265 If their alarm is any guide, the Greeks
Will shortly give you other cause for tears.

ANDROMACHE
And what can be this fear that strikes my heart?
Has some poor Trojan then escaped your blows?

PYRRHUS
Their enmity for Hector has not died.
270 They dread his son.

ANDROMACHE
        A fitting cause for fear!
A wretched child who still is ignorant
That Pyrrhus is his lord, Hector his sire.

PYRRHUS
Such as he is, the Greeks demand his death.
This is why Agamemnon's son is here.

ANDROMACHE
275 And you will utter such a cruel doom?

Is it because of me he's criminal?
Alas, it's not his sire's revenge they fear,
But that one day he'll dry his mother's tears.
He'd have been father, husband to me, but
I must lose all, and always by your hand.   280

PYRRHUS

Lady, my action has forestalled your tears.
The whole of Greece has threatened me with war.
But, even should they cross the seas again
And with a vast armada claim your son,
Should it demand the blood for Helen shed,   285
Ten years of war, my palaces in flames,
I would, unwavering, hasten to his aid.
I would defend him, laying down my life.
But in these dangers courted for your sake
Will you not look on me with kindlier eyes?   290
Hated by Greece, hard pressed on every side,
Must I combat your cruelty as well?
I offer you my sword. May I still hope
That you'll accept a heart that worships you?
Fighting on your behalf, may I aspire   295
Not to include you in my enemies?

ANDROMACHE

My lord, reflect. What will Greece say of you?
Must from so great a heart such weakness flow?
Must such a noble, generous design
Pass for the impulse of a doting heart?   300
A captive, always hateful to herself,
How can you wish me to return your love?
What magic can you find in these sad eyes
Condemned by you to everlasting tears?
No, to respect an enemy's mishaps,   305
To give a son back to his mother's arms,
To fight a hundred nations' cruel will,
Without expecting, as your price, my hea

To give him refuge, even in spite of me,
310 *These* aims are worthy of Achilles' son.

PYRRHUS

What! has your anger not yet run its course?
Must hate and vengeance last for ever? Yes,
I've scattered death, and Phrygia has beheld
A thousand times my hand red with your blood.
315 What havoc, though, your eyes have wrought on me!
How dear they've made me pay the tears they've shed!
And what remorse, through them, has preyed on me.
I've suffered all the ills I did to Troy:
Vanquished, in thrall, devoured by keen regrets,
320 Burned with more blazing fires than e'er I lit,
All my attentions, troubled ardour, tears. . . .
Alas! Was ever I as harsh as you?
But let us end this mutual punishment.
Our common enemies should bring us close.
325 Swear to me only I may hope. I'll give
You back, and be a father to your son.
I'll teach him how to take revenge for Troy.
I'll punish Greece for all your woes and mine.
Fired by a glance, I can accomplish all.
330 Your Ilium can from out its ashes rise;
Swifter than were the Greeks in conquering it,
Within its walls rebuilt I'll crown your son.

ANDROMACHE

My lord, such grandeur touches me no more.
It was his birthright while his father lived.
335 No, you will never look on us again,
Your sacred walls my Hector could not save!
To smaller favours wretches must aspire.
An exile's lot is all I ask of you.
Let me, far from the Greeks and far from you,
340 Weep for my husband and conceal my son.
Your love arouses too much hate for us.
Return, return to Helen's daughter. Go.

PYRRHUS

How can I, lady? Ah! You torture me.
How can I give her back a heart that's yours?
I know my fealty was promised her. 345
I know she came to Epirus to be queen.
Destiny willed you both be present here,
You to bear fetters, she to put them on.
Yet have I been at pains to sue for her?
Does it not seem that, on the contrary, 350
Your spell's all-powerful, and hers disdained?
That she's the captive here and you're the queen?
Ah! Were a single sigh of mine for you
To swerve to her, how happy would she be!

ANDROMACHE

And why should your addresses be repelled? 355
Has she forgotten all your services?
Does Troy, does Hector, make her hate you? Do
A husband's ashes still command her love?
And what a husband! Cruel memory!
His death alone has given your father fame 360
Undying, for it flows from Hector's blood.
And both of you are known but by my tears.

PYRRHUS

Well, then, my lady, you must be obeyed.
I must forget, or rather hate you. Yes,
My passion's violence has gone too far 365
Ever to halt in mere indifference.
Think well. Henceforth, unless my heart can love
With rapture, it must hate with frenzied rage.
I, in my anger, will be merciless.
The son shall answer for the mother's scorn. 370
The Greeks demand him. I do not intend
Always to joy in saving ingrates' lives.

ANDROMACHE

So he will die, alas! His one defence
Lies in his mother's tears, his innocence.
375 And maybe in my present plight his death
Will after all hasten my sorrows' end.
I went on living, suffering for him.
But now I'll join his father in his steps.
So, reunited by your hand, my lord,
380 We three. . . .

PYRRHUS

    Go, lady, go and see your son.
Perhaps your love will be more timorous
And not be guided by resentment still.
To know our fate, I'll call on you again.
As you embrace him, think to save your son.

ACT TWO

Scene One
HERMIONE, CLEONE

HERMIONE
As you desire, I shall receive him. I 385
Am willing to accord him that at least.
Soon Pylades will bring him here to me;
And yet my inner voice discounsels me.

CLEONE
And why are you so loath to see the prince?
Is he not then the same Orestes still 390
For whose return a thousand times you longed,
Whom you regretted for his constant love?

HERMIONE
It is this love so much misprized by me
Which makes his presence here so hard to bear.
How must he triumph, how ashamed I am 395
That my mishaps should equal his distress.
Is this, he'll say, the proud Hermione?
She spurned me once; another casts her off.
She who was wont to rate her heart so high
Learns in her turn what 'tis to be disdained. 400
Ah! God. . . .

CLEONE
      Lady, dispel these baseless fears.
He's felt too deep the power of your spell.
You think a suitor comes to jeer at you?
He brings a heart he could not keep from you.
But what your father writes you do not say. 405

HERMIONE

If Pyrrhus will not cease to temporize,
And not consent to the young Trojan's death,
My father bids me with the Greeks depart.

CLEONE

Well, lady, listen to Orestes, and
410 What Pyrrhus has begun at least conclude.
To act aright you should forestall him now.
Did you not tell me that you hated him?

HERMIONE

Hate him, Cleone? Honour so commands,
After so many favours he forgets.
415 He who was once so dear and has been false!
I've loved too much not to detest him now.

CLEONE

Flee from him, then, and, since Orestes loves ...

HERMIONE

Ah! Give my fury time to swell. Let me
Entrench myself firmly against my foe.
420 I wish to part from him with horror. He
Will ease my path too well, the faithless heart.

CLEONE

What! Are you waiting for some new offence?
To love a captive, and to flaunt his love,
Is not enough to make him odious?
425 What more is needed after what he's done?
If you can hate him, *that* should earn your hate.

HERMIONE

Why must you, cruel one, inflame my wounds?
I fear to look into a heart distraught.
Each thing you witness try to disbelieve.

Believe I love no more. Cry Victory.   430
Believe my heart is steeled against him, and,
If that may be, make me believe it too.
You tell me flee. Well, nothing holds me back.
Envy no more his paltry conquest. Let
His captive over him extend her sway.   435
Let's flee. But if the ingrate felt the call
Of duty and some twinge of faithfulness,
If he came back, sought pardon at my feet;
If you could bind him, Love, to my command,
If . . . But he seeks only to outrage me.   440
Let us stay on to spoil their happiness,
And find some joy in being in their way;
Or, forcing him to break so strong a tie,
Make him a criminal to all the Greeks.
I have already drawn their anger on   445
The son. They must demand the mother too.
I'll pay her back for all she's made me bear.
Let her be *his* downfall or he be hers.

CLEONE

You think her eyes that always flow in tears
Delight to thwart the power of your charms,   450
And that a heart crushed by so many woes
Has sought her persecutor's favour. But
Does she appear to find relief in that?
Why the despair in which her soul is plunged?
Why, if she likes him, is she so aloof?   455

HERMIONE

Alas! I've lent him a too willing ear.
I did not don the cloak of silence, but
Imagined I could safely be sincere,
And, without even a moment of reserve,
Followed the promptings of my heart alone.   460
And who like me would not have ceased to feign,
Strong in the knowledge of a sacred oath?

63

Did he behold me with his present eyes?
Remember, *then* everything spoke for him –
465 My family avenged, Greece overjoyed,
Our vessels laden with the spoils of Troy,
His father's prowess quite eclipsed by his,
His ardour I believed more strong than mine,
My heart, and you, too, dazzled by his fame;
470 Ere he betrayed me, you betrayed me all.
My cup is full. Be Pyrrhus as he is,
Orestes' virtues touch my woman's heart.
At least he loves me, even without return.
Perhaps he'll find a way to conquer me.
475 Well, let him come.

CLEONE

But lady, here he is.

HERMIONE

Ah! Little did I think he was so near.

Scene Two

HERMIONE, ORESTES, CLEONE

HERMIONE

Can I believe your fondness lingers on
And makes you seek a sorrowing princess? Or
Is it your duty only that explains
480 This welcome eagerness to see me here?

ORESTES

Such is the fatal blindness of my love;
You know it, and Orestes' destiny
Is to return unceasingly to you,
While vowing always never to return.
485 I know your looks will open all my wounds,
That every step to you makes me forsworn.
I know. I blush. But I attest the gods,

64

Who saw the frenzy of my last farewell,
I've rushed to every place where certain death
Would free me from misfortune and my vows.   490
I've begged for death of cruel peoples who
Only with mortals' blood assuaged their gods.
They closed their barbarous temples' gates to me
And, miser-like, hoarded my proffered blood.
And now I come to you, and am reduced   495
To seek a death that flees me – in your eyes.
My doom is sure if they will not relent.
They need but banish any trace of hope;
And, to bring on the death for which I crave,
They need but say what they have always said.   500
This has been my obsession for a year.
It's now for you to claim a victim's life.
The Scythians would have saved him from your blows
Had they been as unfeeling as you are.

HERMIONE

Abandon, sir, this gloomy language. Greece   505
To far more urgent matters summons you.
Why talk of Scythians and my cruelty?
Think but of all the kings you represent.
Must their revenge turn on a burst of love?
Is it Orestes' blood they ask of you?   510
Discharge the duties that you are assigned.

ORESTES

Pyrrhus' refusal has discharged me. He
Dismisses me; some other influence
Makes him embrace the cause of Hector's son.

HERMIONE

False-hearted man!   515

ORESTES

    Thus, ready to depart,
I come to hear from you what is my fate.

I seem to hear already the decree,
Pronounced on me, unspoken, by your hate.

HERMIONE

What! Always this unjust and doleful talk!
520 Always complaints of my hostility!
What is this rigour you so oft allege?
I was to Epirus relegated by
My father's will, but who knows if since then
I have not shared in secret your distress?
525 You think you were disquieted alone,
That never did Epirus see my tears?
In short, who tells you that I did not wish
Sometimes, despite my duty, you were here?

ORESTES

That I were here. Ah! my Hermione. . . .
530 But are these words, I beg you, meant for me?
Open your eyes. It's I who speak to you,
Orestes, long the victim of their wrath.

HERMIONE

Yes, it is you whose love, born of their spell,
First made them realize their power, and you,
535 Whom countless virtues forced me to esteem,
You whom I pitied, whom I wished to love.

ORESTES

I understand; such is my baleful lot.
Your heart says Pyrrhus and your reason me.

HERMIONE

Ah! Do not long for Pyrrhus' destiny.
540 I'd hate you.

ORESTES

   You would love me all the more.
Ah! with what different eyes you'd look on me.

You want to love me, and I cannot please;
And, listening then to love's command alone,
You'd love me when you tried to hate me. God!
So much devotion, so much tenderness. . . .   545
Everything pleads for me would you but hear.
It's you alone who argue Pyrrhus' case,
Despite yourself, doubtless despite him too.
For after all he hates you, and he loves
Another. . . .   550

HERMIONE

Who said he despises me?
His eyes, his words, have they informed you so?
Do you feel that my sight inspires contempt,
Or kindles in a heart such fitful fires?
Others may view me in a better light.

ORESTES

Go on. It's noble to insult me thus.   555
Cruel one, is it I who scorn your charms?
Have not your eyes tested my constancy?
Am I a witness of their impotence?
Have I despised them? How they would rejoice
If but my rival scorned their power like me.   560

HERMIONE

What do I care whether he hate or love?
Go. Arm against a rebel all the Greeks,
And bring him the reward of his revolt.
Make of Epirus' land another Troy.
Go. Will you say I love him after that?   565

ORESTES

Lady, do more and come to Greece yourself.
Will you remain a hostage in this town?
Come, let your eyes make every heart beat fast,
And link our hatred in a joint attack.

HERMIONE

570 But meanwhile if he weds Andromache?

ORESTES

What! lady.

HERMIONE

Think of the disgrace to us
Were he to take a Phrygian as his wife.

ORESTES

And yet you say you hate him. Ah! confess.
The flame of passion cannot be confined.
575 Each thing betrays us – silence, voice and eyes;
And fires half-covered the more fiercely blaze.

HERMIONE

My lord, I see your prejudice has poured
Over my words the bane that kills your soul,
Sees all my reasons as but subterfuge,
580 And thinks my hate due to the pull of love.
I must be frank then; later you may act.
You know it was my duty brought me here.
Duty detains me. I can only leave
If ordered by my father or the king.
585 Go in my father's name to Pyrrhus. Say
No foe of Greece can be his son-in-law.
Force him to choose the Trojan boy or me.
Which does he wish to keep, which one give up?
He must hand o'er the boy or send me back.
590 Farewell. If he consents, I'll follow you.

Scene Three

ORESTES (*alone*)

ORESTES

Yes, you will follow me. No doubt of that.

I can already vouch for his consent.
I have no fear of Pyrrhus' keeping her.
His eyes are only for his Trojan love.
Perhaps all other women jar on him.   595
On the first pretext, he will cast her off.
We need but speak. Success is sure. What joy
To rob Epirus of so fine a prey!
Save all that's left of Troy and Hector; keep
His son, his widow – anyone you please,   600
Epirus, if Hermione restored
Never again beholds your king or you.
But, by a lucky chance, he comes this way.
I'll speak. To all her charms, Love, seal his eyes.

Scene Four

PYRRHUS, ORESTES, PHOENIX

PYRRHUS

I looked for you, my lord. A headstrong mood   605
Made me just now combat your arguments.
I readily admit, since leaving you,
I've recognized their force and equity.
I felt like you that I was faithless to
Hellas, my father, and indeed myself.   610
I was reviving Troy, endangering
All that Achilles, all that I had done.
Your indignation I no more condemn,
And soon your victim will be handed you.

ORESTES

My lord, by such a prudent, stern resolve,   615
You purchase peace, but with a wretch's blood.

PYRRHUS

Yes, but I will cement it further still.
Hermione's the pledge of lasting peace;

69

I'm wedding her. It seemed so sweet a sight
620 Awaited but a witness such as you.
You represent the Greeks, her father, too.
Since you're his brother Agamemnon's son.
Go then, and see her. Tell her I await
Tomorrow from your hand her heart – and peace.

ORESTES

625 Ah! God.

Scene Five

PYRRHUS, PHOENIX

PYRRHUS

Well, Phoenix, am I ruled by love?
You still refuse to see me as I am?

PHOENIX

Ah! sir. I recognize you, and your wrath
Restores you to yourself and to the Greeks.
You're not a slavish passion's plaything, but
630 Pyrrhus, Achilles' rival and his son,
Over whom glory has resumed its sway.
You triumph over Troy a second time.

PYRRHUS

Rather my victory begins today.
I revel in my glory only now.
635 My heart, as free as it was once in thrall,
Feels it has crushed in love a thousand foes.
Think, Phoenix, of the troubles I avoid,
And what a host of ills love brings with it.
What friends, what duties I'd have sacrificed,
640 What risks. . . . One look, and they were all forgot
All Greece in league against a rebel. Ah!
I joyed in my undoing for her sake.

70

PHOENIX

I bless, my lord, the timely cruelty
Which gives you back. . . .

PYRRHUS

          Look how she treated me.
I thought, since I had roused a mother's fears,   645
Her son would send her back to me disarmed.
The outcome of their meeting was assured.
But all I found was tears mingled with rage.
Her woes embitter her, make her resist.
Endlessly Hector's name poured from her lips.   650
My promises to help her were in vain.
'It's Hector,' she would say, embracing him;
'His eyes, his mouth, his boldness even now,
It's Hector, you, dear husband, I embrace.'
But what has she in mind? Does she expect   655
I'll let her keep her son to feed her love?

PHOENIX

Yes, this is the reward in store for you.
But let her be.

PYRRHUS

          I see it all. She counts
Upon her beauty and, despite my wrath,
The haughty girl awaits me at her knees.   660
I'd see her at my feet and be unmoved.
She's Hector's widow. I'm Achilles' son.
Far too much hate lies between her and me.

PHOENIX

Then make a start and talk no more of her.
Go to Hermione. Seek but her love.   665
Forget even your anger at her feet.
Go, and yourself prepare her to be wed.
Should you rely upon a rival who
Loves her so deeply?

PYRRHUS

If I marry her,
670 Will not Andromache be jealous?

PHOENIX

What!
Andromache is always in your thoughts!
What is't to you her joy or her chagrin?
What spell despite you draws her to you?

PYRRHUS

No,

I've not yet said all I must say to her.
675 My anger to her is but half revealed.
She does not know how strong's my enmity.
Let us go back. I'll brave her to her face.
And give my hate the very fullest scope.
Come, Phoenix. I'll humiliate her charms.
680 Come!

PHOENIX

My lord, go, cast yourself at her feet.
Go swear to her that you adore her still
And spur her on to one more burst of scorn.

PYRRHUS

I see. You think my heart excuses her,
Seeks to appease her, follows after her.

PHOENIX

685 You love; that is enough.

PYRRHUS

I love her? *I*?
The more I love, the more she hates me. With
No parents, friends or hope except in me,
I can undo her son. Perhaps I should.

An alien in Epirus . . . nay, a slave.
I offer her my heart, my realm, her son,   690
Yet cannot win in her perfidious breast
A higher rank than that of torturer.
No. I have sworn it. I shall take revenge.
I must at some point justify her hate,
Abandoning her son. What tears will flow!   695
What names her grieving heart will call me! What
A tragic scene is being set for her!
'Twill be the death of her, and 'twill be I
Myself who thrust the dagger in her breast.

PHOENIX

Why then so publicly announce your plan?   700
Why did you not foresee how weak you were?

PYRRHUS

You're right, but must forgive an ebbing love.
Fear not this slight encounter's outcome. This
Is the last flicker of a dying fire.
Come, I shall follow blindly your advice.   705
Shall I give up the son and shall I see
Hermione?

PHOENIX

                    Yes, and with heart subdued
Vow to . . .

PYRRHUS

                    Well, what I've promised I shall do.

73

ACT THREE

Scene One

ORESTES, PYLADES

PYLADES

Restrain, my lord, this wild unbridled rage.
710 I do not recognize you. You are not
Yourself. Let . . .

ORESTES

No. I want no more advice.
I'm tired of listening to reason's voice.
Too long my life, my agony's dragged on;
I must abduct her, Pylades, or die.
715 My mind's resolved. I mean to see it through.
Yes, I'm resolved.

PYLADES

Well, if you must, you must.
But meanwhile, sir, think in what place you are.
What will they say when you behave like this?
Dissimulate. Calm your distracted heart.
720 Command your eyes to practise secrecy.
These guards, this court, the air you breathe, depend
On Pyrrhus, and even more Hermione.
Especially from *her* conceal your wrath.
Great God! Why did you see her in this state?

ORESTES

725 I know not. Was I master of myself?
Rage carried me away. Perhaps I went
To threaten both the ingrate and the king.

PYLADES

What was the point of such an outburst?

ORESTES

                          Who,
I ask you, would not be beside himself
At the dread blow from which my reason reels?   730
Tomorrow he will wed Hermione,
Honouring me by receiving her from me.
Ah! sooner will this hand, in his vile blood . . .

PYLADES

You charge him, sir, with this strange turn of fate.
Yet he's tormented by his own designs.   735
Perhaps he's to be pitied just like you.

ORESTES

No. It is my despair that spurs him on.
He'd scorn her but for me and for my love.
Till then he was impassive to her spell.
He takes her to deprive me of her. Ah!   740
The die was cast. Hermione regained
Would have gone off for ever from his sight.
Her heart, wavering between despite and love,
Awaited but his No to yield to me.
Opening her eyes, she listened to me, talked,   745
Pitied me even. A word had done the rest.

PYLADES

You think so?

ORESTES

                What! this molten stream of rage
At Pyrrhus. . . .

PYLADES

             Rage? Never was he more loved.
Think you that, even had he let her go,

750 A flimsy pretext would not keep her here?
Take my advice. Shun her deceptive charms.
Do not abduct her, but for ever flee.
What! you will saddle your existence with
A fury who'll detest you till you die,
755 Regret a marriage just within her grasp,
Who . . .

ORESTES

This is why I *must* carry her off.
If not, then all would smile on her, while *I*
Would take with me only a futile rage,
And, far away, try to forget again.
760 No, I insist she share my agony.
I want no pity, no more lonely tears.
The heartless one must fear me in her turn,
And her unfeeling eyes, condemned to weep,
Must give me back the names I gave to them.

PYLADES

765 So this is how your embassy will end —
Orestes the abductor?

ORESTES

What of that?
Even if I managed to avenge our kings,
The ingrate would enjoy my tears no less.
And what avails me the applause of Greece
770 If I should be Epirus' laughing-stock?
What can I do? But to be frank with you,
My innocence begins to weigh on me.
I do not know what immemorial power
Leaves crime in peace, harasses innocence.
775 Wherever in my life I turn my eyes,
I see misfortunes that condemn the gods.
Let's justify their hate, deserve their wrath.
Let crime's reward precede its punishment.

76

But why will you, misguided one, deflect
On to yourself the anger meant for me.   780
Enough, too long, my friendship weighs you down.
Avoid a wretch, and shun a criminal.
Dear Pylades, whom pity leads astray,
Leave me these perils. All their fruits are mine.
This child that Pyrrhus yields, take to the Greeks.   785
Go off.

PYLADES

Come, we'll abduct Hermione.
In perils, courage shows its mettle. Sir,
What cannot friendship led by love achieve!
Let's go and fire the spirit of your Greeks.
Our ships are ready and the winds blow strong.   790
I know all the dark windings of this place;
The sea below us beats against its walls;
Tonight, without ado, a secret way
Aboard your vessels will conduct your prey.

ORESTES

Dear friend, I trespass on your friendship's zeal.   795
But pardon woes pitied by you alone.
Forgive a wretch who ruins all he loves.
Hated by everyone, who hates himself,
Why cannot I, if fortune smiles, repay... ?

PYLADES

Dissimulate, my lord. It's all I ask.   800
Be sure your plan does not leak out too soon.
Till then, forget Hermione's rebuffs.
Forget you love her. Ah! She's coming.

ORESTES
                                          Go.
Answer for her. I'll answer for myself.

77

ANDROMACHE

Scene Two

HERMIONE, ORESTES, CLEONE

ORESTES

805 Well, so my efforts give you back the king;
I've seen him, and the wedding will be soon.

HERMIONE

So it is said; I have, besides, just learned
You looked for me only to tell me so.

ORESTES

And you will not reject his homage now?

HERMIONE

810 Who would have thought he was not false to me,
His love would wait so long to kindle and
He would come back when I was leaving him?
I'll not contest your view he fears the Greeks.
He's swayed by passion less than interest,
815 And over you I ruled more sovereignly.

ORESTES

No, there's no doubt of it. It's you he loves.
Cannot your eyes do anything they want?
And you were not, doubtless, averse to him.

HERMIONE

What can I do, sir? I was pledged to him?
820 Shall I take back from him what others gave?
Can love decide a princess' destiny?
All we are left with is obedience' crown.
Yet I was ready to depart. You saw
How far I could make light of duty's laws.

ORESTES

825 Ah! cruel one, how well aware. . . . But all

Of us have freedom to bestow our heart;
Yours was your own. I hoped; but after all
You have conferred it without robbing me.
Hence I accuse yourself much less than fate.
But why importune you with my complaints?   830
Your duty is as you declare; mine is
To spare you a depressing interview.

Scene Three

HERMIONE, CLEONE

HERMIONE

Did you expect he would be so restrained?

CLEONE

Unspoken grief's all the more ominous.
I pity him. The more so, as he wrought   835
His own undoing. You need only count
The months since first the wedding was arranged.
Orestes speaks. Pyrrhus makes up his mind.

HERMIONE

Pyrrhus you think's afraid. Afraid of what?
Nations who fled from Hector ten long years,   840
Who, by Achilles' absence terrified,
Took to their burning vessels constantly,
And who would still, but for his mighty son,
Be asking Helen of unpunished Troy.
No, he's himself, and what he does he wills.   845
He marries me because he loves me. Let
Orestes choose to blame his woes on me.
Must we then talk of nothing but his tears?
Pyrrhus comes back to us, Cleone. Well,
Can you conceive my boundless happiness?   850
Know you who Pyrrhus is? Have you heard tell
Of his exploits? But who can count them all?

Fearless, with victory always in his train,
Enchanting, faithful too, the perfect knight.
855 Think of . . .

CLEONE

Dissimulate. Your rival comes
In tears to cast her sorrows at your feet.

HERMIONE

Heavens! Can I not revel in my joy?
Let's leave. What can I say to her?

Scene Four

ANDROMACHE, HERMIONE, CLEONE, CEPHISA

ANDROMACHE

You flee?
Lady, are you not gladdened by the sight
860 Of Hector's widow weeping at your knees?
I do not come to you with jealous tears
To envy you a heart that bows to you.
I saw a cruel hand alas! transfix
The only heart to which my looks aspired.
865 My love was lit by Hector long ago.
With him it's in the tomb imprisoned. But
A son is left to me. One day you'll know
To what extremes a mother's love will go.
But you will never know, at least I hope,
870 Into what anguish we are plunged for him,
When of so much that could rejoice our heart
It's all that's left and we're bereft of it.
Alas! When, tired of ten grim years of war,
The angry Trojans sought your mother's life,
875 I managed to enlist my Hector's aid.
You can win Pyrrhus now as I did him.
Why fear a child who lives when Hector's dead?
Let me conceal him in some desert isle.

His mother's efforts can be counted on;
With me my son will learn only to weep.   880

HERMIONE

I feel for you, but duty's stern command
Bids me be silent when my father speaks.
It's he who sets in motion Pyrrhus' wrath.
If Pyrrhus must be moved, who has more power
Than you? Your eyes have long reigned over him.   885
Make him declare his mind. I will subscribe.

Scene Five

ANDROMACHE, CEPHISA

ANDROMACHE

How her refusal breathes unfeeling scorn!

CEPHISA

Take her advice and go and see the king.
One look would rout Hermione and Greece.
But he himself is seeking you.   890

Scene Six

PYRRHUS, ANDROMACHE, PHOENIX, CEPHISA

PYRRHUS (*to Phoenix*)
                             Where is
Hermione? Did you not say she's here?

PHOENIX

I thought she was.

ANDROMACHE (*to Cephisa*)
                   See how my eyes prevail.

81

PYRRHUS (*to Phoenix*)
What is she saying?

ANDROMACHE
    All abandons me.
Alas!

PHOENIX
Come, Sire, follow Hermione.

CEPHISA
895 What are you waiting for? Silence is vain.

ANDROMACHE
He's sworn to yield my son.

CEPHISA
     But has not yet.

ANDROMACHE
No. What avail my tears? His death's resolved.

PYRRHUS
Will she not deign at least to look on us?
What pride!

ANDROMACHE
    I only make him angrier.
900 I'll leave.

PYRRHUS (*to Phoenix*)
   Come, let us give up Hector's son
To Greece.

ANDROMACHE
   Ah! stop, my lord. What would you do?
If you give up my son, give me up too.

Just now you swore such friendship to me. God!
Can I not touch your clemency at least?
Am I beyond forgiveness, then, condemned?　　　　905

PYRRHUS

Phoenix will tell you. I have given my word.

ANDROMACHE

You who were going to defy for me
So many perils.

PYRRHUS

　　　　　I was blind. My eyes
Are opened now. I would have spared his life
For you. But you did not even ask for it.　　　　910
The die is cast.

ANDROMACHE

　　　　　Ah! sir, you understand
Only too well the sighs that feared rebuff.
Forgive this remnant of my glorious past –
A noble pride that is ashamed to beg.
You know that, but for you, Andromache　　　　915
Would never have embraced a master's knee.

PYRRHUS

No, no. You hate me. In your heart of hearts,
You fear to be indebted to my love.
This very son of yours you cherish so,
If saved by me, would be less dear to you.　　　　920
Hatred, contempt, against me all unite.
You hate me more than all the Greeks combined.
Enjoy at leisure such a noble wrath.
Come, Phoenix.

ANDROMACHE

　　　　　Come, let us rejoin my lord.

CEPHISA

925 Lady . . .

ANDROMACHE (*to Cephisa*)
What more am I to say to him?
Author of my mishaps, he knows them all.

(*to Pyrrhus*)
My lord, see what you have reduced me to.
I've seen my father dead, our walls in flames.
I've seen my kinsmen – all – put to the sword,
930 My husband's bleeding corpse dragged in the dust,
His son alone surviving – but in chains.
Yet for this son I have lived on, a slave.
Indeed sometimes I have consoled myself
That fate exiled me here and not elsewhere,
935 That happily the son of hapless kings
Should, since he must become a slave, be yours.
I thought his prison might become a haven.
Priam's entreaties won Achilles' ear.
I looked for even more kindness from his son.
940 Forgive, dear Hector, my credulity!
I thought your foe incapable of crime;
Despite himself, I thought him generous.
Ah! if at least he'd suffer us to stay
Beside the tomb my love has built for you,
945 And, ending thus his hatred and our woes,
He'd reunite in death two loving hearts!

PYRRHUS
I shall rejoin you, Phoenix.

Scene Seven
PYRRHUS, ANDROMACHE, CEPHISA

PYRRHUS
Lady, stay.
You still may save this son you weep for. Yes,

I fear that, by provoking you to tears,
I merely give you arms against myself.   950
I thought I came here fired with greater hate.
But, lady, turn on me your eyes at least.
Are my looks those of an unbending judge,
Or of a foe who seeks your enmity?
Why do you force me to betray your cause?   955
In your son's name, let's cease this mutual hate.
It's I who conjure you to rescue him.
Must I then plead with you to spare his life?
Must I on his behalf embrace your knees?
For the last time, save him and save yourself.   960
I know what vows I sever for your sake,
What hatred I am calling down on me.
I send Hermione away and set
No crown on her, but everlasting shame.
I lead you to the temple decked for *her*.   965
I place her marriage circlet on your brow.
But this is not an offer you can still
Reject. I tell you you must die or reign.
Despairing of a year's ingratitude,
My heart can bear no more uncertainty.   970
I've had enough of fears and threats and groans.
I die if I undo you; if I wait,
I die. Think well. I leave you. I will come
To take you to the temple where this son
Must be. And there, subdued or wild with rage,   975
Crown you or doom the boy before your eyes.

Scene Eight

ANDROMACHE, CEPHISA

CEPHISA

I told you, lady, that, despite the Greeks,
You would again be mistress of your fate.

ANDROMACHE

Alas! you see the outcome of your words.
980 I had no choice but to condemn my son.

CEPHISA

Lady, you carry faithfulness too far.
Excess of virtue may amount to crime.
Even your husband would advice restraint.

ANDROMACHE

What! give him Pyrrhus as successor? No.

CEPHISA

985 So wills your son whom the Greeks wrest from you.
Think you that, after all, his shade will blush,
Or that he'd scorn a king victorious
Who re-exalts you to your forebears' rank,
Who spurns for you your angry conquerors,
990 Who has forgot he is Achilles' son,
Belies his exploits, makes them meaningless?

ANDROMACHE

Shall I forget these deeds if he does not?
Shall I forget Hector's unburied corpse
Dragged in dishonour round our walls? Shall I
995 Forget his father crumpling at my feet,
Reddening the altar that his arms embraced?
Cephisa, call to mind that cruel night
Which was perpetual night for all our race;
Imagine Pyrrhus as, with flaming eyes,
1000 His path lit by our burning palaces,
He forged a way o'er my dead brothers and
He spurred his men to carnage, dripping blood;
List to the victors shout, the dying shriek,
Choked by the flames, slain by the sword; and see
1005 In this inferno crazed Andromache.
This is how Pyrrhus first appeared to me.

These are the deeds by which he crowned himself;
This is the husband that you offer me!
No, I'll not be his crimes' accomplice. Let
Him take us as his final victims if   1010
He wishes it, and put my wrath in chains.

CEPHISA

Then let us go and see your son expire.
They only wait for you. You shudder.

ANDROMACHE

                                            Ah!
With what a memory you strike my soul,
Cephisa! What! to go and see expire   1015
My son, dear Hector's image, my sole joy!
This son he left me as his passion's pledge!
Ah! I recall, the day his daring soul
Made him seek out Achilles, seek out death,
He asked to see his son and took him in   1020
His arms. 'Dear wife,' he said, drying my tears,
'I know not what may lie in store for me.
I leave my son as token of my troth,
And, if he loses me, he must in you
Find me again. If happiness was ours,   1025
Then show my son how dear I was to you.'
How can I see such precious blood be shed,
And all his glorious forebears die with him?
Must, barbarous king, my crime involve him too?
I hate you. Am I then to blame for that?   1030
Has he reproached you with his kinsmen's death?
Has he complained of ills he does not feel?
But yet, my son, you die unless I stop
The sword the cruel one holds poised to strike.
I could, and yet I offer you to it.   1035
You shall not die. I cannot suffer it.
Let's seek out Pyrrhus. Dear Cephisa, no,
You go and find him.

87

CEPHISA

But what must I say?

ANDROMACHE

That for my son my love is strong enough. . . .
1040 Think you that Pyrrhus' heart has sworn his death?
Can love be guilty of such barbarousness?

CEPHISA

He'll soon come back raging with fury.

ANDROMACHE

Well,
Go and assure him.

CEPHISA

That your troth is his?

ANDROMACHE

Alas! is it still mine to promise him?
1045 O ashes of my husband, father, Troy!
My son, how dear your mother buys your life!
I go. . . .

CEPHISA

Where, lady? What have you resolved?

ANDROMACHE

I shall consult my husband at his tomb.

ACT FOUR

Scene One
ANDROMACHE, CEPHISA

CEPHISA

Ah! there's no doubt of it. It is your lord,
Hector, who's worked this miracle in you.   1050
Troy, with this fortune-favoured son he has
Preserved for you, he wishes to restore.
Pyrrhus has sworn. You heard him speak yourself.
He waited only for a word from you.
But trust his raptures. Father, sceptre, crown,   1055
Content with you, he lays them at your feet.
He makes you sovereign of himself, his land.
Is that this victor who deserves your hate?
Already, full of anger at the Greeks,
He's as concerned about your son as you.   1060
Their fury he forestalls, leaves him his guard.
He hazards his own life to shield the boy.
The temple's ready, and you've given your word.

ANDROMACHE

I shall be there. But now I'll see my son.

CEPHISA

What is the urgency? Is't not enough   1065
That henceforth he will not be kept from you?
Soon you can lavish tenderness on him,
Nor have to count each time you kiss him. Ah!
What joy to rear a child who's growing up
No longer for his master as a slave,   1070
But as the heir of a long line of kings!

ANDROMACHE

Cephisa, let us go. For the last time
I'll look on him.

CEPHISA

God!

ANDROMACHE

O my dear Cephisa!
From you I never have concealed my heart.
1075 You have been faithful in my darkest days.
But I believed you knew me better. What!
Did you believe Andromache could be
False to a husband who relives in her;
And, stirring up the grief of countless dead,
1080 I'd gain my peace of mind by troubling theirs?
Is that the love I promised to his shade?
But his son would have died. I had to act.
By wedding me, Pyrrhus becomes his shield.
That is enough. I'll place my trust in him.
1085 I know my Pyrrhus, headstrong but sincere;
Cephisa, he'll do more than he has sworn.
I still count on the anger of the Greeks.
Their hate will give a father to my son.
And so, since I must sacrifice myself,
1090 I'll pledge to Pyrrhus my remaining days.
When he has made his marriage vows to me,
I'll bind him to my son by deathless bonds.
But then my hand, striking myself alone,
Will end my life and faithlessness, and thus,
1095 Saving my honour, pay what is my due
To Pyrrhus, to my son, my lord and me.
This is the innocent trick my love's devised,
And what my lord himself has ordered me.
I go to Hector and my ancestors
1100 Alone. Cephisa, it's for you to close my eyes.

CEPHISA

Ah! lady, do not ask me to survive. . . .

ANDROMACHE

No, you must not, Cephisa, follow me.
My only treasure I entrust to you.
You lived for me. Live on for Hector's son.
In you alone the Trojans place their hope.   1105
How many future kings have need of you!
Watch over Pyrrhus. Make him keep his word.
If need be, you may talk to him of me,
And stress the marriage I submitted to;
Say I was pledged to him before my death.   1110
But his resentment must be quenched. I showed
Enough esteem by leaving him my son.
Make him admire the heroes of his race,
And try to make him follow in their steps.
Tell him by what exploits they won renown;   1115
Rather what they have done than what they've been.
Relate each day his father's virtues, and
Speak to him sometimes of his mother too.
But let him think no more of our revenge.
He'll have a master. He must humour him,   1120
And not be boastful of his ancestors.
My Hector lives in him, but him alone.
And I myself, for him, in this one day,
Have sacrificed my blood, my hate, my love.

CEPHISA

Alas!   1125

ANDROMACHE

Follow me not, although your heart
Foresees it cannot check its urge to weep.
Someone is coming. Hide your tears. Recall
My fate is in your hands. Hermione
Is here. Let us avoid her temper. Quick.

Scene Two

HERMIONE, CLEONE

CLEONE

1130 No, by this silence I'm astounded. What!
Your lips say nothing, and his cruel scorn
Has not upset your spirits in the least.
You bear unflinchingly this onset. *You*,
Who shuddered at Andromache's mere name,
1135 *You*, who were plunged in bottomless despair
If Pyrrhus deigned to cast a glance at her.
He weds her, gives her, with the diadem,
The troth that you yourself had just received;
And yet your lips, mute to catastrophe,
1140 Have not even opened to complain of him.
Ah! how I fear so ominous a calm!
And how much better . . .

HERMIONE

　　　　　　　　　Have you sent for him?

CLEONE

Orestes comes. He comes. And you will judge
How eagerly he wished to kneel to you,
1145 Always disposed to serve for no reward;
Your eyes are all too sure of dazzling him.
But there he is. . . .

Scene Three

ORESTES, HERMIONE, CLEONE

ORESTES

　　　　Ah! is it true for once
I do your bidding when I come to you?
And by a flattering hope am not deceived?

Did you then really wish my company?　　　　1150
Should I believe your eyes, at last disarmed,
Will . . .

HERMIONE
I would know whether you love me still.

ORESTES
Whether I love you? God! My perjuries,
My insults, my addresses, flight, return,
And my despair, my ever-weeping eyes –　　　1155
What witness will you credit, if not these?

HERMIONE
Avenge me. I'll believe it all.

ORESTES
　　　　　　　Then come.
Let us once more inflame the whole of Greece;
Blazon my valour and your name, and take,
I Agamemnon's and you Helen's place;　　　1160
And in this land revive Troy's sufferings.
People shall talk of us as of our sires.
Let us set out. I'm ready.

HERMIONE
　　　　　　　No, let's stay.
I will not carry vile affronts so far.
Shall I, crowning my foes' base insolence,　　　1165
Go off and wait for slow revenge elsewhere,
Rely on battle as my arbiter,
And in the end perhaps stay unavenged?
I wish to leave Epirus mourning. But,
If you avenge me, do so in an hour.　　　1170
To put me off is to refuse me. Haste.
Haste to the temple. Sacrifice. . . .

ORESTES
　　　　　　　Whom?

HERMIONE

Pyrrhus.

ORESTES

What! Pyrrhus?

HERMIONE

Ah! your hate already flags.
Be quick and go. Fear lest I call you back.
1175 Do not advance rights that I would forget,
Or seek to justify him in my eyes.

ORESTES

What! *I* excuse him? Ah! your kindnesses
Have graven his crimes too deep into my soul.
Avenge ourselves. Yes, but by other ways.
1180 Let's be his foes and not his murderers.
His downfall can be worked by conquest. Must
I bear the Greeks his head as my reply?
Have I assumed a mission for the state
Only by murder to discharge it? No.
1185 In the gods' name, let Greece set forth its case.
Let him succumb under the nation's hate.
Remember that the head that bears the crown . . .

HERMIONE

Is't not enough that I pronounce his doom?
And is it not enough my sullied name
1190 Asks for a victim meant for me alone,
That he who kills a tyrant wins my hand,
That I detest him, that I loved him once?
I'll not deny it. He had won my heart.
Whether my love or father so ordained,
1195 No matter. But be guided by my words.
Despite my feelings shamefully deceived,
Despite the horror that his crime inspires,
While still he lives, fear lest I pardon him.

Suspect my wavering anger till his death.
Tomorrow I may love him if today   1200
He dies not.

ORESTES

    Well, he must be slain before
You pardon him. He must. . . . What must I do?
How can I minister so quickly to
Your anger, how direct my blows to him?
Here in Epirus I have just arrived.   1205
You wish an empire overthrown by me.
You wish a king to die, and, for his death,
A day, an hour, a moment's all you give.
He must be slain before his people's eyes.
Let me escort my victim to the shrine.   1210
I shall resist no more. I only wish
To reconnoitre where to work his doom.
This night I'll act. This night I'll strike him down.

HERMIONE

Meanwhile today he weds Andromache.
The throne's already in the temple raised.   1215
My shame is published, and his crime complete.
What need you more? He offers you his head.
Defenceless to his wedding rite he goes.
Round Hector's son, Pyrrhus arrays his guards.
He's free for an avenging arm to slay.   1220
Will you, despite him, try to shield his life?
Arm with your Greeks all those who've followed me.
Muster your friends. All mine support our cause.
He's false to me, deceives us, scorns us all.
But even now their hate's as fierce as mine;   1225
They're loath to spare a Trojan woman's lord.
Speak. For my enemy can not escape.
Or rather you need only let them strike.
Direct or follow this fine frenzy; and
Come back all covered with the ingrate's blood.   1230
Go. When it's done, be certain of my heart.

ORESTES

But think before you . . .

HERMIONE

Ah! this is too much.
My anger baulks at all this reasoning.
I wished to give your love for me a chance,
1235 To make Orestes happy, but I see
He's undeserving. He can but complain.
Go then. Boast of your constancy elsewhere,
And leave me here to take my own revenge.
My heart's ashamed of its base kindnesses,
1240 And in one day I've been refused too much.
I will, alone, go to their wedding where
You will not venture, to obtain my hand.
There I'll succeed to find a way to him.
I'll pierce the heart that I could never move.
1245 My bleeding hands will, turned against myself,
At once, despite him, link our destinies;
And, ingrate that he is, I would prefer
To die with Pyrrhus than to live with you.

ORESTES

No, I'll deprive you of that baleful joy.
1250 He'll perish by Orestes' hand alone.
It's *I* who'll sacrifice your foes to you,
And you may crown my service if you wish.

HERMIONE

Go. Of your destiny let me be guide;
And all your ships be ready for our flight.

Scene Four

HERMIONE, CLEONE

CLEONE

1255 But this will be your downfall. You should think . . .

96

HERMIONE

Downfall or not, I will avenge myself.
I'm not even sure, despite his promises,
If I should trust in others but myself.
For Pyrrhus' guilt is less to him than me,
And I can strike with surer hand than he.   1260
What pleasure to avenge my slight myself,
Withdraw my arm, stained with the false one's blood,
And, to increase my pleasure and his pain,
To hide my rival from his dying eyes.
Ah! let at least Orestes, slaying him,   1265
Bring home to him I was behind the blow.
Find him. Tell him to let the ingrate know
He's sacrificed to *me*, not to the state.
Run, dear Cleone. My revenge is lost
Unless he knows it's I who strike him down.   1270

CLEONE

I shall obey you, lady, but what's this?
O God! who would have thought it? It's the king.

HERMIONE

Ah! overtake Orestes. Order him
To make no move without consulting me.

Scene Five

PYRRHUS, HERMIONE, PHOENIX

PYRRHUS

My call was unexpected. It is clear   1275
That my arrival interrupted you.
I do not come with shabby artifice
To cloak with fairness my injurious deeds.
I need but listen to my conscience' voice.
I have no art to brazen falsehood out.   1280

97

I take a Trojan wife, yes, and admit
I promised you the troth I vow to her.
It might be claimed that, on the plains of Troy,
Our fathers in our absence forged those bonds,
1285 And that, without consulting you or me,
They made a match in which love played no part.
But I agreed to it. I'll say no more.
By my ambassadors my heart was pledged.
Far from disowning, I endorsed their act.
1290 You landed in Epirus with them, and,
Though the victorious light of other eyes
Had worked before I felt the power of yours,
I did not cling to my new passion. I
Tried to preserve my constancy to you.
1295 You were received as queen, and, till this hour,
I thought my vow would take the place of love.
But love has won the day, and, unkind fate,
Andromache conquers a heart she loathes!
We sweep each other to the altar where
1300 We'll pledge, despite ourselves, eternal love.
Now then, explode against a traitor's heart
Which errs in anguish but errs willingly.
Far from inhibiting your wrath, explode;
It will perhaps ease me as much as you.
1305 Hurl at me all the names for perjurers.
I fear your silence, not your insults, and
A thousand secret witnesses within
Will tell me all the more the less you say.

HERMIONE

In this confession, void of artifice,
1310 At least you do full justice to yourself,
And, firmly bent to break this solemn bond,
You take to crime, sir, as a criminal.
Why should a conqueror stoop, after all,
To keep his word, as slaves are bound to do?
1315 No, perfidy appeals to you, and, if
You sought me out, it was to boast of it.

What! blind to oath and duty, though you love
A Trojan, yet you seek a Grecian's hand!
You leave me, take me back, return again
From Helen's child to Hector's widow. Sir,   1320
To crown a princess and a slave in turn,
Sacrifice Troy to Greece and Greece to Troy,
That shows a heart that's master of itself,
A hero who's not bondsman to his word.
To please your wife, I should perhaps be free   1325
With the sweet names of villain, perjurer.
You came to note the pallor of my brow,
And rush into her arms to mock my grief.
You want me, weeping, to her chariot bound,
But for one day *that* would be too much joy.   1330
Need you seek titles borrowed from elsewhere?
Are not the ones you bear enough for you?
Hector's old father, struck down at the feet
Of his own kin, dying before their eyes,
While your keen sword, deep in his breast, extracts   1335
A trickle of the blood that age has chilled;
In streams of blood Troy's blazing towers plunged,
Polyxenes slaughtered by your own hand
Before the host of the indignant Greeks:
Can aught to such great exploits be denied?   1340

PYRRHUS

I know too well to what excess of rage
Vengeance for Helen carried me away.
I could reproach you with the blood I've shed,
But I am willing to forget the past.
I thank the gods that your indifference   1345
Proves my requited passion innocent.
My heart I see's too scrupulous. It should
Have known you better, better judged itself.
And my remorse offends you mortally.
Where love is not, there's no unfaithfulness.   1350

1343 Pyrrhus could reproach Hermione for Troy since she was Helen's
daughter.

You did not wish to keep me in your chains.
I feared to err. Perhaps I did your will.
Our hearts were not for one another made.
I did my duty. You gave way to yours.
1355 To love me there was no compelling force.

HERMIONE

I did not love you? What then have I done?
For you I scorned the hand of all our kings.
I sought you out myself, deep in your realm.
I still am there despite your faithlessness
1360 And my indulgence which offends the Greeks.
I bid them hide the outrage done to me.
I waited for a perjurer's return.
I thought that, hearkening to duty's call,
One day you'd bring me back a heart that's mine.
1365 I loved you wayward. Faithful, what would I
Have done? Even this instant when I hear
Your cruel lips so calmly speak my doom,
I doubt whether I do not love you still.
But, if it must be so, if the angry heavens
1370 To others grant the glory of your love,
Conclude, my lord, your wedding, but at least
You need not call on me to witness it.
For the last time perhaps I speak to you.
Wait for a day. You will be master then.
1375 You answer not. False-hearted one, I see
You count the moments that you lose with me.
Impatient to rejoin your Trojan love,
You find all others' words grate on your ear.
Your heart communes with her. Your eyes seek hers.
1380 I'll not detain you any more. Be off.
Go. Swear to her the troth you swore to me.
Profane the high gods' sacred majesty;
Those gods, those righteous gods will not forget
That the same vows to *me* united you.
1385 Bear to the shrine this heart that's false to me.
Go. Haste. But fear lest you should find me there.

Scene Six

PYRRHUS, PHOENIX

PHOENIX

My lord, you hear. You cannot disregard
The fury of a proud, revengeful heart.
Her faction here is all too powerful.
Her cause and that of all the Greeks are one.   1390
Orestes loves her still. Perhaps her price . . .

PYRRHUS

Andromache awaits me. Guard her son.

ACT FIVE

Scene One
HERMIONE (*alone*)

HERMIONE

What have I done? What shall I do? Where am I?
What pain devours me? What comes over me?
1395 I wander in the palace aimlessly.
Can I not know whether I love or hate?
How cruelly he cast me off without
A trace of feeling or even feignèd grief.
Did he turn pale or pity me at all?
1400 Could I extract from him a single groan?
Mute to my sighs, unmoved by my distress,
Did he even in the slightest mark my tears?
And I still pity him, and, crowning woe,
My heart, my craven heart, takes sides with him!
1405 I quake to think of the impending blow,
And, thirsting for revenge, I pardon him.
No, I will not revoke my anger's doom.
So let him die! In any case, for us
He lives no more. He triumphs, mocks my rage.
1410 He thinks the tempest will dissolve in tears;
That, always weak and wavering in my heart,
I with one hand will stop the other's blows.
He judges me by favours past. But no,
The villain's thoughts are of a different cast.
1415 In triumph at the altar, what cares he
Whether I wish his life or death elsewhere?
This ghastly choice the ingrate leaves to me.
I say again: No, let Orestes act.
And let him die, since he must have foreseen
1420 The blow, and forced me into willing it.

Willing it? What! It's *I* who order it?
His death will be the outcome of my love?
This king whose exploits, once upon a time,
My ravished ear could not be sated with,
To whom my heart felt it was destined, even   1425
Before my fateful wedding was arranged,
This king, I've traversed all these lands and seas,
Come from so far, but to prepare his death,
Murder, undo him! Ah! before his death . . .

Scene Two

HERMIONE, CLEONE

HERMIONE

What have I done, Cleone? What would you   1430
Report? Is Pyrrhus . . .

CLEONE

        He's the happiest
And proudest man and the most deep in love.
I saw him to the wedding at the shrine
Lead his new conquest with a conqueror's mien.
And, with an eye shining with joy and hope,   1435
Drink in her beauty as he walked with her.
Andromache midst endless shouts of joy
Even to the altar bears the memory
Of Troy; still beyond hate and love, she seems
Joyless and unprotesting to obey.   1440

HERMIONE

And Pyrrhus, was he brazen to the last?
But did you carefully observe his face?
Did he enjoy perfect and tranquil bliss?
Did he not to the palace turn his eyes?
Tell me, did you not show yourself to him?   1445
Did he not blush on recognizing you,

ANDROMACHE

And thus confess his infidelity?
Did to the very end he stay composed?

CLEONE

He's blind to all. His safety and renown
1450 Seem to have fled his memory with you.
Heedless who follows him – subject or foe –
He listens only to the thoughts of love.
Round Hector's son he has arrayed his guard,
And thinks the boy alone is threatened. Him
1455 Phoenix must answer for; he has been placed
By the king's orders in a distant fort.
This in his rapture is his one concern.

HERMIONE

He'll die. What did Orestes say to you?

CLEONE

He with his Greeks entered the temple.

HERMIONE

                                    Well!
1460 And to avenge me is he not prepared?

CLEONE

I know not.

HERMIONE

                You know not? Orestes, too,
Betrays me?

CLEONE

            No, Orestes worships you;
But, with a thousand doubts his mind assailed,
Now heeds his love and now his honour. He
1465 Reveres the crown in Pyrrhus, and reveres
In him Achilles' fame, Pyrrhus himself.

He fears the Greeks; he fears the whole world's wrath.
He fears, he says, himself above all else.
He would in triumph bring you Pyrrhus' head,
But the mere name of murder holds him back.   1470
Finally he went in, uncertain if
He'd come out guilty or an onlooker.

HERMIONE

No, he will not oppose this triumph. He
Will take good care not to disturb this scene;
I know with what remorse his soul is filled.   1475
The coward heart fears death, and only death.
What! without uttering a single word,
My mother roused the whole of Greece to arms.
In ten long years of war she saw for her
Perish a score of kings she did not know.   1480
And all I ask is that a traitor die,
And charge a suitor to redress my wrong.
He wins me without danger at that price.
My hand I offer, yet am not avenged,
Who can do justice for me? I alone.   1485
With cries of grief the temple shall resound.
We'll mar this fateful wedding's outcome, and
Their union shall, if possible, be brief.
I'll strike out blindly in a frenzied rage.
All, even Orestes, will be Pyrrhus for   1490
My hand. I'll die, but die at least avenged,
Nor die alone. Someone will follow me.

Scene Three

ORESTES, HERMIONE, CLEONE

ORESTES

Lady, it's over, and your will is done.
False Pyrrhus at the altar breathes his last.

HERMIONE

1495 He's dead?

ORESTES

He's dying, and our angry Greeks
Have in his blood washed out his faithlessness.
I swore to do so, and, although my heart
Was haunted by the horror of this plot,
I hastened to the temple where our Greeks
1500 Stole to the altar mingling with the crowd.
Pyrrhus caught sight of me, but did not flinch.
Indeed, it seemed I fired his recklessness,
And, flouted in their envoy, all the Greeks
Should but enhance the splendour of the scene.
1505 With rapture taking up the diadem,
He placed it on Andromache himself.
'I give to you,' he said, 'my crown, my troth.
Andromache, reign o'er this land and me.
I will ensure your son a father's care;
1510 The gods are witness of this oath to you.
I here acknowledge all his foes as mine,
And recognize him as the Trojans' king.'
But to these words, which roused the people's cheers,
Our Greeks' sole answer was a cry of rage.
1515 The king was soon besieged on every side,
And I could find no place to strike at him.
They all contended for the final blow.
I saw him struggle with them for a time,
Covered with blood, try to avoid their blows;
1520 But, near the altar, in the end he fell.
I crossed the horror-stricken, surging crowd
To come and carry off my princess, and
Regain the port where soon my friends will come,
Bespattered with the blood I promised you.

HERMIONE

1525 What have they done?

106

ORESTES

Forgive their hastiness.
They have, I see, betrayed your vengeance. You
Wanted my hand to be the first to strike,
And him to feel he died because of you.
But it was I whose ardour spurred them on.
I swept them to the altar for your sake,   1530
And you may rightly pride yourself upon
A death their arm has merely carried out.
You alone dealt the blows. . . .

HERMIONE

Be silent, wretch,
And for this craven murder bear the blame.
Go and parade your fury to the Greeks.   1535
Go, I disown you. You revolt me. Go.
What have you done, barbarian? What mad rage
Made you cut off such splendour in its prime?
How could you sacrifice him, cruel men,
And all your blood not rise on his behalf?   1540
But speak. Who gave you power to seal his doom?
Why did you murder him? What did he do?
Who told you to?

ORESTES

God! did not you yourself
Here, one short hour ago, ordain his death?

HERMIONE

Ah! how could you believe my frantic words?   1545
And should you not have read my inmost thoughts?
Did you not see in my distraction that
My heart belied my mouth at every turn?
Even if I wanted, should you have obeyed,
And not made me repeat it endlessly?   1550
Yourself, before you struck, consult me, and

107

Return again, or rather shun my sight.
Why did you not let me avenge myself?
What brings you here where people flee from you?
1555 This is the cursèd outcome of your love.
You brought the evil star that shines on you.
It's you whose mission, fatal to us both,
Made him prefer my rival, for his doom.
Between us he would still have shared his heart;
1560 Loved me perhaps, at least pretend he did.
Farewell. You may depart. Here I will stay.
I'll have no more of Greece, or Sparta, or
My family, and it's enough for me
That it's produced a monster such as you.

Scene Four

ORESTES (*alone*)

ORESTES

1565 What do I see? Is this Hermione?
For whom then flows the blood that I have shed?
If she speaks true, I am a murderer.
Am I Orestes? Is it Pyrrhus who
Has died? I stifle reason in my heart.
1570 I slay unwillingly a king revered.
I violate in one same day the rights
Of sovereigns, envoys, those of men, and even
Those of the altar where he was besieged.
I am a sacrilegious murderer, regicide.
1575 For whom? An ingrate whom I promise him,
Who'll never see me more even if he lives,
Whose frenzy I've embraced, and, when I've done
Her will, she bids me give her back his life.
She loves him. I am but a maddened brute.
1580 I see her go for ever from my sight,
And, as she flees, she gives me as reward
All the foul names I earned to conquer her.

Scene Five

ORESTES, PYLADES, Orestes' soldiers

PYLADES

Sir, we must go. Let's flee this palace or
Resign ourselves not to emerge alive.
Our Greeks till now defend the palace gates.   1585
The populace pursues us, arm in hand.
Everything here bows to Andromache.
She is their queen, and we their enemies.
And she herself, so heartless to the king,
Renders him all a faithful widow's dues,   1590
Commands them to avenge him, and perhaps
Seeks to avenge Hector and Troy on us.
Let's leave, or we shall be surrounded. Quick!
Our Greeks will join us while Hermione
Still rivets the attention of the mob.   1595
This is your way. Our safety lies in flight.

ORESTES

No, it's Hermione I'll follow, friends.
I shan't survive her last decree. Depart.
The crime is mine. I shall atone for it.

PYLADES

Hermione! you must forget her, sir.   1600
What! still the tool and object of her rage.
Seek you some new affront among the dead?
Because she dies, must then you die with her?

ORESTES

She's dying? Heavens!

PYLADES

                    What! you did not know?
Returning here, we met Hermione   1605
Running towards the temple, wild, distraught.

She came on Pyrrhus, by the soldiers borne,
Whose blood inflamed them to avenge his death.
At sight of him, her frenzy was aroused,
1610 And, from our vantage point, we witnessed her,
A dagger in her hand, bend o'er the king,
Lift her eyes heavenward, stab herself and fall.

ORESTES

The gods be thanked! My woes exceed my hopes.
I praise you, heavens, for your perseverance.
1615 Resolved relentlessly to punish me,
They've raised me to new heights of suffering.
Your hate has joyed in shaping my mishaps.
Yes, I was born to illustrate your wrath,
To be the model of misfortune. Well,
1620 I die contented, and my fate's fulfilled.
Where are these lovers dead? To crown my bliss,
I long to wallow in their blood and mine.
Dying, I want to look on both of them.
Let's join three hearts that could not find accord.
1625 But what thick darkness, sudden, wraps me round?
Where lies escape? Why do I shudder? What
Black horror seizes me? Thank heaven, I glimpse . . .
Great God! What streams of blood flow all around?

PYLADES

Ah! sir.

ORESTES

What! Pyrrhus, so we meet again.
1630 I find my hated rival everywhere.
Pierced through and through, why are you still alive?
Take this! Here is the blow I kept for you.
But what! Hermione embraces him.
She comes to snatch him from the jaws of death.
1635 Great God! What fearful looks she darts at me!
What snakes, what demons follow in her wake?
Daughters of Hades, are you ready now?

For whom these snakes that hiss above your head?
For whom this retinue that follows you?
Come you to bear me off to endless night?   1640
Come, to your rage Orestes yields himself.
Withdraw, and leave it to Hermione.
More savagely than you she'll rend her prey.
I bring my heart. She can devour it now.

PYLADES

He lies unconscious. Now time presses, friends   1645
Let's use the respite that his seizure lends –
To save him. All our efforts would be vain
If frenzy grips him, when he wakes, again.

BRITANNICUS
A Tragedy

INTRODUCTION TO *BRITANNICUS*

With *Andromache* Racine had arrived. But he had not succeeded in making a dent in the prestige of his firmly entrenched rival, Corneille. The partisans of the older playwright
shrugged off the furore over Racine's tragedy by hinting that
the young man might make a hit by portraying passions in the
raw. He could never hope to compete with the master in the
more elevated realm of higher politics, which for the age was
almost synonymous with Roman history.

Stung by the taunt, Racine, sensitive as ever, challenged
Corneille on his own ground. In 1669, after steeping himself
in Tacitus,* he staged *Britannicus*, his first Roman play, and
to ensure that it would stand comparison with his rival's
works, he spared no pains in composing it. Perhaps it is
precisely for this reason that the play lacks the seemingly
effortless fire and mastery of *Andromache*. His genius and
orientation had not entirely absorbed the new material and
technique. Critics havet ermed it 'opaque' and contrived,
marked, by an excessive concern to drag in all the right
historical echoes and references.

The truth is perhaps that, venturing on to the thin ice of
a type of tragedy in which Corneille and Cornelian values
dominated the scene, Racine either did not dare to shape the
work entirely in accordance with his own ideas, or was still
groping his way towards a formula which would reflect them.
The result, as Butler in his *Classicisme et baroque* has so clearly
demonstrated, is a perpetual clash between an ethos ostensibly
lauded in the play and the one built into the fabric of the

* The previous year, Racine had produced, not his usual tragedy, but a
comedy – *The Litigants*. This is a highly amusing but brittle and rather
ferocious comedy, worlds removed from the light-hearted exuberance of
most of Molière's work. It is entirely in line with Louis XIV's efforts at
the time to reform the cumbersome and corrupt apparatus of justice, and
received the monarch's explicit support.

action. Nowhere is this ambiguity more visible than in the case of the main character himself – the youthful Nero.

The situation as the curtain rises is, as in all of Racine's plays, a crisis which is coming to a head. Nero and his mother, Agrippina, are about to meet head on in a struggle for power. The opening scene shows her, alone and unescorted, at the door of Nero's apartment in the early hours of the morning, waiting for the chance to snatch an interview with her son, the emperor. She is clearly out of favour. Yet it was she who, by a horrifying accumulation of crimes, had placed him on the throne, thus displacing Britannicus, the son of the previous ruler Claudius. For the first two years after his accession, Nero had allowed his mother to wield power, but, as popular discontent grew, he had gradually emancipated himself. He is now on the point of taking over. In particular, he is careful not to grant her a private audience, and his closed door symbolizes Agrippina's fall from grace. The motif recurs insistently throughout the play.

Nero refuses to accord the interview. What is more, he has ordered the abduction of June, the fiancée of the previous heir, Britannicus, although it is Agrippina who had given this engagement her blessing.* As the play moves on, it emerges that, to retain her power, Agrippina is intriguing with Britannicus, and the threat to Nero's position becomes clear when he falls in love with June and provokes an outburst of hatred from his rival. Nero decides to take drastic action. He pretends to be reconciled with his mother, grants her an interview, but immediately after confesses to his adviser, Burrus, that he intends to do away with Britannicus, since

While still he breathes, I'm only half alive. (1317)

Horrified, Burrus entreats him to retract, and succeeds. But Narcissus, Nero's confidant, in his turn forces a reversal of this decision, and the play comes to a climax with the poisoning of the wretched Britannicus at a banquet given ostensibly

* In fact, the battle with Agrippina and Britannicus was joined over Aete, a young freedwoman, but, by using June as his starting-point, Racine was able to make the action more taut.

to celebrate the renewal of friendship between the two princes.

The impression created from the outset is that of a youth who, in Racine's own words, is 'becoming a monster', an impression underlined by Agrippina's emphasis on Nero's dubious ancestry on his paternal side:

> The fierce Domitians' wild and sombre mood. (36)

The trait is significant in view of Racine's constant emphasis on hereditary factors. As the play develops, the young emperor is shown in a more and more unfavourable light. The political motives excusing, or at least attenuating, the gravity of the abduction are only hinted at, for example in Agrippina's conjecture (line 58) that the move may be designed to punish June and Britannicus for her support of them. And, when Nero falls in love with June immediately on seeing her arrive at the palace under armed guard, the audience may be excused for imagining that he is merely indulging an amorous caprice which he is using his tyrannical power to satisfy. The traditional picture of the imperial sadist is even more obvious when he tortures June by making her feign indifference to Britannicus while he himself looks on and revels in the sight from his hiding place. The burst of virtuousness induced by Burrus' pathetic appeal not to murder Britannicus is short-lived. Nero's resistance yields rapidly under the insinuating pressure of the villainous Narcissus, and the circle is completed by his callous indifference to Britannicus' death and by the impassioned prophecy of his mother, unfolding a catalogue of the excesses to which the tyrant will be driven by the pangs of remorse and despair, until in the end he will be forced to shed his own blood (1690).

Morality, it would seem, is fully satisfied, particularly since the wicked Narcissus is torn to pieces by the crowd when he tries to stop June from taking refuge with the Vestal Virgins. Against the perverted emperor with his evil genius Narcissus are set the honest and virtuous Burrus and the touching couple of June and Britannicus.

But if we take a closer look at the play, an entirely different picture emerges. First of all there is the question of heredity. Agrippina, to judge from her innumerable crimes (including incest and murder) is hardly in a position to dwell on the ferocity of the Domitians. What is more, the ancestry of Britannicus (though Racine is careful not to raise the point) was no guarantee of virtuous conduct. His father was Claudius, who had an impressive record of atrocities to his credit, and his mother was Messalina, to whom a glancing reference (but not by name) is made in line 1123 and on whose morality it is unnecessary to dilate.

It is strange, too, that the early reign of a man who is embarking on a monstrous career should have been so liberal as to warrant comparison with the golden age of Rome.

However, it is the abduction of June which is the crucial issue. Yet here, reading the play backwards, we can see that the move was in fact dictated by what Burrus (we do not know how sincerely) defines to Agrippina as 'wise policy' (131). June is a descendant of Caesar Augustus, and

> The rights that she inherits, as you know,
> Can of her husband make a rebel prince. (239–40)

However, the political implications of the engagement of Britannicus and June are not underlined, and it is not impossible that Racine started out to portray Nero on traditional lines and only found his real direction as the play gathered momentum. Certainly, to begin with, there is some haziness as to Nero's motives in having June carried off. And even this doubt is almost effaced when we see the young ruler falling in love with June and using his power to press his case with her. It is his rejection at her hands, too, that precipitates the crisis. But it is significant that, at the point where he makes up his mind to do away with Britannicus, his hatred vents itself against Agrippina:

> I recognize the hand that joined these two.
> And Agrippina sought an audience
> And was in her discourse so voluble
> Only to play this odious trick on me. (1086–9)

The point emerges with even greater force after Agrippina

has had her longed-for private talk with her son, who is so outraged by her thirst for power that he exclaims:

> This is too much. Her downfall must
> Free me for ever from my brother's rage. ...
> She's wearied me by harping on his name.
> I'll not allow her wicked recklessness
> To promise him a second time my place. (1315–19)

And, when Burrus asks him what has prompted him to the horrible plan to murder his rival, Nero replies coolly:

> Glory and love, my safety and my life. (1324)

As so often in Racine, personal and political motives are closely intertwined. But in fact love is a secondary consideration. When Narcissus seeks by a crafty allusion to Britannicus's 'marriage with June' to make his master go back on his word, Nero, though nettled, refuses to react:

> You're overmuch concerned. Howe'er that be,
> I do not count him as my enemy. (1412–13)

'There can be no doubt,' notes Butler (op. cit., p. 183). 'Nero has got over his love.* It is at this point that Narcissus speaks the decisive phrase which is to overcome Nero's resistance, or rather revive his dominating passion ...

> Agrippina, my lord, was sure of it.
> She has regained her sovereign hold on you. (1414–15)

There is no dispute about Nero's anger this time. 'Britannicus is lost. It is not to win back June that Nero strikes. It is to humble Agrippina and to deal her the decisive blow which will establish him as master of the State.'

Nor should we regard Narcissus, Butler goes on,

as a sort of devil, or Racinian Iago weaving his web of lies and calumnies to lead the young sovereign astray. The complaints which

---

* The secondary importance of Nero's infatuation is confirmed by the fact that, in all other cases in Racine, passion is shown, not as burgeoning, but as deeply rooted and irresistible.

he stresses had been presented by Nero himself in more moderate
terms in his talk with Agrippina who was unable to reply to them:

> But Rome desires a master, not a mistress.
> You heard the rumours that my weakness roused.
> The senate and the people, daily vexed
> To hear your wishes published by my voice,
> Affirmed that Claudius, dying, with his power
> Had left me too his blind submissiveness.
> You've seen our soldiers bear resentfully
> Their eagles past you time and time again,
> Outraged at slighting by this shameful deed
> The heroes who're depicted on them still. (1239–48)

And Nero is merely repeating the arguments advanced by Burrus
in the first Act. Agrippina's ambition weakens the king; it is the
cause of a dangerous unrest in the army, in the people and in the
State as a whole. The method employed by Nero [to dispose of his
rival] was perhaps not the only one open to him, but the fact is that
it settles the problem, at least on the political plane, which is the
only one that counts in the play. The elimination of Britannicus,
far from proving a boomerang, establishes Nero's power and breaks
Agrippina's.

Moreover, 'it is not by some kind of perversity that Racine
consummates the ruin of Britannicus and accords Nero the
victory. It is because [for the tragedian] success has its techniques, regardless of the aims pursued.' These techniques
may be defined as machiavellianism, which 'appears as the
only method whereby a king can maintain himself in power
and maintain the State . . . this is the *via unica*, beyond which
lie only precipices'. For a *principe nuovo* or newly appointed
king, according to the Italian writer's philosophy, the first
duty is to crush even the slightest stirring of opposition on the
part of any potential successor, and to put it down promptly
and ruthlessly. In *Britannicus*, this is exactly what Nero does.
And he has ample grounds for taking action. As Burrus (an
entirely unmachiavellian character) points out to Nero:

> Your mother's always to be feared, my lord.
> Rome, all your troops, revere her ancestors;
> Germanicus, her father, they recall.
> She knows her power, and you her vigorousness. (768–71)

And Britannicus, whom she is backing (or seeming to back)
has not only a claim (admittedly heightened by Racine on the
misleading analogy of seventeenth-century French conditions)
to succeed his dead father Claudius, but has in fact behind him
'all the chiefs of the nobility' (907–8).

Contemporaries therefore, notes Butler,

were not mistaken when they reproached Racine with having made
his hero 'too good'. . . . It is certain that his Nero has nothing of the
bloodthirsty madman of history. He is becoming a monster, says
Racine. But Nero is definitely less monstrous than Pyrrhus. He does
not attack an innocent child. . . . he does not threaten June to put
her to death. . . . He gets rid of a rival but at the same time he
strikes down an enemy who literally endangers his life and the
security of the State. There is not a single Racinian crime for which
so many excuses can be found. He cannot be said to arouse our
sympathy but . . . beyond his puerile fears [of his mother], his
hesitations, his reversals, and even his repentances there emerges
a character of a redoubtable logic and coherence.

If Nero's personality builds up as the play develops,
Agrippina's disintegrates. And the reason is fairly clear. In the
days of her greatness, she was fighting both for herself and
her son. When he turns against her, and seeks to throw off her
hold, she is divided inwardly by her maternal instincts.* She
had secured the throne for Nero by a mixture of ruthless
crimes, adroit manoeuvres and skilful timing, as is patent
from her account of her ascent in the great speech in Act
Four. But the same speech is a brilliant demonstration of her
complete disorientation when it comes to confronting her son,
and not, as previously, enemies or even those with whom she
was not emotionally involved. She commits blunder after
blunder, motioning Nero to approach and take his place as if
he were still her ward and not the master of Rome, confusing
wise moves such as the banishment by Nero of the freedman,
Pallas, with more serious matters such as his frequentation of
'young libertines' (though there is no other hint of this in the

* It has often been emphasized how typical many of Agrippina's
exclamations are of a mother deploring her son's evil wavs. Cf. e.g. 1270
and 1275–7.

play) and the eviction of Octavia from Nero's heart (though what worries Agrippina is that she herself has been displaced). And in fact it is Nero's infatuation with June which, just as it has envenomed the rivalry between Nero and Britannicus, raises to a paroxysm Agrippina's fear of being excluded from power. For at bottom her relations with Nero are never very far from incest. As she exclaims to her confidante on learning of her son's love for June:

> Do you not see how low they're bringing me?
> It's I to whom they give a rival, I.
> Soon, if I do not break this fateful bond,
> My place is taken, and I count for naught. (879–83)

The colourless and ineffective Octavia whom Agrippina had, as she herself says, placed in Nero's bed, had never worried her as a potential rival for power, but June is a very different matter.

> She'll have the power of mistress and of wife. (888)

The situation is such that Agrippina panics and loses all sense of reality. She scorns the humble attempt of Burrus to form an alliance with her. She reveals her most secret plans in the presence of a known agent of Nero (see Act One, Scene Three and Act Two, Scene Five), and she utters empty threats against her son on two occasions, admittedly to Burrus who is unlikely to repeat them (255–66 and 835–44). She is fatuously overconfident about the effect of her talk with Nero (which, as the spectator knows, has merely enraged him):

> No more. I've spoken. Everything has changed. (1583)

And lastly when (1673–93) she foretells that Nero's crimes will recoil on him, she completely forgets that all these crimes, and in particular the liquidation of Britannicus, were set off by her own infamous actions in ejecting that prince from what appeared to be his rightful place as successor to his father's throne.

Burrus is in a different class. He has no crimes on his conscience such as Agrippina has. And it falls to him to defend the traditional themes (whose absence would have shocked the public) of the need for a king to practice clemency and seek the happiness of his people, and the power of immanent justice which makes the punishment follow the crime.

Yet, if we take a close look at his acts, Burrus appears at the very least naïve, not to say disingenuous. After all, it was he who made the army swear allegiance to Nero when Claudius died. If he knew that the emperor had been poisoned by Agrippina, or was aware of even a fraction of the sordid intrigues which led to Nero assuming power, why is he so indignant and surprised at the turn of subsequent events? If he did not, what weight can be attached to his views? He assures Agrippina that, if she makes public the crimes committed by her to have Nero made emperor, nobody will believe her. He puts forward the official and highly inaccurate version of Nero's having been raised to power by the wishes of Rome. And he swears that Nero's

> generous heart
> Will soon make [her] forget [her] present schemes. (869–70)

Even worse, he urges her to

> Affect a mother's mild indulgence (272)

at a time when, as she herself points out,

> Nero himself [her] downfall has proclaimed. (276)

Indeed, in a scene which Racine had the good sense to excise, Burrus is shown as proposing an alliance between himself and Narcissus to bring Nero back to the strait path of virtue. Candour could go no farther.

Nor is this all. In his pathetic appeal to Nero to abstain from murdering Britannicus, there are a number of transparent fallacies. It is not true that Burrus can answer for the young prince's obedience. Britannicus has never renounced his claim to the empire. He weeps with rage and humiliation at his situation and plots his 'enemy's' downfall (and hence almost certainly assassination). There is not the slightest reason to assume that Agrippina and he would not speedily

resume their plotting to oust their common foe. Burrus'
generous sentiments are in fact based on a completely false
and unrealistic picture of the situation and hence have a hol-
low, abstract ring. The whole scene in which he brings Nero
back to the path of duty is a bravura piece calculated to
elicit the plaudits of the audience (as it did those of Boileau),
but it is in the main a residue of the values and sentiments
inherited from Corneille and the baroque tradition.

Just as Nero triumphs, Agrippina is swept aside, and
Burrus' appeals prove in the end quite ineffective. Britannicus is doomed. It is not that Racine does not pity them. Indeed, the love between the young prince and June is one of
the most touching things in the playwright's work. But, as
Butler observes (op. cit., pp. 186–7), 'their sufferings do not
suffice to cancel the laws to which they fall a victim'. Racine's
plays are not written for candid souls, nor do these prosper
in the plays themselves. Britannicus, for whom

> distrust
> Is the last science of a noble heart (339–40)

survives exactly twelve hours from the time the ruthless battle
of wits at the court begins.

Yet, despite these contradictions between the baroque
ethics of the semi-feudal nobility and the machiavellian approach of the centralizing monarchy, the play has a compact-
ness and a drive which are undeniable. There is a terseness and
an economy of effort rare even in such a master of conciseness
as Racine. The cutting at the end of certain scenes is of a
positively cinematic sharpness, as for example when Nero,
having been won back by Narcissus to his plan to murder
Britannicus, says cryptically:

> Narcissus, come. Let's see what's to be done. (1480)

And some of the entrances are equally forceful. Thus Nero,
at the beginning of Act Two where he might well be taken as
replying to a suggestion by the virtuous Burrus that he should
banish or even liquidate his mother:

No, Burrus, no, despite her wrongful acts,
She is my mother. (359–60)

Yet it may be doubted whether it was this technical virtuosity which ensured the play its triumph shortly after its chequered start. If, in his second Preface (in 1676), Racine was able to write that, 'The critics faded away. The play remained', this was largely if not exclusively the result of the intervention of the all-powerful Sun-King in his favour. And the royal support can hardly be regarded as accidental. The values underlying the work were those of the new absolute monarchy which concentrated its energy on restricting the powers of the nobility and the other forces hampering the creation of a national policy. And these values were the direct antithesis of those that had previously obtained, in real life and in literature, when the nobles had dominated the scene. The tragedy, significantly enough, is dedicated to the son-in-law of Colbert, and through him to Colbert himself, the main architect of the new policy. *Britannicus*, in short, marks a new departure both in Racine's work and in the literature and outlook of the age. And this 'realistic' political orientation was to be amply confirmed in his succeeding plays, in particular *Bajazet*.

RACINE'S DEDICATION TO
BRITANNICUS

TO MY LORD
THE DUKE OF CHEVREUSE

MY LORD,

You will perhaps be astonished at seeing your name at the head of
this work; and, if I had asked your permission to offer the work to
you, I doubt whether I would have obtained it. But it would in a way
be ungrateful to hide any longer from the world the kindness with
which you have always honoured me. What likelihood is there that a
man who works only for glory can keep silent on as glorious a protection as yours? No, MY LORD, it is too much to my advantage for it
to be known that even my friends are not indifferent to you, that you
take an interest in all my works, and that you have procured for me
the honour of reading this one to a man whose every hour is precious.*
You were a witness with what penetration he judged the structure of
the play and how far above anything I have been able to produce is his
idea of what constitutes an excellent tragedy. Have no fears, MY
LORD, that I shall venture farther, and that, not daring to praise
him to his face, I shall address myself to you in order to be able to
praise him with greater liberty. I know that it would be dangerous to
weary him with praise; and I dare to say that this very modesty
which you have in common with him is not one of the least ties that
bind you together. Moderation is but a common virtue when it is
associated with only common qualities. But that, with all the qualities
of heart and mind, that with a judgement which, it seems, should be
the fruit only of the experience of several years, that, with a splendid
grasp of a thousand fields which you are not able to hide from your
close friends, you still have this sagacious modesty that all admire in
you, all this is unquestionably a virtue which is rare in an age in which
people are puffed up on the most slender grounds. But I let myself be

* The French statesman, Colbert.

carried away unconsciously by the temptation to speak of you. It must indeed be very strong, since I have been unable to resist it in a letter in which I had no other intention than to prove to you with how much respect I am

My Lord

Your very humble and very obedient servant,

RACINE

RACINE'S PREFACES TO
BRITANNICUS
*
FIRST PREFACE

Of *all the works which I have given the public, none has earned me more applause or more attacks than this one. However much trouble I have taken to polish this tragedy, it would seem that the more I tried to improve it, the more certain persons made a point of decrying it. There is no intrigue to which they did not resort, no criticism which they did not think up. There are even some who have taken sides with Nero against me. They said I made him too cruel. For my part, I thought that the very name of Nero denoted something more even than cruel. But perhaps they are putting a strained interpretation on his story and mean that he was a man of probity in his earliest years. One need only have read Tacitus to know that, if for a time he was a good emperor, he was always an extremely wicked man. In my tragedy, I do not deal with other than personal matters. Here, Nero is shown in his intimacy and his family. And they will dispense me from citing to them all the passages which could easily prove to them that I have no amends to make to him.*

Others have said, on the contrary, that I had made him too good. I admit that Nero is not my idea of a good man. I always regarded him as a monster. But here he is becoming *a monster. He has not yet set fire to Rome. He has not killed his mother, his wife, his guardians. Apart from that, it seems to me that he lets himself be involved in enough cruelties to prevent anyone from failing to recognize him for what he is.*

Some people have taken up the cudgels for Narcissus and have complained that I have made him a very wicked man and Nero's confidant. I need only quote one passage to answer them. 'Nero,' says Tacitus, 'bore the death of Narcissus impatiently, because that freedman fitted in admirably with the prince's still hidden vices: cujus abditis adhuc vitiis mire congruebat.

Others again were shocked that I chose a man as young as Britannicus as the hero of a tragedy. I referred them, in the preface to Andromache, *to the opinions of Aristotle on the tragic hero; far from being perfect, he must always have some imperfection. But I will add that a young prince of seventeen who has a great deal of spirit, love, frankness, and credulity, the usual qualities of a young man, seemed to me calculated to excite compassion. I need prove no more.*

But they say that this prince was only entering his fifteenth year when he died. He and Narcissus are made to live two more years than they really lived. I would not have mentioned this objection had it not been raised with such vigour by a man* who has taken the liberty of making an emperor† reign twenty years when he reigned for only eight, although this change is much more serious in terms of chronology where time is computed by the years reigned by each emperor.

Nor does June lack censors. They say that out of an old coquette named Junia Silana I have made a virtuous girl. What would they reply if I told them that June is an invented character like Emilia in Cinna,‡ *or like Sabina in* Horace?‡ *But I must inform them that, had they read history at all closely, they would have found a Junia Calvina of the family of Augustus, a sister of Silanus to whom Claudius had promised Octavia. This June was young, beautiful and, as Seneca puts it,* festivissima omnium puellarum [*the most vivacious of girls*]. *She loved her brother tenderly; 'and their enemies,' says Tacitus, 'accused them both of incest, although they were guilty only of a little indiscretion.' If I represent her as being more restrained than she was, I have never heard that we were forbidden to improve a character's morals, especially if that character was not well known.*

People find it strange that she appears on the stage after Britannicus' death. I must say it is being over-scrupulous to object to her saying in four rather touching lines that she is on her way to Octavia's apartments. But they say it was not worth while bringing her back for that. Someone else could have announced it in her stead. They do not realize that one of the rules of the stage is to put into narrative only what cannot take place as action, and that all the ancients often bring

---

* Corneille, Racine's ageing rival.
† Héraclius, in a play of that name by Corneille.
‡ A play by Corneille.

on to the stage characters who have nothing else to say except that they are coming from one place and going back to another.

All that is beside the point, say my censors. The play is finished by the time we reach the narrative of Britannicus' death, and one ought not to listen to the rest. But they do listen to it, and even with as much attention as to the end of any other tragedy. As for me, it was always my understanding that, as the tragedy was the imitation of a complete action in which several persons cooperate, that action is not finished until we know the situation in which it leaves these persons. This is Sophocles' almost general practice. Thus, in Antigone, he uses as many lines to depict Haemon's frenzy and Creon's punishment after that princess's death as I have used for Agrippina's imprecations, June's withdrawal, Narcissus' punishment and Nero's despair after Britannicus' death.

What should one do to content such captious judges? The matter would be easy if only one were prepared to jettison good sense. One need only turn one's back on naturalness, plunge into the extraordinary. Instead of a simple action stripped to the bone, such as an action which takes place in twenty-four hours and which, advancing by degrees to its end, is sustained only by the interests, the feelings and the passions of the characters, one should fill out this action with lots of incidents which could not possibly happen in less than a month, with a large number of stage tricks, the more surprising the less probable they are, and a host of declamations in which one would make the characters say the exact opposite of what they ought to say. One ought, for example, to represent some intoxicated hero who would set out to incur his mistress's hatred for fun; a garrulous Lacedaemonian; a conqueror who would do nothing but reel off maxims of love; a woman who would give lessons in pride to conquerors.* That no doubt would make these gentlemen cry out in admiration. What, however, would be the reaction of the small number of sensible people whom I am anxious to please? How would I dare, so to speak, to come before those great men of old whom I have taken as models? For, to borrow the ideas of a writer in antiquity,† *these are the real*

---

* This passage contains a number of digs at Corneille. The 'intoxicated hero' is Attila, the Lacedaemonian is Agésilas, in plays of these names, the 'conqueror' is Caesar in *La Mort de Pompée*, and the woman who reels off maxims on love is Cornelia in that play.   † Longinus.

spectators whom we ought to select. And we ought ceaselessly to ask ourselves: 'What would Homer and Virgil say, if they were to read these lines? What would Sophocles say, if he saw this scene represented?' However that may be, I have no intention of preventing people from speaking out against my works. In any case it would be pointless to try. Quid de te alii loquantur ipse videant, *says* Cicero; sed loquentur tamen [*It's for others to see how they speak of you; but in any case they will speak*].

I would only beg the reader to forgive this preface which I have composed only to justify my tragedy to him. There is nothing more natural than to defend oneself when one feels that one is unfairly attacked. I see that Terence himself seems to have written prologues only to plead his case against the criticism of an evil-minded old poet, malevoli veteris poetae,* *who had intrigued for votes against him up to the time when his comedies were being put on.*

> . . . Occepta est agi:
> Exclamat, etc.

[*As the performance starts, he cries out, etc.*]

There are no objections which people have not dug up. But what escaped the spectators might be picked up by the readers. The fact is that I make June enter the Vestals, where, according to Aulus Gellius, no one was received below the age of six or over that of ten. But here the people take June under their protection, and I felt that in view of her birth, her virtue and her misfortunes, they could dispense her from the age limits imposed by the laws just as they waived these limits for the consulate in the case of so many great men who deserved that privilege.

To conclude, I am firmly persuaded that there are plenty of other criticisms which would leave me no alternative but to profit from them in future. But how I pity the plight of a man who works for the public. Those who see our weak points most clearly are the very ones who are most willing to overlook them. They forgive the passages they do not like in favour of those by which they are taken. There is nothing, on the contrary, more unfair than an ignoramus. He always believes that admiration denotes a lack of understanding. He even runs

* Corneille again!

down the most striking passages in order to give the impression that he is intelligent, and, if we have the temerity to stand up to him, he taxes us with presumptuousness and with unwillingness to take anyone else's word. It never occurs to him that he is sometimes prouder of expressing a very bad judgement than we are of writing a rather good play:

Homine imperito nunquam quidquam injustius.

[*There is nothing more unfair than an ignoramus.*]

SECOND PREFACE*

THIS *is the tragedy which I can say I have worked over most carefully. Yet I confess that to start with its success was not up to my
expectation. It had hardly made its appearance on the stage than a
host of critics appeared who seemed destined to destroy it. I thought
myself that its fate would be less auspicious than that of my other
tragedies. But in the end what happened to this play was what always
happens to works with something in them. The critics faded away.
The play remained. It is now the work of mine which the court and
the public are keenest to see. And, if I have written something lasting
and which deserves some praise, most of the connoisseurs agree that it
is this very* Britannicus.

To say true, I had worked on models which have been of the utmost
help in the picture I wished to paint of the court of Agrippina and
Nero. I had copied my characters from the greatest painter of ancient
days, I mean Tacitus. And I was at the time so full of this excellent
historian that there is hardly an outstanding trait in my tragedy
which I do not owe to him. I had wanted to include in this collection a
selection of the finest passages which I have tried to imitate, but I
found that this extract would take up almost as much room as the
tragedy. Thus, the reader will pardon me if I refer him to that author,
who in any case is in everybody's hands, and I will content myself with
giving some of the passages from him on each of the characters which I
put on the stage.

To begin with, Nero: it must be remembered that in the play he is
shown in the first years of his reign, which were happy ones, as we
know. Thus, it was not possible for me to represent him as being as
evil as he was later to become. Nor do I depict him as a virtuous man,
for he never was so. He has not yet killed his mother, his wife, his
guardians. But he has in him the seeds of all these crimes. He is
beginning to wish to shake off the yoke. He hates both groups of
people, and he hides his hatred from them under feigned caresses:
factus natura velare odium fallacibus blanditiis [*naturally gifted*

* First published in 1676.

135

in veiling his hate under deceptive caresses]. *In a word, he is here in process of becoming a monster, but he does not yet dare to come out openly, and he seeks pretexts for his evil acts:* Hactenus Nero flagitiis et sceleribus velamenta quaesivit [*Until then Nero sought to veil both debauches and crimes*]. *He could not bear Octavia, a princess of an exemplary goodness and virtuousness,* fato quodam, an quia praevalent illicita; metuebaturque ne in stupra feminarum illustrium prorumperet [*by a sort of fatality or by the attraction of forbidden fruit; and it was feared that he might start to debauch distinguished women*].

I give him Narcissus as his confidant. In this I have followed Tacitus, who says that Nero bore with impatience Narcissus' death because that freedman fitted in admirably with the still hidden vices of the prince: cuius abditis adhuc vitiis mire congruebat. *This passage proves two things. It proves that Nero was already vicious, but that he dissimulated his vices, and that Narcissus furthered these evil inclinations.*

I have chosen Burrus as an upright man in opposition to this court pest. And I have chosen him rather than Seneca. This is the reason: they were both guardians of Nero in his youth, the one for arms, the other for letters. And they were famous, Burrus for his experience in arms and for the severity of his morals, militaribus curis et severitate morum; *Seneca for his eloquence and for his agreeable turn of mind,* Seneca praeceptis eloquentiae et comitate honesta. *Burrus, after his death, was sorely missed because of his virtues,* Civitati grande desiderium ejus mansit per memoriam virtutis.

Their whole trouble was how to resist the pride and ferocity of Agrippina, quae, cunctis malae dominationis cupidinibus flagrans, habebat in partibus Pallantem [*who, burning with all the delirium of maleficent power, had engaged Pallas to further her interests*]. *I quote only this remark about Agrippina, for there are too many things to say about her. It is she whom I have striven most carefully to portray, and my tragedy is no less the downfall of Agrippina than the death of Britannicus. This death was a thunderbolt for her; and 'it seemed,' says Tacitus, 'from her terror and consternation, that she was as innocent of this death as Octavia; Agrippina lost in him her last hope, and this crime made her fear a greater one':* sibi supremum auxilium ereptum, et parricidii exemplum intelligebat.

Britannicus' age was so well known that it was not possible for me to represent him other than as a young prince who had a great deal of spirit, love and frankness, the usual qualities of a young man. He was fifteen, and it is said that he was very intelligent, whether this is true or whether his misfortunes led people to think this of him without his having been able to give proofs of it: neque segnem ei fuisse indolem ferunt; sive verum, seu, periculis commendatus, retinuit famam sine experimento.

One must not be astonished if he has only such an evil man as adviser as Narcissus. For orders had long been given for Britannicus to be allowed to frequent only people bereft of loyalty or honour: nam, ut proximus quisque Britannico, neque fas neque fidem pensi haberet, olim provisum erat.

It remains to speak of June. She must not be confused with an old coquette named Junia Silana. The character in the play is another June, whom Tacitus calls Junia Calvina, of Augustus' family, the sister of Silanus to whom Claudius had promised Octavia. This June was young, beautiful and, as Seneca puts it, festivissima omnium puellarum [*the most vivacious of girls*]. *Her brother and she loved each other tenderly; and their enemies, says Tacitus, 'accused both of them of incest, although they were guilty only of a slight lack of discretion'. She lived on into Vespasian's reign.*

I make her enter the Vestal Virgins, although, according to Aulus Gellius, nobody was ever received by them under the age of six or over the age of ten. But here the people take June under their wing, and I thought that, in view of her birth, her virtue and her misfortunes, the people could dispense her from the prescribed age limits as they dispensed so many great men from the rules affecting the consulate since they deserved that privilege.

CAST

NERO, *emperor, Agrippina's son*
BRITANNICUS, *son of the emperor Claudius and Messalina*
AGRIPPINA, *widow of Domitius Ahenobarbus, Nero's father, and,*
after her second marriage, widow of the emperor Claudius
JUNE, *sweetheart of Britannicus*
BURRUS, *Nero's mentor*
NARCISSUS, *Britannicus' mentor*
ALBINA, *Agrippina's confidante*
GUARDS

The scene is in Rome, in a chamber in Nero's palace

BRITANNICUS

ACT ONE

Scene One
AGRIPPINA, ALBINA

ALBINA

While Nero lies in sleep's abandonment,
What! must you linger here till he awakes?
Must Caesar's mother, without retinue,
Keep solitary vigil at his door?
Withdraw; go back to your apartments.   5

AGRIPPINA

                       No.

Albina, not for even a moment. Here
I'll wait for him. The grief he causes me
Will occupy me all the time he rests.
All I've foretold is only too assured.
Nero has struck against Britannicus.   10
Unbridled Nero banishes constraint;
Tired of respect, he wishes to be feared.
Britannicus lies heavy on his mind
And every day I start to irk him too.

ALBINA

What! you whom Nero owes his very life?   15
You who have raised him from so low to power,
Who, disinheriting even Claudius' son,
Have given lucky Domitius Caesar's name?
All speaks in Agrippina's favour. He
Owes you his love.   20

18 *Domitius:* the family name of Nero before he was adopted by the Emperor Claudius.

AGRIPPINA

He does, Albina. Yes.
All, if he's generous, enjoins him to;
All, if ungrateful, speaks against me, though.

ALBINA

If he's ungrateful? Why, his every act
Proclaims a soul well schooled in duty's laws.
25 For three whole years all he has said or done
Promises Rome a perfect emperor. Rome
For two years under Nero's sceptre seems
To have reverted to its consuls' times;
He rules it like a father. Nero young
30 Has all the virtues of Augustus old.

AGRIPPINA

No, I am interested but not unjust.
He's starting where Augustus ended. Yet
If e'er the future should destroy the past,
Where once Augustus started he may end.
35 His mask is vain. I read upon his face
The fierce Domitians' wild and sombre mood.
He mingles with the pride their blood inspires
The fierceness of the Neroes drawn from me.
Tyranny always starts auspiciously.
40 Caligula was once Rome's favourite.
But, mildness feigned turning to frenzied rage,
Rome's favourite became its incubus.
What care I, after all, if Nero dies
Renowned for long, unchanging virtuousness?
45 Have I then placed him at the empire's helm
To do the people's and the senate's will?
Ah! let him be Rome's father, but recall
That Agrippina is his mother still.
Meanwhile what term is strong enough to brand
50 The outrage dawn has just revealed to us?
He knows, for their love cannot be concealed,

That June is worshipped by Britannicus.
And this same Nero, with his virtuous life,
Has June abducted in the depths of night.
What does he want? Driven by hate or love,   55
Is it alone the joy of harming them?
Or rather does his spitefulness intend
To punish them because of my support?

ALBINA

What! you support them!

AGRIPPINA

                    Dear Albina, stop.
I know I've wrought their downfall, only I;   60
The throne to which his blood entitled him,
Britannicus was swept from it by me.
By me alone robbed of the wedding with
Octavia, June's own brother took his life –
Silanus, he whom Claudius had in mind,   65
Who claimed Augustus as his ancestor.
Nero takes all; I on the contrary
Must keep the balance between them and him,
So that, by the same law, Britannicus
Will one day hold it 'twixt my son and me.   70

ALBINA

What! you . . .

AGRIPPINA

                    I seek to reinsure myself.
I'll lose my hold on Nero otherwise.

ALBINA

But why such needless steps against a son?

AGRIPPINA

I soon would fear him if he feared me not.

ALBINA

75 Perhaps groundless alarm assails your mind.
But if no longer dutiful, at least
His change is not yet visible to us,
And these are secrets between him and you.
Whate'er new titles Rome confers on him,
80 There's none he does not with his mother share;
His generous love keeps nothing for himself.
Your name in Rome's as sacred as his own.
As to Octavia, no one speaks of her.
Augustus did not honour Livia more.
85 Nero was first to sanction, laurel-crowned,
The fasces past his mother to be borne.
What need you more to test his gratitude?

AGRIPPINA

A little less respect, more confidence.
Albina, all these presents rouse my gall;
90 I see my honours grow and credit sink.
No, no, the time is past when Nero young
Passed the court's adoration on to me,
When he relied on me to run the state,
When my command convoked the senate here,
95 When I, behind a veil, invisible,
Was that great body's all-deciding soul.
Nero, of Rome's caprices still unsure,
Was not yet drunk with his imperial power.
That day, that sombre day, still strikes my soul,
100 When he was dazzled with his glory and
On which the envoys of a host of kings
Paid him their homage in the sight of all.
I was about to join him on the throne.
I do not know what paved my downfall, but
105 Nero, the moment he set eyes on me,
Let his annoyance sweep across his face.

84 *honour Livia more:* i.e. more than Nero honours Agrippina. Livia was
Augustus' wife. Cf. 476.

Indeed, a grim foreboding seized my heart.
With false respect cloaking the wrong he planned,
He rose, and, running to embrace me, steered
Me from the throne I was about to mount.   110
Since this dire setback, Agrippina's power
Each day has sped towards its decline. I hold
Only a shadow. People now invoke
Seneca's name alone and Burrus' aid.

ALBINA

If this suspicion's rooted in your thoughts,   115
Why feed a poison that is killing you?
At least tell Caesar what your feelings are.

AGRIPPINA

Caesar no longer sees me by myself.
I'm given a public audience at my hour.
His answer's set, as are his silences.   120
Two guardians, his masters and my own,
Now scrutinize each word exchanged by us.
But I'll pursue him still the more he flees.
I'll take advantage of his troubled heart.
I hear a sound. Come, let's go in at once   125
And for this outrage call him to account.
Bare, if we can, the secrets of his soul.
What's this? Already Burrus issues from the room?

Scene Two
AGRIPPINA, BURRUS, ALBINA

BURRUS

In the emperor's name, I wanted to announce
Orders which might at first seem ominous,   130
But which are prompted by wise policy.
This, Caesar wished to be conveyed to you.

AGRIPPINA (*tries to go in*)
Let him convey it then to me himself.

BURRUS

Caesar has for a time withdrawn from us.
135 Already, using a less public door,
Both consuls had forestalled you, lady. But
Allow me to go back expressly. . . .

AGRIPPINA
No.

I'll not disturb his regal privacy.
Meanwhile, let us, with somewhat less constraint,
140 For once, dropping pretence, exchange our views.

BURRUS

Burrus was always horrified of lies. . . .

AGRIPPINA

You hide the emperor from me. For how long?
Must I intrude to gain an audience?
Have I then raised your fortunes to such heights
145 To put a bar between my son and me?
Do you not dare to let him judge himself?
Do Seneca and you vie as to who
Will first efface me from his memory?
Was it for that I gave you Nero, or
150 For you under his name to rule the state?
The more I think the less I can believe
That you dare count me as your creature, *you*,
Whom I could have allowed to rot, obscure,
As tribune of some legion still, and *I*
155 Who take my forebears' place upon the throne,
Your masters' daughter, sister, mother, wife.
To what do you aspire? Think you I've made
An emperor to have three imposed on me?
Nero is not a child. It's time he reigned.

158 *three:* i.e. Nero, Burrus and Seneca.

How long must the emperor walk in fear of you?   160
Can't he see anything but through your eyes?
And has he not his ancestors as guides –
Augustus or Tiberius? Can he not
Copy Germanicus, my father? I
Among these heroes dare not place myself;   165
But there are virtues I can trace for him.
I can at least instruct him how to keep
Distance between a subject and himself.

BURRUS

I had intended only to excuse
This single one of Caesar's acts, but since,   170
Though not expecting me to plead his case,
You make me surety for his future years,
I'll answer with a soldier's bluntness which
Has not the art of camouflaging truth.
You gave into my keeping Caesar's youth,   175
It's true, and *that* I never should forget.
But did I swear that I'd be false to him?
Or make an emperor fit but to obey?
No, I am answerable not to you.
He's not your son. He's master of the world.   180
Lady, I owe account for him to Rome,
Which thinks I hold its future in my hand.
If he was to be reared in ignorance,
Were there but Seneca and I to choose?
Why was the post not given to flatterers?   185
Why seek in exile tutors to corrupt?
The court of Claudius, rich in former slaves,
Where two were sought could have supplied a score
Coveting the honour of debasing him;
They would have kept him a perpetual child.   190
What then is your complaint? You are revered.
By Caesar, by his mother people swear.
It's true the emperor does not every day
Place at your feet his throne and swell your court.
But should he? Should his gratitude appear   195

Only in his subservience to you?
Must Nero, always humble, always shy,
Dare never to be Caesar but in name?
Shall I be frank? Rome thinks that he is right.
200 Rome to three freedmen for so long enslaved,
Barely recovering from the yoke it bore,
From Nero's reign reckons its liberty.
Nay, virtue seems itself to be reborn.
The empire's ceased to be a tyrant's spoils.
205 The people now appoint its magistrates;
Caesar selects the chiefs the soldiers want;
The army's Corbulon, the senate's Thraseas,
Are innocent despite their dubious fame;
The deserts, peopled once with senators,
210 Are occupied by their informers now.
What matter, then, if Caesar follows us,
Since our advice but heightens his renown;
If Rome, under a prosperous reign, is free
Still, and if Caesar is all-powerful?
215 But Nero needs no help to steer his course.
I do not seek to guide him, but obey.
He can as models take his ancestors;
But, to do well, he need but be himself;
So that his virtues, in an endless chain,
220 Bring back recurrently his first fine years.

AGRIPPINA

And so, doubting the future, you believe
That without you Nero will go astray.
But you, pleased with your handiwork so far,
Who've just born witness to his character,
225 Can you explain why Nero has become
A ravisher and has abducted June?
Is his intent by this disgraceful deed
To sully in her veins my forebears' blood?
What does he charge her with? And what offence

200 *three freedmen:* Pallas, Narcissus, Callistes, who were powerful at
Claudius' court.

Makes of her in one day a criminal,   230
She who, reared in austerity, would not
Have seen him had he not abducted her,
And who would even be grateful to him for
The boon of never setting eyes on him?

BURRUS

I know she's not suspected of a crime,   235
But Caesar still has not condemned her, and,
Lady, here nothing grates upon her eyes;
She's in the palace of her ancestors.
The rights that she inherits, as you know,
Can of her husband make a rebel prince;   240
The blood of Caesar must not be allied
To those whom Caesar has not yet approved;
You yourself would agree he must approve,
Before Augustus' grandchild can be wed.

AGRIPPINA

I understand. Nero informs me thus   245
In vain Britannicus has my support.
In vain, to cheer him in his wretched lot,
I've comforted his love with marriage hopes;
To my confusion, Nero seeks to show
That I make promises beyond my powers.   250
Rome is convinced my favour's great. He wants
To undeceive it now by this affront,
He wants the whole world terror-struck to learn
Not to confuse the emperor and my son.
This he can do. Yet I dare tell him still   255
He must before he strikes strengthen his hold;
And that, by forcing me to this extreme,
To pit against him my weak influence
He must expose his own, and in the scales
My name may well weigh heavier than he thinks.   260

BURRUS

What! must you always question his respect?

147

Can he not take a step but you distrust?
Does the emperor think you side with June or that
You're reconciled now with Britannicus?
265 Have you become his enemies' ally
To find a pretext to complain of him?
Will idle gossip that's retailed to you
Prompt you to split the empire always? Will
You fear each other always? Must it be
270 That your embraces are in fact disputes?
Ah! drop a censor's sombre diligence;
Affect a mother's mild indulgence. Bear
Some coldness without making much of it,
And do not warn the court to shrink from you.

AGRIPPINA

275 Who would be honoured by my credit when
Nero himself my downfall has proclaimed
And from his presence seems to banish me?
When Burrus dares detain me at his door?

BURRUS

Lady, I see it's time I held my tongue,
280 And that my bluntness now begins to jar.
Grief is unjust, and every argument
Which does not pander to it heightens it.
Here is Britannicus. I shall make way.
I'll leave you here to pity his sad plight,
285 And maybe, lady, put the blame upon
Those whom the emperor has consulted least.

Scene Three

AGRIPPINA, BRITANNICUS, NARCISSUS, ALBINA

AGRIPPINA

Where are you running? What impulsive fear
Drives you so blindly midst your enemies?
What do you seek?

BRITANNICUS

What do I seek? Ah! God.
Everything I have lost is in this place.   290
June has been dragged off to this palace by
A rabble of wild soldiers, shamefully.
Alas, how horror-stricken must have been
Her timid spirits at this novel sight!
In short she's snatched from me. A harsh decree   295
Will sever hearts linked by their misery.
They do not want us, mingling our despair,
To help each other to support our woes.

AGRIPPINA

Enough. Like you I feel for all your wrongs;
My protests have forestalled your just complaints.   300
But I do not intend by impotent
Anger to keep my solemn pledge to you.
I'll say but this. If you would hear me, come
To Pallas' chamber where I'll wait for you.

Scene Four

BRITANNICUS, NARCISSUS

BRITANNICUS

Should I, Narcissus, take her at her word   305
As arbiter between her son and me?
What do you feel? Is Agrippina not
She whom my father for my ruin wed,
And who, if you speak true, hastened the course
Of his last days, too slow for her designs?   310

NARCISSUS

It matters not. She's outraged just like you;
She's pledged her word to give you June as wife;
Unite your grievances; your interests link.

149

These halls resound in vain with your regrets;
315 So long as, with a supplicating voice,
You scatter sad complaints and not affright,
And your resentment is confined to words,
Of this be sure, always you will complain.

BRITANNICUS

Narcissus, well you know if I intend
320 To tolerate for long my slavery;
I will not, stunned for ever by my fall,
Renounce the throne that I was destined for.
But I am still alone. My father's friends
Are merely strangers my misfortunes freeze.
325 My very youth averts from me all those
Who in their hearts have kept their loyalty.
Now that a year's modest experience
Has given me some knowledge of my fate,
What do I see round me but venial friends
330 Who keep a watch upon my every step,
Who, chosen by Nero for this odious task,
Make traffic of the secrets of my soul.
Howe'er that be, each day I am betrayed;
He even foresees my plans. He hears my words.
335 Like you he knows what happens in my heart.
Narcissus, is't not so?

NARCISSUS

　　　　Ah! What base soul ...
But *you* must choose confidants who're discreet,
And not be lavish with your secrets.

BRITANNICUS

　　　　　　　Yes.
Narcissus, you say true, but this distrust
340 Is the last science of a noble heart.
It can be long deceived. But you are right,
Or rather I'll believe no one but you.
My father, I recall, once praised your zeal.

Of all his freedmen you alone are true;
Your eyes, that every moment scan my acts,   345
Have so far saved me from a thousand snares.
Go then. See if the news of this new storm
Has roused the spirits of our former friends.
Observe their eyes, and note their utterances;
See if I can expect some loyal aid.   350
Above all in this palace note with skill
How carefully Nero the princess guards.
Find out if she's recovered from the shock,
And if I'm still allowed to speak to her.
At Pallas' place I'll seek out Nero's mother,   355
Pallas, like you my father's freedman. Then
I'll see, embitter, follow her, and try
To involve her more with me than she intends.

ACT TWO

Scene One
NERO, BURRUS, NARCISSUS, GUARDS

NERO

No, Burrus, no, despite her wrongful acts,
360 She is my mother. I'll ignore her whims.
But I'll no longer suffer or ignore
The insolent rogue who dares to foster them.
Pallas poisons my mother with advice;
Britannicus, my brother, too, he leads
365 Astray. He *only* has their ear, and now
You'd find them all gathered at Pallas' place.
This is too much. I must keep him away
From both. For the last time let him depart.
This is my wish, my order. Let the night
370 Find him no more at Rome or at the court.

(to Burrus)

Go; this command affects the empire's weal.

(to Narcissus)

Narcissus, you, approach.

(to the guards)

And you, withdraw.

Scene Two
NERO, NARCISSUS

NARCISSUS
Thanks to the gods, my lord, June in your hands

Now answers to you for the rest of Rome.
Your enemies, shorn of their empty hopes,   375
At Pallas' place bemoan their impotence.
But what's this? You yourself seem stunned, unnerved,
More even than Britannicus himself.
What does this sombre melancholy bode,
And these dark looks that wander restlessly?   380
All smiles on you. Fortune obeys your will.

NERO

Narcissus, all is lost. I've fallen in love.

NARCISSUS

You?

NERO

Only now, but it's for all my life.
I love, nay, I adore, I worship June.

NARCISSUS

You love her?   385

NERO

Driven by curiosity,
Last night I saw her just as she arrived,
Sad, raising to heaven her tear-filled eyes,
That shone amid the torches and the arms;
Fair, unadorned, and in the négligé
Of a fair lady just aroused from sleep.   390
Well then. I know not if this disarray,
The shadows, torches, silence and the shouts,
The grim demeanour of her ravishers,
Enhanced the timid sweetness of her eyes.
Whate'er the truth, ravished by this fair sight,   395
I tried to speak to her but lost my voice.
Motionless, and by long amazement seized,
I let her go to her apartment while
I went to mine. There in my loneliness
I tried in vain to blot her image out.   400

It still came back. I thought I spoke to her.
I loved even the tears I made her shed.
Sometimes I asked her pardon, but too late.
I had recourse to sighs and even to threats.
405 And this is how, wrapped in my new-found love,
My eyes unsleeping waited for the dawn.
But I perhaps exaggerate her charms.
I've seen her in too flattering a light.
What do you feel?

NARCISSUS

Is it to be believed
410 That she could hide from Nero for so long?

NERO

You know it well. And whether she imputes
The mishap of her brother's death to me,
Whether her heart, so studiedly aloof,
Begrudged my eyes her budding beauty's sight,
415 Nursing her grief and prisoned in the dark,
She even avoided her deserved renown.
And it's this virtue so unknown at court
Whose constance whets my love. Narcissus, think.
There is no Roman beauty whom my love
420 Does not make proud and honoured, who, as soon
As she feels able to sustain his gaze,
Does not at once on Caesar try her charms.
Locked in her palace, modest June alone
Regards these honours as a source of shame,
425 Flees, and perhaps dares not deign to inquire
If Caesar merits love or if he loves.
But is Britannicus in love with her?

NARCISSUS

Most sure.

NERO

So young, does he yet know himself,
And know the poison of bewitching looks?

NARCISSUS

Love does not always wait for reason's dawn.　　430
He loves her, doubt it not. Schooled by her charms,
His eyes already are inured to tears.
Her slightest wishes are commands for him;
Perhaps he even has persuasion's art.

NERO

Indeed? He has some sway over her heart?　　435

NARCISSUS

I know not, but, my lord, I can say this.
I've seen him sometimes fleeing from these halls,
His heart full of an anger he concealed,
Complaining of the court's ingratitude,
Tired of your power and of his slavery,　　440
And wavering between turbulence and fear. N
He called on June and he came back content.

NERO

So much the worse for him, Narcissus. It
Were better far if he incurred her wrath.
Nero will not be jealous unavenged.　　445

NARCISSUS

You! and at what, my lord, are you concerned?
June may have pitied him and shared his woes;
The only tears that she has seen were his.
But now her eyes have been unsealed, my lord.
Looking more closely at your splendour, she　　450
Will see around you kings undiademed
Lost in the crowd, and even her sweetheart too,
Glued to your eyes, be honoured by a glance
That you, my lord, have chanced to cast on them.
When she will see you, from your glory's height,　　455
Come yearning to admit her victory,

Doubt it not, master of a heart subdued,
Command but to be loved, and you'll be loved.

NERO

For how much trouble must I be prepared!
460 And what reproofs!

NARCISSUS

But what is stopping you?

NERO

All – Agrippina, Burrus, Seneca,
Octavia, all of Rome, three virtuous years.
Not that a trace of feeling for my wife
Binds me to her in pity of her youth.
465 My eyes, long since of her devotion tired,
Deign rarely to be witness of her tears,
Too happy if the boon of a divorce
Relieves me of a marriage forced on me.
The heavens themselves seem to condemn her, since
470 In vain she has invoked them four long years.
The gods are by her virtue still unmoved;
They have with offspring never blessed her couch.
The empire still in vain demands an heir.

NARCISSUS

Why hesitate, my lord, to cast her off?
475 The empire and your heart condemn your wife.
Augustus pined for Livia. He and she
Were by a joint divorce united, and
You owe the empire to this kind divorce.
Tiberius, as Augustus' son-in-law,
480 Dared to repudiate his daughter. You
Alone, so far curbing your own desires,
Do not dare win your pleasure by divorce.

NERO

And Agrippina, the implacable?

My love, uneasy, sees her even now
Bring me Octavia and with flaming eye   485
Attest the sanctity of bonds she formed,
And, dealing at my heart even heavier blows,
Reproving me for my ingratitude.
How can I suffer such unpleasantness?

NARCISSUS

Are you not your own master, and hers too?   490
Are you to cringe before her always? Live.
Reign for yourself. Too long you've reigned for her.
What do you fear? You're not afraid of her.
Just now you've banished haughty Pallas, he
Whose proud audacity you know she backs.   495

NERO

Far from her eyes, I threaten, I command.
I listen to your council and approve.
I spur myself to try and flout her will.
But (I lay bare my soul entire to you)
As soon as ill-luck brings me back to her,   500
Whether I dare not yet deny the power
Of eyes wherein I long my duty read,
Whether because of all her benefits,
All that she's given me I submit to her.
In short my efforts are of no avail.   505
My genius trembles, stupefied, at hers;
And it's to free myself from this her hold
That I avoid her and offend her even,
And that from time to time I rouse her gall
To make her flee just as I flee from her.   510
But I detain you. Go, Narcissus, or
Britannicus might charge you with deceit.

NARCISSUS

No, no. He has blind faith in me. He thinks
I see you by his orders, and my aim
Is to inquire of all that touches him.   515

Through me he seeks to learn your secret thoughts.
To see his love he's all impatience, and
Expects to do so through my services.

NERO

Well. I agree. Bear him this welcome news.
520 He'll see her now.

NARCISSUS

Banish him far from her.

NERO

I have my reasons, and you may be sure
I'll sell him dear the joy of seeing her.
Meanwhile, boast to him of your stratagem;
Tell him you've tricked me, and he's seeing her
525 Without my orders. Someone's at the door.
It's she. Go seek your master. Bring him here.

Scene Three

NERO, JUNE

NERO

You lose composure, lady, and turn pale.
Do you read some sad presage in my eyes?

JUNE

I cannot hide from you that I have erred.
530 I sought Octavia, not the emperor.

NERO

I realize it, but I cannot hear
Without a twinge of envy it was she.

JUNE

Envy, my lord?

NERO

       Think you that in these halls
Only Octavia has eyes for you?

JUNE

Whom else, my lord, could I implore? Of whom   535
Should I inquire about an unknown crime?
You, who are punishing me, you must know.
My lord, I beg you, tell me my offence.

NERO

What! is your misdemeanour then so slight –
To hide your presence from me for so long?   540
These treasures that the heavens endowed you with,
Were they received only to bury them?
Shall then Britannicus untroubled see
His love and your enchantment blossoming?
Why from such glory banished until now   545
Have you confined me, cruel, to the court?
It's even asserted that, without offence,
You let him pay you his addresses. For
I cannot think, without consulting me,
That virtuous June has given him groundless hopes,   550
Or that you're willing to be loved or love
Without my knowing but by rumour's voice.

JUNE

I'll not deny, my lord, his words and sighs
Have sometimes been his heart's interpreter.
Nor has he shown disdain for me, alas!   555
The sole survivor of a glorious line,
Perhaps recalling that in happier times
His father named me as his future wife.
He loves me; he obeys his father, and
I dare to add, you and your mother too.   560
For your desires always accord with hers. . . .

NERO

My mother has her plans, and I have mine.
Let's talk no more of Claudius or of her;
Their choice is not what I am guided by.
565 No, I alone will answer for you, and
I wish myself to choose your husband.

JUNE

                                    Ah!
My lord, reflect that any other match
Will shame the Caesars, they from whom I spring.

NERO

Lady, the husband whom I have in mind
570 Can fitly link your ancestors with his.
You need not blush to listen to his suit.

JUNE

And who then is, my lord, this husband?

NERO

                                    I.

JUNE

You?

NERO

          I would indicate another name
If I knew someone greater than myself.
575 To offer you a choice you could accept
I've scoured the whole wide empire, Rome, the court.
The more I sought, the more I seek even now
Into whose hands this treasure to commit,
The more I see that Caesar, he alone,
580 Deserves to please you and take charge of it,
And can entrust you only to the hands
Assigned by Rome dominion of the world.
Yourself look backward to your earliest years.

Claudius had destined you, then, to his son,
But that was at a time when he had planned   585
To make him heir to the whole empire. Now
The gods have spoken. Far from flouting them,
You ought to rally to the empire's side.
They with this gift have honoured me in vain
If it is disunited from your heart;   590
If all my cares are not beguiled by you;
If, while I give to vigils and alarms
Days to be pitied, days always begrudged,
I cannot sometimes at your feet unbend.
Let not Octavia seem an obstacle;   595
Rome gives you its assent as well as I,
Repudiates her and invites me to
Dissolve a marriage heaven disavows.
Therefore reflect. Weigh carefully my choice
Worthy of a great prince who worships you,   600
Worthy of your fair eyes so long concealed,
And of the world to which you owe yourself.

JUNE

I am, my lord, not without reason dazed.
I in the compass of a single day
See myself dragged here like a criminal,   605
And, when I come before you terror-struck,
When I can hardly trust my innocence,
You offer me at once Octavia's place.
I dare to tell you I have not deserved
This undue honour or indignity.   610
And can you wish, my lord, that I who saw
Almost at birth my family extinct,
Who in obscurity nursing my grief
Attune my virtue to my wretched state,
Can suddenly emerge from darkest night   615
Into a rank full in the public eye
Whose brightness from afar I could not bear
And with whose majesty another's clothed?

599 *my choice:* the choice made by me.

NERO

I have already said I'll cast her off.
620 Show less affright, or else less modesty.
Accuse me not of blindness in my choice;
I'll answer for you to yourself. Consent.
Be mindful of the blood from which you spring.
Prefer a solid glory based upon
625 The honours Caesar means to grant you to
The glory of a No you will regret.

JUNE

The heavens see, my lord, my inmost thoughts.
I have no dreams of insane glory and
I realize the vastness of your gifts.
630 But the more splendour it would cast on me,
The more the rank would shame me, and enhance
The crime of having robbed the heir to it.

NERO

You take her interest far too much to heart.
Friendship can go no further, lady. But
635 Let's not deceive ourselves, and face the facts.
The brother, not the sister, touches you.
Britannicus . . .

JUNE

He's touched my heart, my lord.
This I have never troubled to conceal.
This frankness, I am certain, is unwise.
640 But my lips always speak what's in my heart.
Far from the court, my lord, I never thought
That I would have to learn to feign. I love
Britannicus. I was to marry him
When he was destined to the empire's throne.
645 But these misfortunes which have lost him it,
His honours cancelled and his palace shunned,
A court his downfall keeps away from him,

All these are ties that bind me fast to him.
Everything ministers to your desires.
Your days, in pleasure spent, flow by, serene.   650
The empire is their never-ending fount.
Or, if some sorrow interrupts their flow,
The whole world, eager for your happiness,
Hastes to efface them from your memory.
Britannicus has no one. I alone,   655
Whate'er torments him, I can care for him.
His pleasures are confined to these few tears
Which sometimes help him to forget his woes.

NERO

It is these tears and pleasures I begrudge.
All else but *he* would pay for them by death.   660
But in his case I'll show more clemency.
He'll soon appear before you.

JUNE

                    Ah! my lord,
Your virtues always reassured my fears.

NERO

I could have had him barred the entry here;
But I am anxious to avert the snares   665
Which his resentment might involve him in.
I do not seek his downfall. Better if
He hears his sentence from the lips he loves.
If his life's dear to you, send him away
Without his thinking I am jealous. Take   670
The burden of his exile on yourself;
And, if not by your words and silences,
At least by coldness make him realize
That he must bear his hopes in love elsewhere.

JUNE

I must pronounce to him this harsh decree!   675

163

I swore a thousand times the opposite.
Even if I could forget myself so far,
My eyes, my lord, would make him disobey.

NERO

Hidden near by, I shall observe you. So
680 Prison your love deep in your heart. There is
No secret language you can keep from me.
Looks you think silent I shall intercept.
His ruin is infallible if you
Let slip a gesture or a sigh for him.

JUNE

685 Alas! if still I dare to express a wish,
Allow me never to set eyes on him.

Scene Four

NERO, JUNE, NARCISSUS

NARCISSUS

Britannicus is seeking June, my lord.
He's near.

NERO

Let him come.

JUNE

Ah!

NERO

                    I'm leaving you.
His fate depends on you more than on me.
690 Remember, when you meet, I'm watching you.

Scene Five
JUNE, NARCISSUS

JUNE
Ah! dear Narcissus, haste to meet your lord;
Tell him ... I'm lost, for here I see him come.

Scene Six
JUNE, BRITANNICUS, NARCISSUS

BRITANNICUS (*to June*)
Ah! what good fortune brings me back to you?
What! I can now enjoy such sweet discourse.
But midst this pleasure grief devours me. Can   695
I hope alas! to see you once again?
Must I by endless devious paths purloin
Bliss that you once vouchsafed me every day?
What an awakening! What a night! Your tears
Did not disarm their cruel insolence.   700
Where was I then? What envious deity
Refused to let me die before your eyes?
Alas! in the affright that seized your soul,
Did you address some mute complaint to me?
My princess, did you deign to wish me there,   705
Or think how I would suffer for your sake?
You're silent. What an icy welcome! Is
It thus your eyes console my wretched plight?
Speak. We're alone. Our enemy deceived
While we are speaking is engaged elsewhere.   710
Let's use this happy absence to the full.

JUNE
You are in places echoing with his power.
These very walls, my lord, they may have eyes,

713 The literal translation – *eyes* – has been retained since it is the fact
that Nero *sees* June which is so sinister. See line 682 above.

And never is the emperor far from here.

BRITANNICUS

715 Since when are you so apprehensive? What!
Your love already lets itself be caged?
Where is this heart that always swore to me
To make even Nero envious of our love?
But banish, lady, such a groundless fear.
720 Loyalty's not yet dead in every heart;
All seem to approve my anger by their looks;
The emperor's mother has come out for us.
Indignant with his conduct, Rome itself. . . .

JUNE

My lord, you speak against your inmost thoughts.
725 You have repeatedly yourself confessed
That Rome spoke with one voice in praising him;
You always paid some homage to his deeds.
No doubt your language is inspired by grief.

BRITANNICUS

These words astonish me, I must admit.
730 I did not seek you out to hear him praised.
What! to confide to you my killing care,
I steal a favourable moment, and
This very moment, dearly bought, is spent
In praising Nero who oppresses us!
735 What has transformed you so in one short day?
Why! Ev'n your looks have learned how to be mute.
What do I see? You fear to meet my eyes?
Does Nero please you? Do you shrink from me?
Ah! if I thought so. . . . In God's name, dispel
740 The anguish into which you cast my soul.
Speak. Am I no more in your memory?

JUNE

Withdraw, my lord, the emperor is at hand.

BRITANNICUS

Narcissus, after this whom can I trust?

Scene Seven

NERO, JUNE, NARCISSUS

NERO

Lady. . . .

JUNE

My lord, I will hear nothing more.
You are obeyed. At least let me indulge   745
In tears his eyes will not be witness of.

Scene Eight

NERO, NARCISSUS

NERO

Well, then, you see how violent is their love,
Narcissus; even in her silences
It showed. She loves my rival. That is sure.
But I'll delight in making him despair.   750
I revel in imagining his grief;
I've seen him doubt the heart of his beloved.
I'll follow her. My rival waits for *you.*
By new suspicions haste to torture him;
And, while I see him wept for and adored,   755
Make him pay dear this bliss he knows not of.

NARCISSUS (*alone*)

Fortune is beckoning you a second time,
Narcissus. Will you now resist its voice?
Let's follow to the end its orders and
Let's ruin wretches to attain our goal.   760

ACT THREE

Scene One
NERO, BURRUS

BURRUS

Pallas obeys, my lord.

NERO

               And with what eye
Does Agrippina see her pride abased?

BURRUS

Ah! doubt it not. The blow's struck home, my lord.
Soon in reproaches she will vent her grief.
765 Her feelings long have started to explode.
May they in useless cries exhaust themselves!

NERO

What! think you she might stoop to plotting?

BURRUS

                              Well,
Your mother's always to be feared, my lord.
Rome, all your troops, revere her ancestors;
770 Germanicus, her father, they recall.
She knows her power, and you her vigorousness;
And what makes me redoubt her even more
Is that you feed more fuel to her wrath
And that you give her arms against you thus.

NERO

775 I, Burrus?

BURRUS

Yes, this love that masters you . . .

NERO

I understand, but that's past remedy.
I've blamed myself more than you ever will.
I *must* love, come what may.

BURRUS

You *think* you must,
My lord, and, with a token fight content,
You dread an evil that is weak at birth.   780
But if, buttressed by duty, you resolved
Never to come to terms with love, your foe;
If you consulted your first glorious years;
If you would deign, my lord, to call to mind
Octavia who deserves a better fate,   785
And her devotion which has risen above
Your scorn; if, more than all, avoiding June,
You weaned your eyes of her for some few days;
Despite this love by which you seem bewitched,
We love not if there's no desire to love.   790

NERO

I'll take your word, Burrus, when in the field
I must sustain the glory of our arms;
Or when, more tranquil, in the senate house
I must decide the nation's destinies,
I shall rely on your experience.   795
Believe me, though, love is a different art,
And I would scruple somewhat to compel
Your austere character to stoop that far.
Farewell. I suffer anguish without June.

Scene Two
BURRUS (*alone*)

800 Nero discloses his true self at last.
This cold ferocity I thought to tame
Is ready to shake off your feeble bonds.
In what excesses may it vent itself?
God! in this crisis, which way shall I turn?
805 Seneca who should ease the strain on me
Knows not this danger, busied far from Rome.
Stay. If, arousing Agrippina's love,
I could . . . But look. Good luck brings her this way.

Scene Three
AGRIPPINA, BURRUS, ALBINA

AGRIPPINA

Well, was I wrong in my suspicions, sir?
810 Your lessons are indeed remarkable!
Pallas is exiled, he whose crime perhaps
Was to have raised your master to the throne.
Nor, as you know, would Claudius whom he ruled
Have, but for him, adopted Nero. Nay
815 A rival has been given to his wife;
My son is from his wedding pledges freed.
Fine mission for the scourge of flatterers,
Chosen to curb his youthful ardour! You
Pander to it yourself. Nero can now
820 Despise his mother and forget his wife.

BURRUS

No, as of now, the charge is premature.
Nero's done naught that cannot be excused.

Blame Pallas' exile on himself alone;
Long has his pride invited punishment.
The emperor only does regretfully   825
What all the court demanded in their hearts.
The rest's a pity, but is not beyond
Repair. Somehow we'll dry Octavia's tears.
But calm your outburst. By a gentler path
You'll bring back Nero sooner to her. Cries   830
And menaces will merely frighten him.

AGRIPPINA

In vain you try to seal my lips. I see
My silence stimulates your scornfulness;
I'm too respectful of my handiwork.
My backing does not crumble, Pallas gone;   835
Heaven leaves me plenty to avenge my fall.
Now Claudius' son is starting to resent
Crimes which have brought me nothing but regret.
I'll show him to the army, doubt it not,
And rouse the soldiers' pity for his wrongs,   840
Make them like me atone for their mistakes.
On the one hand you'll see an emperor's son
Ask back the loyalty sworn to his race,
And hear the daughter of Germanicus;
And, on the other, Ahenobarbus' son   845
By tribune Burrus backed and Seneca,
Who, both recalled from exile by myself,
Share, in my eyes, supreme authority.
Our common crimes I mean to spread abroad;
I'll tell the paths by which I guided him.   850
To stir up hatred for his power and yours
I shall admit to the most foul reports.
I'll avow all, exiles and murders, even
Poison. . . .

827 *The rest*: a euphemistic allusion to June's abduction.
837 *Claudius' son*: Britannicus. Cf. also 842.
845 *Ahenobarbus' son*: Nero.

BURRUS

Lady, they'll not believe your words.
855 They will see through your stratagems and you –
A witness self-accusing out of spite.
For me, who was the first to aid your plans,
Who even made the army take the oath
To him, I'll not repent my honest zeal.
860 He is a son who takes his father's place.
Adopting Nero, Claudius, by that choice,
Mingled the rights of his own son and yours.
To choose him Rome was free. Tiberius too,
Adopted by Augustus, was their choice,
865 And young Agrippa, from Augustus sprung,
Was barred the sceptre which in vain he claimed.
His power, established on so firm a base,
By you yourself cannot be undermined;
And, if I've still his ear, his generous heart
870 Will soon make you forget your present schemes.
I have begun my task. I'll see it through.

Scene Four

AGRIPPINA, ALBINA

ALBINA

To what impulsive moves grief drives you on!
How can the emperor fail to learn of them?

AGRIPPINA

Ah! let him now appear to me himself.

ALBINA

875 Lady, in the gods' name, abate your wrath.
What! to the brother or the sister must
You sacrifice your peace of mind? Will you
Confine great Caesar even in his amours?

867 *His power:* Nero's power.

AGRIPPINA

Do you not see how low they're bringing me?
It's I to whom they give a rival, I.   880
Soon, if I do not break this fateful bond,
My place is taken, and I count for naught.
Till now Octavia, honoured but in name,
Was useless to the court, and hence ignored.
Favours and honours flowed from me alone,   885
Won me all mortals' interested desires.
This girl has taken Caesar by surprise.
She'll have the power of mistress and of wife.
The fruit of so much care, the Caesars' pomp,
All will hang on a single look of hers.   890
Nay, I am shunned. Already I'm cast off. . . .
Albina, I can not endure the thought.
Even should I hasten on heaven's firm decree,
Ungrateful Nero . . . Here his rival comes.

Scene Five

BRITANNICUS, AGRIPPINA, NARCISSUS, ALBINA

BRITANNICUS

Our common foes are not invincible,   895
And our misfortunes find responsive hearts.
Your friends and mine, till now so reticent,
While we were losing time in vain regrets,
Have, fired by anger at iniquity,
Confided to Narcissus their dismay.   900
Nero is not yet firm possessor of
The ingrate whom he scorns my sister for.
If you still feel the wrong that's done to her,
He can be guided back to duty's path.
Half of the senate will espouse our cause —   905
Sylla and Piso, Plautus . . .

893 *heaven's firm decree:* allusion to predictions by the Chaldean augurs
who had prophesied to Agrippina that her son would kill her.

AGRIPPINA

                    Prince, what's that?
Sylla and Piso, Plautus, all the chiefs
Of the nobility!

BRITANNICUS

            This wounds you and
I see your wrath, wavering, irresolute,
910 Already fears to win what it desires.
No, you have made my downfall too secure;
Fear no friend's daring now on my behalf.
I have no friends. Your too far-sighted moves
Lost me them or seduced them long ago.

AGRIPPINA

915 My lord, to your suspicions give less heed;
Our safety hangs on working hand in glove.
I've pledged my word. Despite your enemies,
I take back nothing that I've promised you.
Guilt-stricken Nero flees in vain my wrath;
920 Sooner or later he must listen to
His mother. I'll in turns be strong and mild;
Or with your sister I myself will go
And broadcast both my fear and her distress,
Winning all Romans over to her tears.
925 Farewell. I shall lay siege to Nero. You,
Take my advice and stay away from him.

Scene Six

BRITANNICUS, NARCISSUS

BRITANNICUS

Have you not lured me with deceiving hopes?
Is your account to be relied upon,
Narcissus?

NARCISSUS
Yes, but this is not the place
To pour this secret matter in your ear.   930
Let us go out. What are you waiting for?

BRITANNICUS
Alas!

NARCISSUS
What do you mean?

BRITANNICUS
                          If, by your art,
I could again see. . . .

NARCISSUS
                    Whom?

BRITANNICUS
                                I am ashamed.
But I'd await my fate with greater calm.

NARCISSUS
You think her faithful after all I've said?   935

BRITANNICUS
No, I believe her ingrate, criminal,
Deserving all my wrath. And yet I feel
I'm not convinced as deeply as I ought.
Persisting in its wilfulness, my heart
Excuses, justifies and worships her.   940
I'd like at last to rout my unbelief,
And like to hate her with a tranquil mind.
For who'll believe a heart that seems so great,
Opposed from childhood to a treacherous court,
Renounces so much glory and at once   945
Hatches vile plots unheard of even at court?

NARCISSUS

And who knows whether in her long retreat
She did not plan the emperor's conquest, sure
That she would not remain concealed for long?
950 Perhaps she fled, to stimulate pursuit,
To spur on Nero to the glorious feat
Of winning one till then invincible.

BRITANNICUS

I cannot see her then?

NARCISSUS

My lord, even now
She listens to her new admirer's suit.

BRITANNICUS

955 Well then, let's go, Narcissus. Look, it's she.

NARCISSUS (*aside*)

God! Quick, to the emperor and report this news.

Scene Seven

BRITANNICUS, JUNE

JUNE

Withdraw, my lord, and flee a frantic rage
Kindled against you by my steadfastness.
Nero is furious. I have stolen away
960 While Agrippina is detaining him.
Farewell. Doubt not my love, and be prepared
To hear me justify myself one day.
Your image, always present in my soul,
Can never be effaced.

BRITANNICUS

I understand.
965 I am to flee, safeguarding your desires,

And leave the field free for your new amours.
Doubtless, on seeing me, deep down, your shame
Allows you only an uneasy joy.
Well, I must leave.

JUNE

Do not impute to me . . .

BRITANNICUS

You might at least have held out longer. I   970
Do not complain that mere affection's bond
Should yield to those that fortune favours or
That you've been dazzled by the empire's pomp,
Even if it meant my sister's sacrifice;
But that, thirsting for greatness like the next,   975
You seemed to me so long averse to it,
No, I admit my heart is in despair
And unprepared for this one tragedy.
I've seen injustice rising on my fall
And heaven in league with my persecutors.   980
Heaven's wrath was not exhausted, for it still
Remained for me to be forgot by you.

JUNE

My just impatience would in happier times
Force you to make amends for your distrust.
But Nero threatens you. In this extreme   985
I've other worries than to harass you.
Come, sir, be reassured. Cease to complain.
Nero was listening then and bid me feign.

BRITANNICUS

What! cruel Nero . . .

JUNE

Witness of each word,
With a stern aspect kept his eyes on mine,   990
Ready to let his vengeance fall on you
For any gesture which betrayed our love.

177

BRITANNICUS

Nero was listening to you. But alas!
Could not your eyes have tried not to mislead,
995 And hinted at the author of this crime?
Must love have but one language or be mute?
What pain a single look could have dispelled!
You should have . . .

JUNE

        Sealed my lips and rescued you.
How oft, alas! since I must speak the truth,
1000 My heart began to tell how it was wracked!
Ah! cutting short innumerable sighs,
How I avoided eyes I always sought!
What torment not to speak to the beloved,
To hear him groan, to torture him oneself,
1005 When with a look I could console him! But
How many tears that one look would have cost!
Ah! when I think of it, unnerved, distraught,
I did not feel that I had feigned enough.
I feared the anguished pallor of my brow!
1010 I felt my looks betrayed my agony.
Ceaselessly angry, Nero seemed to me
To blame my eagerness in pleasing you;
I feared my love I could not keep within;
In short, I wished that I had never loved.
1015 Alas for his good fortune and for ours,
He sees only too clear into our hearts!
I say again conceal yourself from him;
At greater leisure I'll enlighten you,
And countless other secrets I'll report.

BRITANNICUS

1020 This is too much. I see only too well
Your kindness, my good fortune and my crime.
And do you know all that you leave for me?

(throwing himself at June's feet)

Ah! let me now atone for my mistake.

JUNE

What are you doing? Look. Your rival's here.

Scene Eight
NERO, BRITANNICUS, JUNE

NERO (*to Britannicus*)

Continue, Prince, these charming ecstasies.   1025

(*to June*)

I measure your indulgence by his thanks,
Lady; I've just surprised him at your feet.
But he might render thanks to me as well,
For this place favours him. I keep you here
Only to make such trysts easier for him.   1030

BRITANNICUS

I'll offer her my sorrow or my joy
Wherever she deigns to allow me to.
And this same palace where you prison her
Has nothing which should strke my soul with awe.

NERO

What docs it show you but admonishes   1035
That I should be respected and obeyed?

BRITANNICUS

It did not see the two of us brought up,
Me to obey you, you to brave me so,
And did not reckon when it saw us born
Domitius was to lord it over me.   1040

1034 Since he is in a palace where he was born and which he was to have inherited.
1040 Domitius was Nero's original name before Claudius adopted him. Its use by Britannicus is deliberately insulting. Cf. 18 and 1147.

NERO

Thus are our wishes crossed by destiny;
Then I obeyed. Now *you* have to obey.
If you have not yet learned to let yourself
Be guided, you are young and can be taught.

BRITANNICUS

1045 And who will teach me?

NERO

                    The whole empire, Rome.

BRITANNICUS

Does Rome imagine that your rights include
Force and injustice's full cruelty,
Poisoning and abduction and divorce?

NERO

Rome does not venture with inquiring eyes
1050 To pry out secrets that I hide from it.
Respect them too.

BRITANNICUS

                    Rome's views on them are known.

NERO

At least Rome does not speak. Be silent too.

BRITANNICUS

Nero begins to throw off all constraint.

NERO

Nero begins to weary of your words.

BRITANNICUS

1055 So everyone should bless his happy reign.

NERO

Happy or not, I want but to be feared.

BRITANNICUS

If I know aught of June, such sentiments
Are hardly such as merit her applause.

NERO

At least, lacking the secret how to please,
I can chastise a rival's hardihood.   1060

BRITANNICUS

But as for me, whatever perils lower,
Only her enmity can make me quail.

NERO

Pray for it, I can only say to you.

BRITANNICUS

My one ambition lies in pleasing her.

NERO

This she has promised you. You'll always please.   1065

BRITANNICUS

At least I do not spy upon her words.
I let her speak on all that touches me,
And do not hide, to force her to be mute.

NERO

I understand. Ho, guards!

JUNE
               What do you do?
He is your brother. He is jealous, Sire.   1070
A thousand woes harass his wretched life.
Can his good fortune make you envious?

Allow me to unite your hearts estranged.
I'll hide from you and steal away from him.
1075 My flight will terminate your direful strife;
My lord, I'll go and swell the vestals' throng.
Do not contend with him for my poor love,
And let the gods alone be vexed by it.

NERO

The plan is strange and suddenly conceived.
1080 To her apartments, guards, escort her back.
Britannicus keep in his sister's suite.

BRITANNICUS

Is this how Nero battles for a heart?

JUNE

Prince, without crossing him, bow to the storm.

NERO

Guards, do my bidding with no more delay.

Scene Nine

NERO, BURRUS

BURRUS

1085 What is this? God!

NERO (*without seeing Burrus*)

        Their love is twice as strong.
I recognize the hand that joined these two.
And Agrippina sought an audience
And was in her discourse so voluble
Only to play this odious trick on me.

(*seeing Burrus*)

1090 Find out whether my mother still is here.

She is confined within this palace. She,
Instead of *her* guards, shall be given mine.

BURRUS

What! without hearing her? Your mother?

NERO

                                        Stop.
I know not, Burrus, what you have in mind;
But, for these last few days, my every wish   1095
Has found you thwarting me censoriously.
Answer for it, I tell you. Otherwise
Others will answer both for you and her.

ACT FOUR

Scene One
AGRIPPINA, BURRUS

BURRUS

Yes, at your leisure, you can plead your case;
1100 Caesar himself deigns to receive you here.
If to the palace you're confined by him,
Perhaps the purpose was to talk to you.
Howe'er that be, if I dare speak my mind,
Forget that he may have offended you:
1105 Rather prepare to open wide your arms;
Defend yourself without accusing him.
The court looks, as you see, to him alone.
Though he's your son, and even your handiwork,
He is your emperor. And you must like us
1110 Bow to the power that he received from you.
Depending on his favour or his frown,
The court will crowd around or hold aloof;
It's his support that's sought in seeking yours.
But here the emperor comes.

AGRIPPINA
                            Leave me with him.

Scene Two
AGRIPPINA, NERO

AGRIPPINA (*sitting down*)
1115 Come hither, Nero, and assume your seat.
They summon me to clear myself with you.
    1116 *They:* a contemptuous reference to Burrus.

184

I know not with what crime I'm vilified;
All those I'm guilty of I shall expound.
You reign. You know how wide a gulf your birth
Had placed between imperial rule and you.   1120
Even my forebears' rights, that Rome endorsed,
Were stepping-stones to nowhere but for me.
The mother of Britannicus condemned,
The battle was begun for Claudius' hand.
Among all those intriguing for this prize   1125
And who implored his freedmen for their votes,
I coveted his bed with the sole thought
Of leaving you the throne I would ascend.
Swallowing my pride, I begged for Pallas' aid.
His master, each day fondled in my arms,   1130
Insensibly drank, in his niece's eyes,
The love towards which I sought to guide his heart.
But this blood bond that linked the two of us
Barred him the way to an incestuous bed.
He dared not wed his sister's daughter. But   1135
The senate was seduced. A milder law
Put Claudius in my bed, Rome at my feet.
It meant a lot for me, nothing for you.
You followed me into his family;
I had you given his daughter as your wife.   1140
Silanus loved her. She abandoned him,
And with his blood he marked that fatal day.
That still was nothing. How could you have hoped
To be preferred by Claudius to his son?
Pallas I once again implored to help.   1145
Won by my pleas, Claudius adopted you.
He called you Nero, and himself desired,
Before the time, to make you rule supreme.
Everyone *then*, calling to mind the past,
Unmasked my plot, already far advanced.   1150

1123 *The mother of Britannicus:* Messalina, who is never referred to by
name in the play in order, presumably, not to diminish sympathy for
Nero's rival. The construction of the line is a Latinism, the sense being:
Once the mother of Britannicus had been condemned.

Britannicus' impending downfall stirred
His father's friends to counteract my move.
My promises dazzled the eyes of some,
And exile freed me from the worst of them;
1155 Claudius, exhausted by my endless plaints,
Dispatched far from his son all those whose zeal,
Long tried and tested in his cause, could still
Unblock a pathway to the throne. Nay, more,
From my own retinue I chose the men
1160 I wished his education handed to.
And on the contrary I made a point
Of choosing tutors Rome revered for *you*.
Deaf to intrigue I went by good report,
I brought in Burrus from the army and
1165 Recalled from exile this same Seneca
Who since . . . Rome *then* esteemed their qualities.
At the same time exhausting Claudius' wealth,
My hand was spreading largesse in your name;
Gifts, circuses, these irresistibly
1170 Won you the people's and the soldiers' hearts.
The troops recalling earlier loyalties
Favoured in you Germanicus, my father.
But meanwhile Claudius started to decline.
His eyes, long closed, were opened in the end.
1175 He recognized his error. In his fear,
He even let slip some pity for his son,
And wished to rally all his former friends.
His guards, his palace, and his bed were mine.
I let his heart yearn unavailingly.
1180 I gained control of his last moments, and
My moves, ostensibly sparing his grief,
Concealed from him, dying, his own son's tears.
He died. What shameful rumours went the rounds.
I killed the news, too sudden, of his death;
1185 While Burrus went in secret to demand
The garrison's allegiance to you and

1166 *Who since* . . .: i.e. who have since used their position to intrigue
against me. See 142–161.

You reached the camp under my auspices,
In Rome the altars smoked with sacrifice;
Impelled by my false orders, all the town
Prayed for the health of one already dead.   1190
Finally, when the legions' firm support
Had reinforced your rule, Claudius was seen;
And, at his fate astounded, people learned
At the same time of your reign and his death.
This my sincere confession is to you.   1195
These are my crimes and this is my reward.
You had enjoyed the fruit of so much care
With seeming gratitude for six bare months
When, tired of a respect that rankled, you
Pretended not to know me any more.   1200
Burrus and Seneca poisoned your ear,
Giving you lessons in ingratitude
And pleased at being in their art outshone.
I've seen you favour with your confidence
Otho, Senecio, young libertines,   1205
Pandering to all your pleasures deferently.
And when, resentful at your deep contempt,
I asked account of all these wrongful deeds,
You answered me merely with new affronts –
The sole recourse of ingrates when exposed.   1210
June I affiance to your brother; they
Are both delighted with your mother's move.
What do you do? June is abducted, and
Becomes at once the object of your love.
I see Octavia cancelled from your heart,   1215
About to leave the bed I placed her in.
Pallas is banished and your brother seized;
To crown it all, you curb my liberty;
Burrus dares lay presumptuous hands on me.
And when, convicted of such perfidy,   1220

1183 *Shameful rumours:* that she had poisoned him (as indeed was the case).
1192 *Claudius was seen:* a literal translation. The sense is: People were allowed to see Claudius.

You should have seen me to atone for it,
It's you who bid me justify myself.

NERO

I'm well aware I owe the throne to you,
And, without troubling to repeat yourself,
1225 You could have, lady, with a tranquil mind,
Kindly relied upon my gratitude.
Moreover, these incessant, loud complaints
Have given all those who heard them to believe
That formerly (I speak between ourselves)
1230 You for yourself had worked under my name.
'Such honours and such deference,' they said,
'Are these such slight rewards for her support?
What are his crimes, this son she so condemns?
And has she crowned him only to obey?
1235 Is then his power only held in trust?'
Not that, could I have stretched a point so far,
I would not have been glad to yield to you
This power your cries seem to demand of me.
But Rome desires a master, not a mistress.
1240 You heard the rumours that my weakness roused.
The senate and the people, daily vexed
To hear your wishes published by my voice,
Affirmed that Claudius, dying, with his power
Had left me too his blind submissiveness.
1245 You've seen our soldiers bear resentfully
Their eagles past you time and time again,
Outraged at slighting by this shameful deed
The heroes who're depicted on them still.
Another would have yielded to the storm.
1250 But always, if you rule not, you complain.
In league against me with Britannicus,
You strengthen him by June's affiancement;
And all these plots are hatched by Pallas' hand.
And when reluctantly I would secure
1255 My peace of mind, spurred on by hate and fear,

You wish to show my rival to the troops;
Even in the camp the rumour goes the rounds.

AGRIPPINA

I make him emperor? *That*'s what you believed?
With what intent? What would it profit me?
What honours in his court could I expect?   1260
If, when you reign, I'm given scant respect,
If my accusers watch my every step,
If even their emperor's mother they molest,
What can I hope for in a stranger's court?
They would reproach me, not with feeble cries,   1265
With intrigues scotched the moment they are hatched,
But crimes committed for, in front of you,
Of which I'd be convicted all too soon.
I know you now. I see through all your shifts;
You are an ingrate and you always were.   1270
Even in the cradle all my loving care
Evoked only a feigned response from you.
Nothing could move you. Your hard-heartedness
Should have cut short my flow of kindliness.
How wretched am I, and by what ill luck   1275
Must all my efforts lead but to rebuffs.
I have one son alone. O you just heavens,
Have I made vows for anyone but him?
Remorse, fear, perils – nothing's held me back.
I rose above his scorn. I turned my gaze   1280
Away from ills foretold me even then.
I did my best. You reign. That is enough.
Take, with the freedom you've deprived me of,
My life as well, if you desire it so,
And may the people, by my death enraged,   1285
Not wrest from you what I've so dearly bought.

NERO

Well then, pronounce. What would you have me do?

AGRIPPINA

Punish my vile accusers' boldness; let
Britannicus' resentment be assuaged;
1290 Let June accept the husband of her choice;
Let both of them be free; let Pallas stay;
Grant me an audience at any time;

(seeing Burrus at the back of the stage)

Let Burrus, come to eavesdrop on us both,
No longer dare to stop me at your door.

NERO

1295 Yes, lady, in my gratitude I wish
Henceforth in people's hearts to engrave your power.
This happy coolness I already bless
Which has rekindled our affection's flame.
Whatever Pallas did I shall forget,
1300 And with Britannicus be reconciled.
As to this love that has divided us,
You shall be arbiter and judge the case.
Go then, and bear my brother this good news.
Ho! there, obey my mother's orders, guards.

Scene Three
NERO, BURRUS

BURRUS

1305 My lord, what an enchanting vision will
This peace and these embraces offer me.
You know if ever I denounced her, if
I tried to come between you and her love,
And if I've merited this unjust wrath.

1281 *ills foretold me:* that Nero would murder her. Cf. 893.
1286 *what I've so dearly bought:* Nero's rule as emperor.

NERO

I'll not mislead you. I complained of you,   1310
Burrus; I thought you were in league with her;
Her enmity restores my trust in you.
She triumphs, Burrus, all too early. I
Embrace my rival but to stifle him.

BURRUS

My lord?   1315

NERO

      This is too much. His downfall must
Free me for ever from my mother's rage.
While still he breathes, I'm only half alive.
She's wearied me by harping on his name.
I'll not allow her wicked recklessness
To promise him a second time my place   1320

BURRUS

So she will soon mourn for Britannicus.

NERO

Before the day is done I'll fear him not.

BURRUS

And what has made you harbour this design?

NERO

Glory and love, my safety and my life.

BURRUS

Whate'er you say, this horrible design   1325
Was never, Sire, engendered in your breast.

NERO

Burrus!

BURRUS

Must I, O heaven! learn this from you?
Could you without a shudder hear these words?
Think in what blood you are about to plunge?
1330 Is Nero tired of reigning in all hearts?
What will they say of you? What's your intent?

NERO

What! always prisoner of my past renown,
I'll have before my eyes this magic love
Which fortune gives and takes in one short day?
1335 Slave to their wishes, foe of my desires,
Am I their emperor just to humour them?

BURRUS

And is it not enough, my lord, for you
That public happiness on *you* depends?
It is for *you* to choose. You're master still.
1340 Virtuous, so far, you always can be so;
The path's marked out. Nothing now holds you back;
You've but to mount virtue's ascending scale.
But, if you listen to your flatterers,
You needs, my lord, must plunge from crime to crime,
1345 Buttress your deeds by other cruel acts,
And wash in blood your blood-stained arms. In death,
Britannicus will stimulate the zeal
Of friends who're ready to take up his cause.
And these avengers then will be avenged
1350 By men who, even on death, will be replaced.
You light a fire that cannot be put out.
Dreaded by all, you'll go in fear of all,
Always oppress, and tremble in your plans,
And number all your subjects as your foes.
1355 Ah! does the happy time of your first years
Make you, my lord, abhor your innocence?
Think of the happiness that shone in them.
How peacefully, O heaven! did they flow by.

What joy to think, to say within oneself:
'Everywhere, at this hour, I'm blessed, I'm loved;   1360
The people do not shudder at my name;
In all their sorrows I am never named;
They do not, darkly hostile, flee from me;
And hearts leap, everywhere, as I go by!'
Such were your pleasures. What a change, O God!   1365
The humblest was most precious in your eyes.
One day, I well recall, the senators
Urged you to underwrite a felon's death.
You would not yield to their severe demands;
You taxed yourself with too much cruelty,   1370
And, mourning the misfortunes empire brings,
'I wished,' you said, 'I had not learned to write.'
No. Either you'll be guided by me, or
My death will save me from the grievous sight;
I'll not survive the end of your good name,   1375
If you intend to do so foul a deed.

(throwing himself at Nero's feet)

I am prepared, my lord. Before you leave,
Bid them transfix this heart that won't consent.
Summon the cruel men who've prompted you;
Let them try out their still unsteady hand.   1380
But my tears touch my emperor, and I see
His virtue shudder at their frenzied rage,
Ah! lose no time. Tell me the wretches' names
Who dare to give you murderous advice.
Summon your brother. In his arms forget. . . .   1385

NERO

What do you ask!

BURRUS

He does not hate you. No.
He is betrayed. I know he's innocent.
I guarantee his loyalty to you.
I'll haste to him, press him to talk to you.

NERO

1390 In my apartment let him wait with you.

Scene Four
NERO, NARCISSUS

NARCISSUS

Everything's ready for this rightful death.
The poison's here. Famous Locusta has
Redoubled her devoted care for me;
She made a slave expire before my eyes;
1395 The sword is not less quick to end a life
Than the new poison she entrusts to me.

NERO

Narcissus, good. I'm grateful for your care,
But I do not desire you to proceed.

NARCISSUS

Your flagging hatred for Britannicus
1400 Forbids me. . . .

NERO

Yes, we're being reconciled.

NARCISSUS

Far be't from me to unpersuade you, but
Just now, my lord, he was your prisoner.
This slight will rankle in his heart for long;
There are no secrets time does not reveal.
1405 He'll know my hand was to administer
A poison you had had prepared for him.
May the gods turn his mind from this design.
But maybe he'll do what *you* dare not do.

NERO

His heart is vouched for, and I'll conquer mine.

NARCISSUS

Marriage with June, is that what seals the bond? 1410
You'll make this sacrifice as well, my lord?

NERO

You're overmuch concerned. Howe'er that be,
I do not count him as my enemy.

NARCISSUS

Yes, Agrippina, sir, was sure of it.
She has regained her sovereign hold on you. 1415

NERO

What's that? What did she say? What do you mean?

NARCISSUS

She boasted of it fairly openly.

NERO

Of what?

NARCISSUS

      She needed but a moment's speech
For all this sound and fury to subside
Into an unassuming silence. You, 1420
She said, would be the first to sue for peace,
Only too glad that she'd forget the past.

NERO

But, dear Narcissus, what am I to do?
I'm only too inclined to punish her
And to make sure her triumph's fond excess 1425
Is followed soon by lifelong, keen regret.
But what would Rome, the whole world, say? Am I

To follow in a tyrant's footsteps now?
Will Rome, effacing all my honoured deeds,
1430 Leave me as only title poisoner?
They'll stamp my vengeance as a fratricide.

NARCISSUS

And will you, Sire, be led by their caprice?
Did you imagine they would never talk?
Is it for you to heed their idle words?
1435 Are you unmindful of your own desires?
Are you the only one you dare not trust?
The Romans are not known to you, my lord.
No. In their utterances they're more reserved.
Such caution only undermines your rule.
1440 They'll think they really merit to be feared.
They've long been moulded to subjection's yoke.
They love the hand that keeps them firmly chained.
You'll see them always hankering to please.
Their slavishness wearied Tiberius. I
1445 Myself arrayed in robes of borrowed powers,
Given me by Claudius with my liberty,
A hundred times at my past glory's height,
I've tried their patience and not wearied it.
You fear the stigma of a poisoning.
1450 The brother kill; forsake the sister. Rome,
Lavishing victims on its altars, will
Find crimes for them even when they're innocent.
You'll see ranked as ill-augured both the days
On which brother and sister once were born.

NERO

1455 Narcissus, once again, I can't go on.
I've promised Burrus. I was forced to yield.
I do not want, breaking my word once more,
To give his virtue arms against me now.
My spirit flags, fighting his arguments.
1460 I hear his words with an uneasy mind.

NARCISSUS

Burrus, my lord, does not think all he says,
His virtue's shrewd, and husbands his prestige.
Or rather all of them have but one thought.
They'd see their power humbled by this move.
Then, Sire, you would be free, and, just like us, 1465
These haughty lords would bow the knee to you.
What! know you not all that they dare to say?
'Nero,' they whisper, 'is not born to rule.
He only says and does what he is bid.
Seneca guides his mind, Burrus his heart. 1470
His one ambition, his one quality,
Is in excelling as a charioteer,
Contending for unworthy prizes and
Exhibiting his prowesses to Rome,
And, lavishing his voice upon the stage, 1475
Reciting songs he wishes to be praised,
While soldiers go the rounds from time to time
Extracting tribute of applause for him.'
Ah! will you not force them to hold their tongue?

NERO

Narcissus, come. Let's see what's to be done. 1480

ACT FIVE

Scene One
BRITANNICUS, JUNE

BRITANNICUS

Yes, Nero – who would have imagined it? –
Awaits me to embrace me in his suite.
He has invited all his gilded youth.
He wishes festive pomp and gaiety
1485 To underwite his pledges publicly,
And render even more ardent our embrace.
Extinguishing this love, that caused such hate,
He makes you now my sovereign arbiter.
And I, though banished from my forebears' rank,
1490 And though he flaunts their spoils in front of me,
Since, ceasing to be hostile to my love,
He seems to me to yield this glorious prize,
.My heart, deep down, forgives him, I confess,
And leaves the rest to him with less regret.
1495 What! I need not be parted from you? I
Can in this moment, tranquil, look upon
These eyes unmoved by sighs or terror, which
Empire and emperor sacrificed to me?
Ah! lady . . . but what newly formed alarm
1500 Amidst our ecstasies constrains your joy?
Why, as you listen, do your saddened eyes,
These eyes with long-drawn looks gaze heavenward?
                                              What
Is it you fear?

JUNE
              I do not know myself.
But I'm afraid.

BRITANNICUS

You love me?

JUNE

Yes, alas!

BRITANNICUS

Nero no longer mars our happiness.   1505

JUNE

But do you vouch for his sincerity?

BRITANNICUS

What! you suspect him of a hate concealed?

JUNE

A moment past he loved me, swore your end.
He flees me, courts you. Such an utter change
Can hardly be a single moment's work.   1510

BRITANNICUS

This work was wrought by Agrippina's hand.
She thought my fall would spell her ruin too.
Thanks to her quick, forestalling enterprise,
Our greatest enemies have fought for us.
I trust the feelings she displayed to me.   1515
Burrus I trust. I trust his master even.
Like me, it is not in him to deceive.
His hate is frank, or he desists from hate.

JUNE

My lord, you should not judge his heart by yours.
Each of you goes his way by different paths.   1520
I've known the court and Nero for a day,
But, in this court, if I dare speak my mind,
How distant thought is from the spoken word!

1494 *the rest:* the empire.

BRITANNICUS

How little do the lips and heart agree!
1525 How joyfully do people break their word!
We both are strangers in a foreign land.

BRITANNICUS

Whether his friendship's genuine or feigned,
If *you* fear Nero, has *he* nought to fear?
No, he will not, by underhand attack,
1530 Provoke the people and the senators.
Nay, he admits the latest wrong he's done.
Even to Narcissus his remorse was clear.
If he had told you, Princess, the extent. . . .

JUNE

But does Narcissus not deceive you?

BRITANNICUS

                                        Why?
1535 What reason to distrust him has my heart?

JUNE

How can I say? Your life my lord's at stake.
All's suspect to me. *All* I fear's corrupt.
Nero I fear. I fear my evil star.
Despite myself, with dark forebodings filled,
1540 I see you go from me regretfully.
Alas! perhaps this peace in which you joy
Conceals some snare to rob you of your life.
Ah! what if Nero, angered by our love,
Had chosen the night to cloak his vengeance, if,
1545 Even as I look at you, prepared to strike.
Perhaps I speak to you for the last time!
Ah! Prince!

BRITANNICUS

                        You're crying! Ah! my dearest love,
Your heart can feel for me so deeply? In
A day when Nero, filled with sense of power,

Thinks he can blind you with the splendour here, 1550
Where everyone flees me and honours him,
You could prefer my plight to all the court?
What! in this very day, this very place,
Refuse an empire, weep in front of me!
But, lady, pray you, end these precious tears; 1555
Soon my return will dissipate your fears.
I would be suspect if I still delayed.
Farewell. My heart bursting with love, I go,
Amidst the transports of the blinded young,
To see, to talk to, my fair love alone. 1560
Farewell.

JUNE

Prince. . . .

BRITANNICUS

I must go. I'm waited for.

JUNE

But wait at least till you are summoned hence.

Scene Two

AGRIPPINA, BRITANNICUS, JUNE

AGRIPPINA

Prince, wherefore this delay? Leave with dispatch;
Nero impatiently complains you stay.
The joy and the delight of all the guests 1565
Waits, to burst forth, for you two to embrace.
Let not their wishes go unsatisfied.

(*to June*)

Go. Let us, lady, to Octavia.

BRITANNICUS

Go
Fair June, and hasten, with a carefree mind,

1570 To greet my sister who's awaiting you.

(*to Agrippina*)

As soon as possible, I'll follow you
And come and thank you for your services.

Scene Three

AGRIPPINA, JUNE

AGRIPPINA

Lady, I err, or during your farewell
Some tears of grief have moistened your fair eyes.
1575 May I not know what care has cast this cloud?
You harbour doubts about the peace I've wrought?

JUNE

After the anguish that this day has brought,
How could I calm the turmoil in my mind?
I still can hardly grasp the miracle.
1580 I fear your efforts may be thwarted, for,
Lady, some change is common at the court;
And some alarm always attends on love.

AGRIPPINA

No more. I've spoken. Everything has changed.
There is no room for your suspicions now.
1585 I answer for a peace that's sworn to me;
Nero has given too definite a pledge.
Ah! had you seen him when, caressing me,
He reaffirmed to me his promises!
By what embraces did he keep me here!
1590 His loving arms could not take leave of me;
His loving kindness, written on his face,
Descended to the slightest details. He
Confided like a son who trustingly
Forgets his pride upon a mother's breast.

But soon, resuming a severer mien,   1595
As of an emperor who consults his mother,
His august confidence placed in my hands
Secrets on which the empire's fate depends.
No, it must to his glory be confessed,
His heart is not inclined to wickedness.   1600
Only our foes, leading his heart astray,
Abused his kindliness against us both.
But now at last *their* power's on the wane.
Rome will know Agrippina once again;
Already my return to favour's hailed.   1605
But let us not wait here for night to fall.
Let's see Octavia, giving her the rest
Of an auspicious day I thought ill-starred.
But what's this noise? What these tumultuous cries?
What can it be?   1610

JUNE

God, save Britannicus!

Scene Four
AGRIPPINA, JUNE, BURRUS

AGRIPPINA

Where are you running, Burrus? Stop. What means . . .

BURRUS

Britannicus is dying. It's the end.

JUNE

Ah! my beloved!

AGRIPPINA

He's dying?

BURRUS

                    He is dead,
Lady.

JUNE
Forgive this burst of grief. I'll go
1615 And help him if I can, or follow him.

Scene Five
AGRIPPINA, BURRUS

AGRIPPINA
What a vile outrage!

BURRUS
I can not survive.
I must forsake the court, the emperor.

AGRIPPINA
What!
He did not shrink even from his brother's blood?

BURRUS
The plot was carried out more cunningly.
1620 As soon as Caesar saw his brother, he
Rises, embraces him. There is a hush.
Suddenly Caesar takes a goblet up:
'To give this day a more auspicious end,
My hand pours out the first drops of this cup.
1625 Gods, from whom this libation flows,' he says,
'Be present at our new-found harmony.'
Britannicus swears the same binding oaths.
Narcissus fills the goblet in his hands;
But hardly did his lips approach the rim,
1630 The sword is not more powerful to strike;
Lady, the light is ravished from his eyes;
He falls upon his couch, inert and cold.
Imagine how this blow dumbfounds us all.

1619 i.e. no blood was shed.

Half of us, terror-struck, run screaming out.
But those with longer knowledge of the court   1635
Compose their face in line with Caesar's eyes.
He still remains reclining on his couch.
Astonishment appears to pass him by,
'This malady, whose violence you fear,
Has oft in vain attacked him as a child,'   1640
He says. Narcissus makes a show of grief,
But his false joy bursts out in spite of him.
For me, even should the emperor punish me,
I made my way through a detested court,
Prostrated by this crime, to go and mourn   1645
Britannicus, Caesar and all the state.

AGRIPPINA

He comes. You'll see if I'm behind his deed.

Scene Six

AGRIPPINA, NERO, BURRUS, NARCISSUS

NERO (*seeing Agrippina*)

God!

AGRIPPINA

    Nero, stop. I want a word with you.
Britannicus is dead. I see by whom.
I know the murderer.   1650

NERO

    Who is it?

AGRIPPINA

            You.

NERO

                    I?
How can you harbour such suspicions? Ah!

There are no ills but I'm to blame for them.
And, if one were to listen to your words,
It was *my* hand that cut short Claudius' life.
1655 You loved his son. His death leaves you distraught.
But can I answer for the blows of fate?

AGRIPPINA

No, no. Britannicus was poisoned, and
Narcissus did the deed. You ordered it.

NERO

Lady . . . Who can have said such things to you?

NARCISSUS

1660 My lord, does this suspicion wound you so?
Britannicus, lady, had secret plans
That would have given you greater cause for pain.
Marriage with June was but a minor goal.
For your own help he would have made you pay.
1665 He was deceiving you. His slighted heart
Was bent, some day, on calling back the past.
Whether, despite you, fate has served you, or
Whether, informed of plots against his life,
Caesar relied upon my loyalty,
1670 Leave weeping to your enemies alone.
Let this misfortune bode most ill for them.
But you . . .

AGRIPPINA

Go on with such lieutenants. You
By glorious deeds will make yourself renowned.
Go on. After this step, you'll not turn back.
1675 Your hand has started with your brother's blood,
And one day it will strike your mother too.
Deep in your heart, I know you hate me. For
You wish your freedom from your debt to me.
My death itself, though, will avail you nought.

1666 *calling back the past:* advancing his earlier claims to the empire.

Think not that, dying, you'll be left in peace.   1680
These heavens, this Rome, this life you owe to me,
Will rise unendingly to haunt your dreams.
Like furies, your remorse will dog your steps;
You'll think to calm them by some other crimes;
Your frenzy, feeding on its violence,   1685
With bloodshed ever fresh will mark your days.
But in the end I hope the outraged heavens
Will add, to all your other victims, *you*;
And, having wallowed in their blood and mine,
You will yourself be forced to shed your own.   1690
And in the days to come your name will seem
To cruel tyrants a most cruel slight.
This does my heart presage for you. Farewell
Now you may go.

NERO

Narcissus, follow me.

Scene Seven

AGRIPPINA, BURRUS

AGRIPPINA

Ah! My suspicions were unjust! I blamed   1695
Burrus, and to Narcissus lent my ear.
Did you see, Burrus, what a furious gaze,
In leaving Nero gave me as farewell?
All's over. Nothing more can stop him now.
The blow foretold will fall upon my head.   1700
And you yourself will in your turn be crushed.

BURRUS

Ah! lady, I have lived a day too long.
Would that his hand, with happy cruelty,
Had tried his new-found frenzy out on me;

1705 That he had not, by this foul outrage, given
Too sure a pledge of ills that plague the state.
His crime alone is not what makes me quail.
Jealousy could have driven him to the deed.
But, if I must explain my grief to you,
1710 Nero beheld him die unblenchingly.
His eyes already have the impassive look
Of tyrants who're inured to crime since youth.
Let him conclude, and let him send to death
A tiresome, disapproving minister.
1715 Far from my wanting to avoid his wrath,
The swiftest death would be most dear to me.

Scene Eight

AGRIPPINA, BURRUS, ALBINA

ALBINA

Lady, my lord, haste to the emperor. Come
And rescue Caesar from his frenzied rage.
He's forced to part from June eternally.

AGRIPPINA

1720 What! June herself has ended her own life?

ALBINA

To weigh the emperor down with endless grief,
Now, without dying, she is dead for him.
Thus did she dash to liberty from here:
She feigned to go to sad Octavia's rooms,
1725 But soon she took a less familiar path,
On which my eyes followed her hasty steps.
Out of the palace gates she went distraught.
Augustus' statue struck her eyes at once,
And, moistening with her tears his marble feet
1730 Which she encircled with her fervent arms:

1700 *The blow foretòld:* cf. 1281 above.
1714 *minister:* used in the Latin sense of lieutenant, assistant.

'Prince, by these knees,' she says, 'I hold embraced,
Protect at once the remnants of your line.
Here in your palace has been sacrificed
Your one descendant that resembled you.
They want me, on his death, to be forsworn.   1735
But, to be true to him perpetually,
I dedicate myself to these high gods
Whose altars by your virtue now you share.'
Meanwhile the people, whom this sight astounds,
Run up and crowd around her on all sides;   1740
Moved by her tears and pitying her woes,
With one accord take her beneath their wing.
They lead her to the shrine where from of old
Our virgins destined to the altars' cult
Guard so devotedly the precious trust –   1745
The flame undying, burning for our gods.
Caesar watches them go, but dares not act.
Narcissus, bolder, and intent to please,
Makes for fair June, and unabashed begins
To stop her in her flight with impious hand.   1750
This recklessness is punished by a hail
Of deadly blows. His blood spurts out on June.
Caesar, struck by so many sights at once,
Abandons him to his avengers' hands.
He goes back home. All flee his silence grim.   1755
Only the name of June comes from his lips.
Aimless he walks, and with unsteady gaze
Dares not to heaven raise his eyes distraught.
And it is feared, if night and solitude
Will stimulate the anguish of despair,   1760
If any longer you refuse him aid,
His grief is such that he will take his life.
Time presses. Haste. It needs a passing mood,
And it will be his end.

AGRIPPINA

      As he deserves.
But Burrus, let us go and see how far   1765

His wild fits go, what change remorse will bring,
And if henceforth he'll follow other ways.

BURRUS

Would God it were the last of his foul crimes!

BERENICE

A Tragedy

INTRODUCTION TO *BERENICE*

THE subject of *Berenice* is simple. It is the agonizing parting of a man and a woman who have been everything to each other for five years. With unwonted terseness, Victor Hugo summarized the action by ticking off the five acts on the fingers of one hand: *Titus / Reginam Berenicem / invitus / invitam / dimisit.* This neat formula, based on a quotation from the Latin historian, Suetonius, means literally: Titus / Queen Berenice / he unwilling / her unwilling / sent away.

Racine's contemporaries did not take to the play, and their unfavourable judgement was not, as in the case of *Britannicus*, speedily reversed. Most famous critics of later ages were harsh in their condemnation. Voltaire pronounced that the work was merely 'an eclogue in dialogues' and was 'unworthy of the tragic stage'. 'A lover and his mistress' (the words are used in the platonic seventeenth-century sense), he declared, 'cannot possibly provide a fit subject for tragedy. This is unquestionably the weakest of Racine's works still being performed.' For Sainte-Beuve, writing in the same hostile vein, *Berenice* is 'a charming and melodious weakness in Racine's work'. It is 'a ravishing elegy'. There is no action to speak of. 'Every act is more or less the same all over again.' And most other critics up to 1900, and even a few of the more recent ones, have been equally unkind.*

It is difficult to avoid the impression that the great men just quoted and their less eminent *confrères* are yielding, consciously or unconsciously, to the preference for violence which seems to be ineradicably implanted in mankind, and which is so amply satisfied by spectacles such as that of Hermione, seeking in a fine frenzy of unrequited passion to engineer the execution of Andromache's infant son, ordering the wretched Orestes to assassinate Pyrrhus, disowning the horrible deed

* For a convenient summary of the critics' views of the play, readers are referred to Michaut, *La Bérénice de Racine* (pp. 145–71), Paris, 1907.

when it has been done, and finally stabbing herself to death over the corpse of the man whom she so insanely adored. The voluntary parting of the royal lovers seems tame by comparison.

Yet, in his Preface, Racine replied in advance to such criticisms and to the mentality underlying them. 'It is not essential,' he wrote, 'that there should be blood and corpses in a tragedy.' All that is needed is that 'the theme [be] elevated, the passions aroused, and all the play breathe . . . that majestic sadness which is the whole pleasure of tragedy'. And he buttresses his plea for an 'aesthetic of simplicity' by reference to Sophocles' *Ajax* and *Philoctetes*, which revolve round an internal conflict and are practically devoid of external or complicated episodes.

Paradoxically, it is the very nakedness of the structure of *Berenice* that has obscured its dramatic intensity. Only recently, thanks to such writers as Michaut, Dubech, Butler and especially Picard, has the play's mechanism been explained and the way laid open for an understanding of its true essence and greatness.

The central issue is whether Titus will have the strength and courage to carry out his decision to banish Berenice. Long before he inherited power, he had been aware of the Roman prejudice (amounting to a veto) against a foreign woman ascending the throne of the Caesars, a hostility infinitely more unrelenting in the case of a queen, such as Berenice.*

But, if Titus had foreseen the opposition to marriage with her, he had, with blatant wishful thinking, waved aside any doubts as to his ability to enforce his wishes. It is only when he loses his father and is crowned emperor,

When the whole empire bows the knee to [him] (1085)

that he is forced to shed his illusions and that he realizes:

The great gulf fixed between the throne and [her] (1396)

* Racine does not explain why, in these blissful years preceding the crisis, Titus did not simply marry his beloved. The equally surprising fact that she did not become his mistress, as Racine explicitly assures us she did not, is doubtless to be put down to the stern proprieties which are an integral part of the French classical aesthetics.

and the inevitability of sacrificing Berenice to his imperial mission.

Between the new ruler and his happiness stands the majesty of Rome which resounds through the play like a ground bass. The empire is, in effect, co-terminous with the known world (for a European) at the time. But it is symbolized by its nerve centre, Rome. The city is represented as being not only the heart of the empire, but almost a living entity. It may in reality have been 'an insensate mob', as Berenice terms it contemptuously, a rabble reduced to dependence on *panem et circenses*, and its detestation of Titus' beautiful and virtuous sweetheart may be simply an irrational taboo. But, even if this were so, its hostility would still constitute a key factor which no responsible ruler could afford to disregard. As Titus realistically foresees (but rather late in the day), any weakening on his part over Berenice would force him into making dangerous political concessions, which would jeopardize future stability. The Roman empire was never very far from anarchy at the time. With the exception of his father, Vespasian, the previous four emperors had all been murdered and replaced in quick succession.

Whatever the real maturity or influence of the Roman masses, Racine shows them as being justified in opposing Titus' projected marriage. It is significant that the main spokesman of this opposition is the emperor's own confidant, Paulinus, a man of transparent integrity. The Romans for their part are portrayed as a powerfully articulated and politically responsible force represented by 'the tribunes, consuls, senate'. The tribunes, it will be noted, come first. Every detail in Racine counts. Indeed, it is a piquant commentary on his meticulous handling of historical material that he mentions the consuls as part of the deputation to Titus, though well aware that the consuls for the year were no other than the deceased Vespasian and Titus himself. It was essential for the needs of the drama to build up an impressive alliance of the various orders speaking for Rome, and all speaking with one voice.

The clash, then, between Titus' desire to marry Berenice

and his imperial responsibilities is real, profound and un-bridgeable.

But why, it may be asked, does he not simply renounce the throne and go off and live with his beloved Berenice far away from the power politics of Rome? The answer is that he is prompted not so much by fear of the people's hatred of a foreign empress as by his determination to do what he regards as his duty and save the empire. Any evasion of his imperial mission appears to him unmanly. When he is tempted to succumb, he quickly lashes himself back to the path of self-sacrifice:

> Coward, renounce the empire and make love! (1024)

As Raymond Picard has so lucidly explained, in his preface to the play in the Pléiade edition of Racine, 'his accession to the imperial dignity has been a kind of baptism; his eyes are opened. He is enlightened.'

> Renown,
> Inexorable, haunts [his] every step. (1394)

Titus, having seen the light, will now serve his glory in the same way as the believer, touched by grace, consecrates himself to his faith. He pays no need either to his strength or to the obstacles.

> I'll not reflect whether I can survive. (552)

He feels that he has been called. He responds to the summons.

However,

since this salvation presupposes death and more than death, there is scope for all the suffering and heroism of which a man is capable. It is in this specifically dramatic interval, between the decision and the conversion, that the action of *Berenice* takes place.

And it is by no means certain that he will have the super-human strength of will to carry through his resolve to the bitter end.

Thrice Titus is on the point of giving in, and thrice he pulls back. The hero is constantly on the verge of collapse, and tragic tension never flags.

The first ordeal is to break the news of his decision to Berenice. He does not dare to do so himself and falls back on the services of an intermediary – his unfortunate rival, Antiochus. Berenice's reaction is naturally simply to blast the messenger of doom, but she has been shaken in her assurance that the future is hers. Shortly afterwards, when Berenice bursts in on him, Titus can do no better than stammer:

The empire, Rome . . . (623)

before making a precipitous exit. It is only in Scene Four of Act Five that he can finally bring himself to tell her that she must leave Rome for good.

But the second and stiffest hurdle to be surmounted is Berenice's unwillingness to accept her banishment. Titus, she argues forcefully, is all-powerful. Why can he not override the veto of the Roman mob? And, when he musters up all his energy and insists that she must go, she ends the discussion by threatening to take her life. If she were really to commit suicide, Titus would have no option but to do likewise. Only if she can rise above her feelings can he steel himself to rule the empire without her at his side. It is not until the final scene of the play that Titus wins his battle, and his victory is possible only because Berenice, convinced that he really loves her, makes the supreme sacrifice of her feelings. In short, the tragedy pivots on her decision, and hence bears her name.

As with Titus, her ascent to grace is slow and uncertain. Her evolution has been succinctly described by Michaut (op. cit., p. 213) as: 'Act I: Berenice's illusion; Act II: Berenice's doubts; Act III: Berenice's disillusion; Act IV: Berenice's despair; Act V: Berenice's resignation.' Her hesitating advance is entirely understandable. *She* has no prospect of imperial grandeur to fill the void created by a love suppressed.

But her final renunciation is in no way the fruit of weakness or passiveness. With every fibre of her being, in each of her highly varied moods, she is a moving and attractive figure, well worthy to rank beside Andromache, Iphigenia and Monime (in *Bajazet*) in Racine's rich gallery of virtuous women.

There is no bloodshed in her final parting from Titus, but the separation is as fearful as any of the more violent endings in Racine. For, by a tragic irony, it is Berenice who has instilled into Titus, the erstwhile profligate, the thirst to serve the empire which has led to his enlightenment on his accession to the throne. As Titus puts it himself,

> I owe her everything. Cruel reward!
> All that I owe her will recoil on her. (519–20)

Thus, the tragic situation from which there is no way out has been fashioned by her own idealism.

Berenice, then, is a tragedy, and a highly dramatic one, rather than an elegy. What is more, it is utterly Racinian and not an attempt to absorb or copy Corneille's ethos as is often contended because of the play's glorification of the will over passion. This erroneous view has been disposed of in some admirable pages of Butler's *Classicisme et baroque* (pp. 233 *et seq.*). As he points out, the Preface to *Berenice* (and also the Preface to *Britannicus*) amounts to a declaration of war on Corneille and that writer's principles. Racine is making a plea for the utmost simplicity in plot-machinery, for the avoidance of complicated and far-fetched episodes, for naturalness in psychology. Never was he to give a more extreme illustration of this aesthetic than in the present tragedy.

Moreover, the main characters in the play could not have behaved in a way which clashed more sharply with baroque (and hence Cornelian) canons.

Titus is as unpleasant a character as could be imagined. He is ... neither *galant* [i.e. courtly] nor heroic. The public insult to Berenice, whom he has promised to marry and whom he drives out of Rome, is the act of a perjurer and a scoundrel; it arouses only revulsion and contempt. ... Nor is he able to overcome his love, however mediocre that may be; he is incapable of rising above his passion, and he does not know the proud satisfaction of being 'lord of himself as of the universe'.

And Berenice offends even more against the baroque code.

As queen and woman, the poet places her in the falsest, most numiliating light ... yet she does not stop loving [the man who insults her], and she admits it to his face! She has neither pride nor reserve nor restraint. She does not know what *la gloire* [i.e. honour, concern for her good name] is. How different from all the proud baroque heroines from whom the most passionate respect or prayers of their 'swains' does not succeed in extracting 'that confession which is so hard to make'.

And, if it is objected that this is history, then, as Saint-Evremond and Boileau agreed, this subject is not fit matter for a tragedy. The work should never have been written.

True, Titus and Berenice sacrifice their love.

But, in Corneille, the sacrifice carries its own reward. The characters are elevated by it to soaring heights of freedom and joy. In Racine, on the contrary, the characters are maimed by it, condemned to a living death. They hate themselves, whereas in Corneille, even when going to their death, they glory in the prospect.

This persistence in reading Cornelian overtones into *Berenice* is all the more strange since Corneille himself wrote a tragedy on the same theme and at exactly the same time as Racine. His work is called *Titus and Berenice*. The two plays could hardly be more different. Corneille eliminates the offensive scene in which Berenice is scorned by Titus and banished. In defiance of all political realism, Titus leaves the decision as to her future to Berenice herself. In an even wilder burst of fantasy, Corneille makes Rome and the Senate confer Roman citizenship on her. And then, but only then, does she decide to leave Rome, head erect and in triumph. Titus himself emerges from the tussle somewhat battered but a gentleman!

Corneille's tragedy is too, as almost always, extremely complex and involved. It has other characters who play such a prominent part in the plan as to detract attention from the two central figures. The contrast between this over-elaborate work and Racine's starkly simple play could hardly be more striking.

Indeed, the antithesis is not confined to the general structure of the plays. There are numerous passages in which the opposition is so marked as to be clearly deliberate.* It now seems probably that Racine, having learned that Corneille was working on the subject, deliberately chose to issue the most direct possible challenge to his ageing rival.

The outcome is an extreme example of Racine's almost geometrical simplicity of construction, but above all a masterpiece of tragic beauty bathed in a luminous pathos of passion, grandeur and renunciation.

* See Michaut, op. cit., pp. 126–31.

DEDICATORY EPISTLE

To My Lord Colbert
Secretary of State, Comptroller General of Finance, Supervisor of Works, Grand Treasurer of the King's Orders, Marquis de Seignelay, etc.

My Lord,

Whatever well-founded mistrust I have of myself and my works, I dare to hope that you will not condemn the liberty which I take of dedicating this tragedy to you. You did not deem it entirely unworthy of your approval. But what constitutes its greatest merit in your eyes is, My Lord, *that you have been the witness of its good fortune of not displeasing His Majesty.*

It is known that the smallest things become worthy of being considered by you provided they serve his glory or pleasure; and this is why, amidst so many important occupations to which zeal for your king and the public weal keep you continually riveted, you do not sometimes disdain to stoop to our level* to ask us to give account of our leisure.

I would at this point have a splendid opportunity of singing your praises, if you allowed me to praise you. And what could I not say of so many rare qualities which have won you the admiration of the whole of France; of this penetrating mind which lets nothing pass; of this encyclopedic knowledge which comprehends and executes simultaneously so many great things; of this soul that nothing disconcerts, that nothing tires!

But, My Lord, *one must be more moderate in speaking to you of yourself; and I would be afraid, by undesired praise, to make you repent of the favourable attention with which you have honoured me; it is better to try to deserve it by writing new works. In any case, this*

---

* i.e. of men of letters.

is the most agreeable thanks that you can be given. I am, with profound respect,

MY LORD,

Your very humble and very obedient servant,

RACINE

RACINE'S PREFACE TO *BERENICE*

Titus, reginam Berenicem ... cum etiam nuptias pollicitus ferebatur ... statim ab Urbe dimisit invitus invitam.*

This is to say: 'Titus, who loved Berenice passionately, and who even, it was believed, had promised to marry her, sent her away from Rome, against his will and against hers, in the very first days of his rule.' *This action is famous in history. And I found it most suitable for the stage, because of the violence of the passions which it was capable of exciting. In fact, there is nothing more touching in any of the poets than the separation of Dido and Aeneas in Virgil. And who can doubt that what provided matter for a whole canto of a heroic poem, where the action lasts several days, is not sufficient for a tragedy which should not take up more than a few hours? It is true that I have not driven Berenice to kill herself, like Dido, because Berenice, not having with Titus the ultimate commitments that Dido had with Aeneas, is not obliged, like Dido, to take her life. Apart from that, her last farewell to Titus, and the efforts she makes to part from him, are not the least tragic aspect of the play. And I dare to affirm that it whips up, in the hearts of the spectators, the emotion which the rest of the play aroused in it. It is not essential for there to be blood and corpses in a tragedy. It is enough if the action is elevated, the characters heroic, the passions aroused, and if all the play breathes that majestic sadness which is the whole pleasure of tragedy.*

I thought that I could find all these ingredients in my subject; but what pleased me more was that I found it extremely simple. I had long desired to try if I could write a tragedy of that simplicity of action which was so much to the Ancients' taste. For it is one of the basic precepts which they have left us: 'Let what you do,' *says Horace,* 'be always simple and a whole.' *They admired Sophocles' Ajax, who kills himself out of chagrin, because of the madness which seized him after the refusal to give him Achilles' arms. They admired the Philoctetes,† of which the whole subject is that Ulysses tries to take Hercules' arrows by surprise. Even Oedipus,† although full of recog-*

* Suetonius, *Titus*, Chapter VII.   † Other tragedies by Sophocles.

nition scenes, is less burdened with matter than the simplest tragedy of our time. We see, to conclude, that the supporters of Terence, who rightly put him above all comic poets for the elegance of his diction and the vraisemblance* *of his characters, nevertheless confess that Plautus scores over him by the simplicity of most of his subjects. And no doubt it is this wonderful simplicity which won Plautus all the praise lavished on him by the Ancients. How much simpler even than he was Menander, since Terence is forced to take two of that poet's comedies to make one of his!*

And it must not be thought that this rule is just a product of the fantasy of those who made it. Only the vraisemblable *touches in tragedy, and what likelihood is there that in one day a host of things takes place which could hardly happen in several weeks? There are people who think that this simplicity is a sign of poor inventive capacity. It does not occur to them that, on the contrary, the essence of inventive capacity consists in making something out of nothing, and that all this accumulation of incidents has always been the refuge of poets who did not feel they had enough imaginativeness or enough vigour to hold their spectators' attention for five acts by a simple action supported by the violence of the passions, the beauty of the feelings and the elegance of their style. I am far from imagining that all these qualities are to be found in my work; but neither can I believe that the public takes it amiss that I have given it a tragedy which has been honoured by so many tears and the thirtieth performance of which was as well attended as the first.*

It is not that some people have not reproached me with this simplicity which I had sought with such care to achieve. They thought that a tragedy which had such a slender plot could not measure up to the rules of playwriting. I inquired whether they complained of being bored. I was told that they all admitted that they were not bored, indeed that several passages in it touched them and that they would be happy to see it again. What more do they want? I would urge them to have a good enough opinion of their judgement not to believe that a play which touches and delights them can be absolutely contrary to the rules. The golden rule is to delight and to touch. All the rest are only designed to observe this central rule. But all these other rules go into

* *Vraisemblance:* verisimilitude, i.e. conformity to life – one of the main standards of all French classical writing.

great detail, which I do not advise them to bother about. They have more important things to do. Let them rely on us to take upon ourselves the chore of expounding the difficulties in Aristotle's Poetics; *let them stick to the pleasure of weeping and being moved; and let them allow me to say to them what a musician said to Philip of Macedonia, who asserted that a song was not according to the rules: 'God forbid, my lord, that you should ever be so unfortunate as to know these things better than I!'*

This is all I have to say to those persons whom I shall always be proud to please. For, as for the pamphlet* attacking me, I think that the readers will be only too glad to dispense me from replying to it. And what in fact can I reply to a man who does not think at all and who does not even know how to set out what he thinks? He speaks of protasis as if he understood what the word meant, and asserts that this first of the four parts of the tragedy should always be clos est to the last one, which is the catastrophe! He complains that his excessive knowledge of the rules prevents him from enjoying himself at the play. Certainly, to judge from his dissertation, never was a complaint less well-founded. It seems that he has never read Sophocles, whom he most incorrectly praises for a great multiplicity of incidents *and that he has never even read any poetics except in the prefaces to some tragedies. But I forgive him for not knowing the rules of play-writing, since, fortunately for the public, he does not go in for this kind of writing. What I do not forgive him is for being so unfamiliar with the laws of wit, particularly as he insists on seasoning every word with a joke. Does he think he amuses polite society by these* pocket alases *and a host of other cheap witticisms which he will find condemned in all the good authors if he ever gets round to reading them.*

All these criticisms are the monopoly of four or five wretched little scribblers who have never been able to arouse the interest of the public by themselves. They always look out for some work which succeeds in order to attack it, not out of jealousy, for what grounds would they have for jealousy? But in the hope that the writer will take the trouble to reply to them and that they will thus be lifted out of the obscurity in which their own works, were it not for these attacks, would leave them for their whole lives.

* *La critique de Bérénice,* by the abbé Montfaucon de Villars.

CAST

TITUS, *Emperor of Rome*
BERENICE,* *Queen of Palestine*
ANTIOCHUS, *King of Commagene*
PAULINUS, *confidant of Titus*
ARSACES, *confidant of Antiochus*
PHOENISSA, *confidante of Berenice*
RUTILUS, *a Roman*
TITUS' RETINUE

The scene is in Rome, in a chamber between Titus' apartments and those of Berenice

* For convenience of the rhythm, this name is pronounced in three syllables, as in French.

BERENICE

ACT ONE

Scene One
ANTIOCHUS, ARSACES

ANTIOCHUS

Here let us pause. The splendour of these halls
Is, I can see, Arsaces, new to you.
Oft to this chamber, stately and withdrawn,
The Emperor entrusts his secrets. Here
It is that sometimes, hiding from his court,   5
He comes and to the queen unfolds his love.
This is the door to his apartments, and
This other entrance leads into the queen's.
Go. Tell her that, loath to intrude on her,
I dare to ask her for a private talk.   10

ARSACES

Intrude on her, sir? you, her faithful friend,
With such a fine solicitude for her?
Antiochus, you, who once sought her hand?
Whom the East counts among its greatest kings?
Is there already such a gulf between   15
The queen, as Titus' future wife, and you?

ANTIOCHUS

Go, go, I say, and without more ado,
See if I soon can speak to her alone.

Scene Two
ANTIOCHUS (*alone*)

Well, are you still the same, Antiochus?
Can I, untrembling, say: 'I love you'? Why!   20

227

Already I am trembling. My wild heart
Fears and desires this moment equally.
Berenice once bereft me of all hope;
She even sealed my lips eternally.
25 For five long years I have been silent and
Under a cloak of friendship hid my love.
Destined to lofty rank by Titus, why
Should she be kinder than in Palestine?
He weds her. Have I waited all this time
30 To once again declare my love for her?
What will a rash confession profit me?
Since I must leave, leave without angering her,
Withdraw, and without pouring out my heart,
Go far away from her, forget or die.
35 What! always suffer pangs she knows not of!
Always shed tears that I must swallow down?
Even when I lose her, must I dread her wrath?
Fair queen, why should you be displeased? Do I
Bid you abandon the imperial throne?
40 Or love me? No, I come only to say
That, after long, deluding hopes to find
Obstacles fatal to my rival's suit,
Now he's all-powerful, your marriage nears,
Ill-starred example of long constancy,
45 After five years of love and fruitless hope,
I leave, still faithful, though all hope is gone.
Instead of frowning, she may pity me.
In any case, constraint is useless now.
What does a luckless suitor have to fear
50 Who can resolve never to see her more?

Scene Three

ANTIOCHUS, ARSACES

ANTIOCHUS

Can I go in, Arsaces?

ARSACES

Sir, I've seen
The queen, but had to force a way to her
Through ever swelling waves of worshippers
Drawn by her coming greatness in her wake.
Titus, after a week's austere retreat,   55
At last ceases to mourn Vespasian,
His father; and this lover turns to love
Again. And if, my lord, the court speaks true,
Perhaps by nightfall, happy Berenice
Will change the name of queen for empress.   60

ANTIOCHUS (*sadly*)
                                                    Ah!

ARSACES

What! can it be these words distress you, sir?

ANTIOCHUS

And so I cannot speak to her alone?

ARSACES

You'll see her, sir. Berenice is informed
You wish to have a private audience.
The queen has deigned to signal with a glance   65
Her willingness to grant you your request;
And doubtless but awaits the moment when
She can avoid an all-invading court.

ANTIOCHUS

'Tis well. Meanwhile, have you neglected nought
Of my important orders to you?   70

ARSACES

                                              Sir,
You know how prompt I am to do your will.
Vessels in Ostia speedily equipped,

72 Ostia was the port of Rome.

229

At any moment ready to set sail,
Await but your command to leave. But whom
75 Will you send back home to Commagene?

ANTIOCHUS

We must depart after I've seen the queen.

ARSACES

Who must?

ANTIOCHUS

I

ARSACES

You?

ANTIOCHUS

Leaving the palace, I
Shall leave Rome, and, Arsaces, leave for good.

ARSACES

I am, and with good reason, much surprised.
80 What! Berenice has wrested you, my lord,
For so long from the bosom of your states;
She has detained you for three years in Rome;
And when the queen, her triumph now assured,
Counts on you to attend her marriage feast,
85 When Titus, deep in love, by wedding her,
Will cast reflected glory on you, sir . . .

ANTIOCHUS

Arsaces, let her revel in her lot,
And leave a subject that displeases me.

ARSACES

I understand. These very dignities

75 Commagene: a small province in the north-east of Syria.

Have driven your devotion from her mind.   90
Friendship betrayed gives way to enmity.

ANTIOCHUS

Arsaces, never did I hate her less.

ARSACES

What then? Already eaten up by pride,
Does the new emperor feign to know you not?
Does some foreboding of his unconcern   95
Make you avoid his presence far from Rome?

ANTIOCHUS

Titus has not appeared false to himself.
I have no cause for discontent.

ARSACES

                    Why leave?
What whim turns you into your enemy?
Heaven places on the throne a loving prince,   100
A prince who once witnessed your prowess, saw
Your search for death and glory in his wake,
And whose own valour, seconded by yours,
At last subdued rebel Judaea's might.
He still recalls that glorious, grievous day,   105
Decisive for a long and doubtful siege.
Upon their triple walls, the untroubled foe
Gazed without peril on our vain assaults,
And laughed the powerless battering-ram to scorn.
You alone, you, a ladder in your hand,   110
You carried death up to their very walls.
That day wellnigh shone on your funeral.
Titus embraced you dying in my arms,
And the whole camp, victorious, mourned your death.
This is the time, sir, when you may expect   115
The fruit of so much blood they saw you shed.
If, eager to inspect your realm again,

You're tired of living where you do not reign,
Must you, unhonoured, seek the Euphrates' shore?
120 Do not depart till Caesar sends you there,
Triumphant, laden with sovereign dignities
With which Rome's friendship graces even kings.
Can nothing alter your resolve, my lord?
You do not answer?

ANTIOCHUS

What can I reply?
125 I wait for a brief audience with the queen.

ARSACES

What then, my lord?

ANTIOCHUS

Her fate will settle mine.

ARSACES

How?

ANTIOCHUS

I desire to know if she will wed.
If what she says agrees with rumour's voice,
If she's exalted to the Caesars' throne,
130 If Titus is to marry her, I leave.

ARSACES

What is so fearful about this report?

ANTIOCHUS

When we have left, I'll tell you all the rest.

ARSACES

Into what turmoil you have cast my soul!

ANTIOCHUS

Here is the queen. Farewell. Do my commands.

Scene Four
BERENICE, ANTIOCHUS, PHOENISSA

BERENICE
At last I can escape the tedious joy 135
Of all these new fortune-created friends;
I flee their pointless, long-drawn-out respects
To seek a friend whose words come from the heart.
I must be frank. I had, impatiently,
Already charged you with forgetfulness. 140
What! this Antiochus, I said, whose zeal
Had all the East and Rome as witnesses,
Who, always constant in adversity,
Followed, unchanging, my vicissitudes,
Today when heaven seems to presage for me 145
An honour which I mean to share with you,
Hiding from sight, this same Antiochus
Now leaves me at the mercy of a crowd
Of strangers.

ANTIOCHUS
                    So it's true. From what you say
Marriage will crown your many years of love. 150

BERENICE
My lord, I will confide my fears to you.
These days have seen me shed some tears. This long
Mourning imposed by Titus on his court
Had even frozen his passion at the root.
No longer had he that assiduous love 155
When he would spend days hanging on my eyes.
Care-laden, silent now, with tearful gaze,
He only took a sad farewell of me.
Judge of my grief, I, who have sworn to you
So oft I loved him for himself alone; 160
I who would have, far from imperial pomp,
Chosen his heart, sought out his qualities.

233

ANTIOCHUS
Has he resumed his earlier tenderness?

BERENICE
You were a witness of this night gone by
165 When, in response to his religious wish,
The senate placed his father midst the gods.
This duty done, his filial piety
Was, my lord, by a lover's care replaced.
This very moment, without telling me,
170 He's in the senate he himself convoked.
There he extends the bounds of Palestine;
He adds Arabia and all Syria.
And, if I can believe his friends' reports,
If I believe his oft-repeated vows,
175 He'll over all these states crown Berenice,
And to these titles add an empress' name.
He will come here himself to tell me so.

ANTIOCHUS
And hence I come to say farewell to you
For ever. . . .

BERENICE
What! Farewell! What words are these?
180 You look dismayed and you change countenance.

ANTIOCHUS
I must go, lady.

BERENICE
What! Can I not know . . .

ANTIOCHUS (*aside*)
I should have gone before I saw her.

BERENICE

What

Do you fear? Come. End your long silence. Speak.
What is the secret of your leaving Rome?

ANTIOCHUS

At least remember I but do your will,   185
And that for the last time you hear me speak.
If, in the power and glory of your rank,
You still recall the place where you were born,
You will remember it was there my heart
Was wounded by you first. I fell in love.   190
I won your brother, King Agrippa's ear.
He spoke to you for me. Who knows, perhaps
You were disposed to listen to my pleas.
Titus, alas, came, saw and pleased. To you
He then appeared with all the might of one   195
Who bore the empire's vengeance in his hands.
Judaea paled. Ill-starred Antiochus
Was numbered first among the vanquished. Soon,
My sorry plight's heartless interpreter,
Your lips bade mine be silent. But I long   200
Held out and used the language of the eyes.
My tears and sighs followed you everywhere.
Your rigour in the end carried the day.
You made me choose: Exile or silence. I
Was forced to promise silence, nay, to swear.   205
But, since I now dare to reveal my heart,
When you extracted so unfair a pledge,
I vowed never to cease from loving you.

BERENICE

What say you?

ANTIOCHUS

I've been silent five long years,
And shall be silent even longer. I   210

Followed my lucky rival into war.
After my tears, I hoped to shed my blood,
Or hoped my fame, borne by a thousand deeds,
At least would reach you if my voice could not.
215 Heaven seemed inclined to end my sufferings.
You wept for my alas! uncertain death.
Vain perils! And how grievously I erred!
Titus' élan outdid my frenzied feats.
I must do justice to his valour. For,
220 Though he was born to rule the universe,
The darling of all hearts, and loved by you,
He seemed to draw all blows to him alone;
Whereas, unhoping, hated, tired of life,
His rival seemed only to follow him.
225 I see your heart applauds me secretly;
I see I'm listened to with less regret,
And that, attentive to this tale of woe,
In Titus' favour you forgive the rest.
At last, after a cruel, long-drawn siege,
230 He quelled the haggard, bloodstained rebels spared
By hunger, flames and internecine broils,
And left a plain where ramparts once had stood.
Imperial Rome saw you arrive with him.
The East was one vast desert where I pined.
235 I wandered long in Caesarea where,
Drinking enchantment, I had worshipped you.
I asked you back again of your sad realms;
I sought in tears the traces of your steps.
But, in the end, succumbing to my gloom,
240 Despair guided my steps to Italy.
Fate dealt me there the shrewdest blow of all.
Titus, embracing me, led me to you.
A veil of friendship tricked both you and him;
My love became your love's confidant then,
245 But always some hope dulled my suffering –
Rome and Vespasian thwarted your desire;
With such resistance Titus might give way.
Vespasian's dead; Titus is master now.

Why did I not then flee? Because I wished
To follow his new reign for some few days.   250
My fate's fulfilled; your glory is at hand.
Others enough, your nuptials' witnesses,
Will come and add their raptures to your joy.
For me, who could but mingle tears with it,
Too constant victim of a pointless love,   255
Happy in my mishaps to be allowed
To tell my story to the cause of them,
I leave deeper in love than ever.

BERENICE

                              Sir,
I never thought that on the very day
Which will with Caesar's link my destiny   260
A mortal man could with impunity
Come and declare he was in love with me.
My friendship will ensure my silence, though,
And I'll forget all your outrageous words.
I did not hinder their injurious flow.   265
I'll even regretfully take leave of you.
Amidst these honours heaven bestows on me,
I wished but you as witness of my joy.
I honoured, like the world, your qualities.
You admired Titus. Titus cherished *you*.   270
A hundred times I had the sweet delight
Of talking to another Titus.

ANTIOCHUS

                              Ah!
It's this I flee. I shun, alas! too late,
These cruel talks in which I have no part.
I flee the name – Titus – that tortures me,   275
The name that endlessly your lips repeat.
What shall I say? I flee your vacant eyes
Which never saw me, staring into mine.
Farewell. I go, my heart too full of you,
To wait, still loving you, my longed-for death.   280

237

Above all, fear not that blind suffering
Will trumpet my misfortune round the world.
You will, only on learning of my death,
Remember I was still alive. Farewell.

Scene Five

BERENICE, PHOENISSA

PHOENISSA

285 Ah! how I pity him. Fidelity
So great deserved a better recompense.
Do you not pity him?

BERENICE

This sudden flight
Leaves me, I must confess, a secret wound.

PHOENISSA

I would have kept him.

BERENICE

Who should keep him? *I*?
290 I should suppress his very memory.
Should I encourage his insensate love?

PHOENISSA

Titus has not yet said what he will do.
Rome sees you, lady, with suspicious eyes;
I dread the rigour of its laws for you:
295 Marriage for Romans is with Roman maids;
Rome hates all kings. Berenice is a queen.

BERENICE

The time for trembling's past. I've Titus' love.
He can do anything. He's but to speak.
He'll see the senate bow the knee to me,

The people crown his images with flowers. 300
The splendour of that night did you behold?
Are not your eyes full of his majesty?
This pyre, these torches, this inflamèd night,
These eagles, fasces, people, army, and
This host of kings, consuls and senators, 305
Borrowing their radiance from my beloved;
This gold, this purple that his glory gilds,
These laurels, witness of his victory;
And all these eyes gazing from every side
Focused on him alone their eager looks; 310
This royal carriage and this gentleness.
Heaven! how gladly, how respectfully,
All hearts assured him of their loyalty!
Speak, can one see him and not think like me
The world would straight acclaim him as their lord 315
On seeing him, even were he born obscure?
But memory's magic carries me away.
Meanwhile, this very moment, all of Rome
Makes vows for Titus, and by sacrifice
Celebrates the beginning of his reign. 320
Why tarry? For his rule's prosperity
Offer our vows to the protecting heavens.
And then, unwaiting and unwaited for,
I'll seek him out at once and say to him
Everything happiness so long restrained 325
Inspires in mutually enamoured hearts.

301 *that night:* the previous night. Cf. 164 above.

ACT TWO

Scene One
TITUS, PAULINUS, RETINUE

TITUS

Has the king of Commagene been told?
Does he know I am waiting for him?

PAULINUS

                         Sire,
I hastened to the queen's apartment where
330 He had been seen. He was already gone;
But I left word to tell him of your wish.

TITUS

Then it is well. What of Queen Berenice?

PAULINUS

For all that you have done for her she loads
Heaven with vows for your prosperity.
335 I saw her going out.

TITUS

                   What kindly thoughts!
Alas!

PAULINUS

Whence springs this sadness for the queen?
The East, almost entire, will bow to her.
You pity her?

TITUS (*motions to the retinue to go*)
Paulinus, stay behind.

240

Scene Two
TITUS, PAULINUS

TITUS

Well, of my plans Rome still uncertain waits
To learn the fate, Paulinus, of the queen;   340
And all the secrets of her heart and mine
Have now become the talk of the wide world.
The time has come for me at last to speak.
What is reported of the queen and me?
Speak. What do you hear?   345

PAULINUS

               I hear on every side
Your virtues published and, my lord, her charms.

TITUS

What do they say of all I feel for her?
What do they augur of such constancy?

PAULINUS

You can do all. Love or fall out of love –
The court will always side with your desires.   350

TITUS

And I have seen it too, this feigning court,
Always too keen to do its master's will,
Approve the horrors that were Nero's crimes.
I've seen it kneeling bless his frenzied rage.
I do not take as judge a fawning court,   355
Paulinus, but a nobler audience;
And, heedless of the voice of flatterers,
I wish through you to hear what all hearts feel.
This you have sworn to do. Respect and fear
Around me bar the passage to complaint.   360
To see and hear the better, I have asked
You, dear Paulinus, for both eyes and ears.

I've even on my friendship put that price.
I wanted you to read men's hearts for me
365 And your sincerity to cut a path
For truth to me, always, through flatterers.
Speak then. What hope is there for Berenice?
Is Rome indulgent or severe to her?
Think you that, seated on the Caesars' throne,
370 So fair a queen might earn Rome's enmity?

PAULINUS

No doubt of that. Be it reason or caprice,
Rome does not see her as its empress. She
Is known to be enchanting. Such fair hands
Seem to demand of you the empire's crown;
375 She even has, they say, a Roman heart;
She's every virtue, but she is a queen.
Rome, by a law that never can be changed
Admits no foreign blood to blend with it,
And does not recognize the offspring born
380 Of such a marriage which its laws condemn.
By banishing its kings, as well you know,
Rome to this title that it once revered
For ever vowed an unrelenting hate;
And, though obedient to its Caesars still,
385 This hate, my lord, a vestige of its pride,
Survives in all their hearts since freedom came.
Caesar, who first subdued it by his arms,
Who silenced laws in the alarms of war,
For Cleopatra burned, but gave no pledge.
390 Alone in the far East he let her pine.
Antony loved her to idolatry,
Forgot, with her, glory and fatherland,
But never called himself her wedded lord.
Rome sought him out and forced him to his knees,
395 And did not stay its frenzy of revenge
Till it had crushed both lover and beloved.
Since then, my lord, Nero, Caligula,
Monsters whose names I hesitate to cite,

With nothing but the figure of a man,
Trod underfoot all the grave laws of Rome,   400
But feared this law alone, and did not light
The torch of a detested marriage feast.
You bade me be, above all else, sincere.
The freedman Pallas' brother, Felix, still
Bearing the marks, the brand, of Claudius' chains,   405
Became the husband of two queens; and, if
I must obey you to the bitter end,
These two queens were of Berenice's stock.
And yet you think you might without offence
Now bring a queen into our Caesars' bed,   410
While the East witnesses a slave ascend,
Fresh from our chains, the couches of their queens.
This is the Romans' judgement of your love.
And it may be that soon, before night falls,
The senate, speaking with the empire's voice,   415
Will here repeat to you what I have said,
And that Rome also, falling at your knees,
Will beg a choice worthy of it and you.
You may, my lord, prepare to make reply.

TITUS

Alas! how great a love they ask me to   420
Forego.

PAULINUS

That love is ardent, I confess.

TITUS

A thousand times more ardent than you think.
I've made my happiness depend on this –
To see her, love her, please her every day.
I have done more. Nothing is hid from you.   425
Daily I've thanked the gods for her that they

406 *two queens:* Drusilla I, Berenice's sister, and Drusilla II, granddaughter
of Antony and Cleopatra.
408 Berenice was also descended from Cleopatra.

In Idumaea sought my father out,
Placed under him the army and the East,
And, stirring up the other lands as well,
430 Placed Rome still bleeding in his peaceful hands.
I even coveted my father's place,
I who, Paulinus, had relenting fate
Postponed the destined day, would, every hour,
Have gladly died if that prolonged his life.
435 All this (how little lovers know themselves!),
In hopes to share the throne with Berenice,
To recognize one day her love and troth,
And at her feet see the whole world and me.
Yet, despite all my love and all her charms,
440 After a thousand vows backed by my tears,
Now that at last her beauty can be crowned,
Now that I love her more than e'er I did,
That marriage ties, linking our destinies
Can in one day reward five years' desires,
445 I shall ... O God, I cannot speak the word.

PAULINUS

Shall what, my lord?

TITUS

                    For ever part from her.
My heart's not waited until now to yield.
If I have sought and listened to your words,
I wanted inwardly to make you crown
450 The ruin of a love that's loath to die.
Berenice long kept victory in doubt.
If in the end my honour tips the scales,
Battles were fought to conquer so much love
From which my heart will bleed for many a day.
455 I loved, I yearned in the profoundest peace –
Another was assigned to rule the world.
Lord of my destiny and free to love,

427 Vespasian was in Idumaea, a province bordering on Judaea, engaged in suppressing the Jews' revolt, when he was proclaimed emperor.

I owed account to no one but myself.
But hardly had my father passed away,
As soon as my sad hand had closed his eyes,   460
Of my fond error I was undeceived.
I felt the burden that was thrust on me.
I knew that, far from being my beloved's,
I would be forced soon to renounce myself,
And that the gods, frowning upon my love,   465
Delivered me thenceforth up to the world.
Rome in my new career is watching me.
How vile for me, how ominous for her,
If, from the first, setting at nought its rights,
I built upon their wreck my happiness!   470
Resolved to make this cruel sacrifice,
I tried to school poor Berenice for it.
But where should I begin? For a whole week,
I've tried to broach the question to the queen.
A hundred times, at the first word, my tongue   475
Clove to my mouth, speechless, a hundred times.
I hoped at least my troubled heart, my grief,
Would bring our common sorrows home to her.
But, unsuspecting, sensing my distress,
She lifts her hand to wipe away my tears,   480
And never in her ignorance foresees
The ending of a love so much deserved.
At last today I summoned up my will.
See her I must, Paulinus, and speak out.
I'm waiting for Antiochus, to give   485
This precious trust to him I cannot keep.
He must escort the queen back to the East.
Tomorrow Rome will see her leave with him.
Soon she'll be so informed by me myself;
For the last time I go to speak to her.   490

PAULINUS

I knew your love of glory would prevail
Which everywhere made vict'ry follow you.
Enslaved Judaea and its reeking walls,

That noble ardour's deathless monument,
495 Were guarantee enough that your great heart
Would not, my lord, destroy its handiwork;
And that the conqueror of so many lands
Would now or later quell his passions too.

TITUS

Ah! under what fine trappings is concealed
500 This cruel glory! Better far for me
If all that still awaited me were death!
Nay this consuming zeal for glorious deeds,
Berenice fired me with it long ago.
As well you know, fame did not always shine
505 With the same lustre on my name as now.
My youth, Paulinus, spent at Nero's court,
Was by corrupt example led astray,
Following the primrose path of dalliance.
Berenice pleased me. What does one not do
510 To please one's love and win one's conqueror?
I carried all before me on the field.
In triumph I returned. But blood and tears
Were not sufficient to deserve her smile.
I sought a thousand wretches' happiness.
515 My charities were lavished far and wide,
Happy far more than you can understand
When I could come before her laden with
A thousand hearts that my good deeds had won.
I owe her all. Ah! cruel recompense.
520 All that I owe her will recoil on her.
As thanks for all these virtues and renown,
I'll tell her: 'Go and never see me more.'

PAULINUS

What, after all this liberality,
Which to the Euphrates will extend her power,
525 After this spate of honours that surprised
The senate, need you fear an ingrate's name?
A hundred lands are added to her realm.

TITUS

Weak efforts to beguile a boundless grief!
I know my Berenice. I realize
That all she ever asked for was my heart.   530
I loved her and was loved. And since that day
(Was it ill-starred alas! or fortunate?)
With no aim in her love than love itself,
A foreigner in Rome, unknown at court,
She spends her days with no thought but to claim   535
Some hours with me, the rest to wait for me.
Even so, if sometimes my attentions flag
And I let pass the moment I am due,
I see her soon again, all bathed in tears;
My hand is long employed in drying them.   540
In short, all the most powerful bonds of love,
Gentle reproaches, ever welling bliss,
Artless desire to please and constant fear,
Charm, honour, virtue – I find all in her.
For five long years I've seen her every day,   545
And every time is splendid like the first.
Enough of this. The more I think of it,
The more my cruel constancy gives way.
What news, O heaven! I have to break to her!
Yet once again. I'll think of it no more.   550
I know my duty. I must follow it.
I'll not reflect whether I can survive.

Scene Three

TITUS, PAULINUS, RUTILUS

RUTILUS

Berenice would, my lord, have speech with you.

TITUS (*sighs*)

Paulinus!

PAULINUS

What! You are prepared to yield
555 Already? Sire, recall your great designs.
Now is the time.

TITUS

Well then, let her come in.

Scene Four

BERENICE, TITUS, PAULINUS, PHOENISSA

BERENICE

Forgive me if my tactless eagerness
Intrudes upon your privacy. And yet,
While all around your court assembled rings
560 With benefactions lavished on my head,
Can it be right, my lord, that I alone
Should never voice my gratitude to you?
But, sir (because I know that this true friend
Is privy to the secrets of our hearts),
565 Your mourning's over. Nothing holds you back.
You are alone at last and seek me not.
I hear you offer me new diadems,
And yet I cannot hear you, sir, yourself.
Alas! less care for pomp and more repose.
570 Can your love only in the senate shine?
Ah Titus! for love banishes constraint,
Of all these names coined by respect and fear,
What worries do you take upon yourself?
Do you have only states to give to me?
575 Since when, think you, my greatness touches me?
A sigh, a look, a single word from you,
That's the ambition of a heart like mine.
See more of me. Don't give me anything.
Must you spend all your time in ruling Rome?

Has your heart nought to say after a week? 580
A word would reassure my fearfulness.
But was the talk of me when I burst in?
Did your discussions have to do with me?
Was I at least the subject of your thoughts?

TITUS

Doubt it not, lady. I attest the gods 585
That Berenice is always in my mind.
Nor time nor absence, this I swear again,
Can ever rob you of this loving heart.

BERENICE

What! you can swear eternal love to me,
And swear it to me in this icy tone? 590
Why call to witness heaven's majesty?
Must my distrust be overcome by oaths?
My heart does not presume to doubt your word,
And I'm persuaded by a single sigh.

TITUS

Lady. . . . 595

BERENICE

      Well. What! my lord, without reply
You flee my gaze, seem to lose countenance.
Will you not banish this dumbfounded look?
Your father's death still overclouds your mind?
Can nothing charm away your carking care?

TITUS

Would that my father had not passed away! 600
How happily I lived!

BERENICE

      All these regrets
Are prompted by your filial piety.
But you have shed, to mourn him, tears enough.

You owe to Rome and glory some concern.
605 Of my own wishes I'll not even speak.
Berenice could console you formerly.
With more delight you listened to me then.
Harassed on your account by countless ills
I for a word from you forewent my tears!
610 You mourn alas! a father. Feeble grief!
They tried (and I still tremble at the thought)
To ravish from me all that I adore;
I whose distraction and alarm you know
When you but for a moment go from me;
615 I who would die the day I was forbid
To speak to you. . . .

TITUS

       Ah! what words left your lips?
What moment have you chosen? Have pity. Stop.
You lavish kindness on an ingrate.

BERENICE

          On
An ingrate? How can you be one, my lord?
620 Perhaps you find my kindness wearisome?

TITUS

No, never, lady, since I must speak out,
Was my fond heart devoured by keener flames.
But . . .

BERENICE

Go on.

TITUS

   Alas!

BERENICE
Speak.

TITUS
The empire, Rome . . .

BERENICE

Well?

TITUS (*to Paulinus*)
Let us go. I can say nought to her.

Scene Five
BERENICE, PHOENISSA

BERENICE

What! leave so soon, and not say anything?   625
Alas! what deadly words! What have I done?
What does he want? What does this silence mean?

PHOENISSA

Like you, the more I think, the more I'm lost.
But is there nothing that you can recall
Which might against you prejudice him. Search   630
Your memory.

BERENICE
                    Ah! you can take my word.
The more I try to summon up the past
From when I met him till this sombre day,
The more I see my fault is too much love.
You heard his words though. Now you must be frank.   635
Tell me. Did I say aught he might resent?
Who knows? Perhaps I have with too much warmth
Made little of his gifts, chided his grief.
May it not be he dreads the Romans' hate?
He fears, perhaps he fears to wed a queen.   640
If that were it. . . . But no. A hundred times

He's braced my love against their cruel laws.
Let him explain this dismal silence. Ah!
I cannot breathe in this uncertainty.
645 *I* should live, *I*, Phoenissa, and yet think
He now neglects me or I've given offence?
Let's follow him. But, when I scan my heart,
I think I see why he is so upset.
He must have known all that has just transpired;
650 His rival's love may have offended him.
He has, I'm told, sent for Antiochus.
Let's seek no more the cause of my distress.
It's sure. This worry that has ravaged me
Is a suspicion easy to dispel.
655 I shall not vaunt this easy victory,
Titus. Would that, without offence to you,
A mightier rival still would tempt my troth
And place more empires at my feet than you,
And with unnumbered sceptres seek my love;
660 That you had nought to offer but your soul!
Then, my dear Titus, loved, victorious,
You'd see what price I put upon your heart.
Phoenissa, come. A word will calm his wrath.
Be reassured, my heart, you're still adored.
665 I was too quick in thinking all was lost.
Titus is jealous, but he is in love.

ACT THREE

Scene One
TITUS, ANTIOCHUS, ARSACES

TITUS

What! you were leaving, prince? Wherefore this haste,
This unforeseen departure, nay, this flight?
Would you conceal even your farewell from me?
Is't as an enemy that you go hence?   670
What will they say – the court, the empire, Rome?
But, as a friend, what cannot I *not* say?
What do you charge me with? That you have been
Merged up till now among the crowd of kings?
My heart, the only present I could make,   675
Was open to you while my father lived.
And now my hand can pour out gifts as well,
You flee my eager benefactions. Come,
Think you that I, forgetful of my past,
Only upon my greatness fix my thoughts?   680
And all my friends, registered distantly,
Are merely strangers that have served their time?
And you who wanted to avoid my glance,
Prince, more than ever I have need of you.

ANTIOCHUS
I?   685

TITUS
You.

ANTIOCHUS
Alas! from an unhappy prince,
What can you hope for but good wishes, sir?

253

TITUS

I've not forgotten that my victory
Owed to your exploits half its glory; Rome
Among its vanquished enemies beheld
690 More than one captive laden with your chains;
And in the Capitol it sees displayed
The spoils you wrested from the rebel Jews.
I do not ask such bloody feats again.
All that I wish to borrow is your voice.
695 I know that Berenice is in your debt.
She thinks she has a loyal friend in you.
She sees and hears no one but you in Rome.
You are but one in heart and soul with us.
For such a noble, constant friendship's sake,
700 Employ the influence you have on her.
See her on my behalf.

ANTIOCHUS

I see her? No.
I have for ever taken leave of her.

TITUS

Prince, you must speak to her for me again.

ANTIOCHUS

You speak to her. You're worshipped by the queen.
705 Why at this very moment forfeit, sir,
The pleasure of a sweet confession. She
Is waiting for it now impatiently.
I vouch for her agreement, as I leave.
Indeed she said you plan to marry her
710 And wish to see her but to tell her so.

TITUS

Ah! how enchanting a confession, and
How happy I should be if it were so.
Today my joy was ready to explode,
And yet today, prince, I must leave her.

ANTIOCHUS

You!

Leave her! my lord!

715

TITUS

Such is my destiny.
For her, for Titus, marriage cannot be.
In this fond hope I lulled myself in vain.
Tomorrow, Prince, the queen must leave with you.

ANTIOCHUS

What words are these? O God!

TITUS

Pity my rank.
Lord of the world, I guide its destiny.
I can make kings and can unsceptre them,
Yet cannot give my heart to whom I choose.
Rome against kings from all time in revolt
Disdains a consort in the purple raised.
The crown, a hundred kings as ancestors,
Brand my devotion and offend all eyes.
My heart, without arousing discontent,
Can freely yearn for maidens lowly born,
And Rome would joyfully accept from me
The most unworthy of her daughters. Why,
Even Caesar yielded to the torrent. If
The people does not see the queen go off
Tomorrow, she will hear this frenzied mob
Ask me to banish her before her eyes.
Save from affront my name, her memory.
Since we must yield, let's yield to honour's voice.
My silent lips and looks for one whole week
Will have prepared her for this sombre news.
And even now, alarmed, insistently
She wants me to convey my thoughts to her.
Relieve the torment of a prostrate heart.

720

725

730

735

740

Spare me the need for this encounter. Go,
Explain to her my troubled silences.
But above all she *must* leave me alone.
745 Be the sole witness of her tears and mine.
Bear my farewell to her. Take hers for me.
Let her and me shun such a meeting, for
It would submerge our wavering constancy,
If living on and reigning in my heart,
750 Can mitigate the rigour of her fate,
Swear to her, prince, that, always true to her,
With sorrowing heart, and exiled more than she,
Bearing even to the grave a lover's name,
My reign will be one long, long banishment.
755 If, not content with robbing me of her,
Heaven still desires to force long life on me,
You, bound to me by friendship's ties alone,
Must not desert her in her misery.
Let the East see you landing in her wake.
760 Arrive in triumph, not as fugitives.
Let such a friendship forge eternal bonds.
Let my name always echo in your talk.
To give a common frontier to your states,
I'll bound them both by the Euphrates' banks.
765 I know the senate, ringing with your name,
Will with one voice confirm this gift to you.
I join Cilicia to Commagene.
Farewell. Do not desert my dearest queen,
She whom my heart has made its one desire,
770 All that I love until the day I die.

Scene Two

ANTIOCHUS, ARSACES

ARSACES

Thus, heaven prepares to do you justice, Sire.
You will leave Rome, but leave with Berenice.
She's thrust into your arms, not snatched from you.

ANTIOCHUS

Give me a moment to compose myself.
Great is this change, unbounded my surprise.   775
Titus entrusts to me his all in love.
Should I believe, great gods, what I have heard?
And, even if I believed, should I rejoice?

ARSACES

But I myself, what must I think of it?
What is it now obstructs your happiness?   780
Did you, my lord, deceive me when, just now,
Leaving, still shaken by your last farewell,
Trembling at having bared your thoughts to her,
You told me of your new-found boldness? Then
You fled a marriage that distracted you.   785
But that is broken off. What troubles you?
Enjoy the raptures to which love invites.

ANTIOCHUS

Arsaces, I am bid escort her back.
I'll long enjoy delightful talks with her.
Indeed, her eyes may even get used to mine.   790
Perhaps she'll see the difference between
Titus' remoteness and my constancy.
Here Titus overwhelms me with his rank.
His might eclipses everything in Rome.
But, though the East rings with his memory,   795
There she will see traces of *my* renown.

ARSACES

Doubt it not, Sire, everything favours you.

ANTIOCHUS

Ah! how we both love to deceive ourselves.

ARSACES

Deceive ourselves?

ANTIOCHUS

What! I might win her still?
800 Berenice might no longer frown on me?
She would beguile my sorrow with a word?
Think you that, even if fate rained blows on her,
If the whole world were to neglect her charms,
The ingrate would accept my tears for her,
805 Or that she'd ever deign to tolerate
Attentions she would think flowed from my love?

ARSACES

And who better than you can comfort her?
My lord, her fortunes are about to change.
Titus is leaving her.

ANTIOCHUS

From that great change
810 My only gain will be new torments when
Her tears reveal how much she worships him.
I'll see her moan. I'll pity her myself.
As fruit of so much love my fate will be
To harvest tears that are not shed for me.

ARSACES

815 What! will you never cease to rack yourself?
Was ever such a mighty heart so weak?
Open your eyes, my lord, and ponder well
The many grounds why Berenice is yours.
Since now Titus no longer seeks her hand
820 It is for her vital to marry you.

ANTIOCHUS

Vital?

ARSACES

Allow her tears a few more days,
Letting their early violence spend itself.
Everything speaks for you, vengeance and pique,

And Titus' absence, your own presence, time,
Three sceptres that alone she cannot wield,   825
Your two adjoining states that seek to merge.
Self-interest, reason, friendship, all combine
To link you.

ANTIOCHUS

            Yes, you bring me back to life.
I joyfully accept this sweet presage.
Let's do what is expected. Why delay?   830
Let's go to her, and, since we're ordered to,
Announce to her Titus abandons her.
But stay. What would I do? Is it for me
To take this cruel mission on myself?
Be it love or honour, I recoil from it.   835
Should dearest Berenice hear from my lips
That she's abandoned. Ah! who would have thought,
Queen, that this word would ever strike your ears?

ARSACES

But all her hate should fall on Titus, sir,
You speak only because he begged you to.   840

ANTIOCHUS

No. Let's not see her. Let's respect her grief.
Others enough will tell her of her fate.
Does it not seem indignity enough
To learn what Titus has condemned her to,
Without my dealing her the crowning blow   845
Of learning through his rival of this slight?
No, no, let's flee and not expose ourselves
By this encounter to undying hate.

ARSACES

Ah! here she is, my lord; make up your mind.

ANTIOCHUS

God!   85c

Scene Three

BERENICE, ANTIOCHUS, ARSACES, PHOENISSA

BERENICE

What is this, my lord, you have not gone?

ANTIOCHUS

Lady, your disappointment's all too clear,
Since it was Titus you were looking for.
But he alone must be accused if I,
Despite our parting, still intrude on you.
855 Perhaps I'd be in Ostia by now
If he had not forbidden me to go.

BERENICE

He sends for you alone. He shuns us all.

ANTIOCHUS

He kept me back only to speak of you.

BERENICE

Of me, prince?

ANTIOCHUS

Yes.

BERENICE

What could he say to you?

ANTIOCHUS

860 Others better than I can tell you that.

BERENICE

What, sir?

ANTIOCHUS

Suspend your indignation. Far
From being silent, others would perhaps

Go on in overweening triumph and
Comply with your insistence joyfully.
But I, in fear and trembling, well you know,   865
Who put your peace of mind before my own,
Would rather cause displeasure than distress,
And fear to grieve more than to anger you.
You'll do me justice ere the day is done.
Farewell.   870

BERENICE

     O God! what fearful words. Come back.
I cannot hide my consternation. Prince,
You see before you a distracted queen
Who, sick at heart, asks you to speak one word.
You fear, you say, to wreck my peace of mind.
Your harsh refusal, far from sparing me,   875
Only excites my anger, grief and hate.
Sir, if you value aught my peace of mind,
If I myself was ever dear to you,
Dispel the anguish that assails my soul.
Tell me what Titus said.   880

ANTIOCHUS

     In the gods' name . . .

BERENICE

What! you are not afraid to disobey?

ANTIOCHUS

I've but to speak to make myself abhorred.

BERENICE

I wish it. Speak.

ANTIOCHUS

     You do me violence.
I say again, you'll praise my silence.

BERENICE

Sir,

885 This very moment, satisfy my wish,
Or be assured for ever of my hate.

ANTIOCHUS

Then, lady, I must now unseal my lips.
You wish it, and your bidding must be done.
But have no fond illusions. You will learn
890 Horrors of which perhaps you dare not think.
I know your inner heart. You must expect
That I shall strike it at its tenderest spot.
Titus has ordered me . . .

BERENICE

What?

ANTIOCHUS

To declare
That now, for ever, you and he must part.

BERENICE

895 Must part? Who? I? Titus and Berenice?

ANTIOCHUS

I must, speaking to you, be fair to him.
All things that in a tender, noble heart
Can make despair in love more hideous,
I saw in his. He weeps. He worships you.
900 But what avails it that he loves you still?
The Roman empire will not brook a queen.
You two must part. Tomorrow you will leave.

BERENICE

Us part? Alas! Phoenissa.

PHOENISSA

Lady, come.
Display your proud nobility of soul.
The blow is hard, and comes with stunning force.   905

BERENICE

After so many oaths, forsake me? No.
Titus who vowed . . . This I can not believe.
He'll not desert me. His renown's at stake.
They wish to poison my belief in him.
This trap is set only to sever us.   910
For Titus loves me. Titus does not want
My death. I'll see him, speak to him at once.
Come.

ANTIOCHUS

What! you're capable of thinking that . . .

BERENICE

You wish it too much to pèrsuade me. No.
I don't believe you. But, whate'er the truth,   915
Take care for ever to avoid my sight. (*exit Antiochus*)
(*to Phoenissa*)
Do not desert me in my present plight.
Alas! how vainly I deceive myself!

Scene Four

ANTIOCHUS, ARSACES

ANTIOCHUS

Was I mistaken? Did I hear aright?
I must take care, *I*, to avoid her sight!   920
Most certainly I shall. I would have left
Had Titus not, despite me, kept me back.
Yes. I must go. Let's do as I had planned.

913 *thinking that* . . .: i.e. thinking that I would deliberately deceive you.

Her hate, that thinks to hurt, obliges me.
925 You saw me disconcerted and distraught;
I would have left, fond, jealous, in despair;
And now that she has banned me from her sight,
Perhaps I'll leave with an indifferent heart.

ARSACES

Now less than ever, sir, must you go hence.

ANTIOCHUS

930 *I*? *I* should stay to see myself disdained?
For Titus' coldness *I* be held to blame?
I shall be punished when the guilt is his?
With what injustice, how insultingly,
She, to my face, doubts my sincerity!
935 So Titus loves her. I'm deceiving her.
She dares accuse me of such treachery.
At what a moment, too? The very time
When I display to her my rival's tears;
When, to console her, I even picture him
940 Constant in love more than he is perhaps.

ARSACES

But why, my lord, this groundless worry? Come,
Allow this spate of tears time to abate.
A week, a month. No matter. It will pass.
Stay.

ANTIOCHUS

No, Arsaces, I shall leave her now.
945 I feel that I might sympathize with her.
My honour, peace of mind, all point that way.
Let's go. Let's flee far from the cruel one.
For long let no one speak to me of her.
Yet fading daylight lingers in the air,
950 I'll in my palace wait for your return.
Go. See if she's not overcome by grief.
Haste, and let's leave, at least assured she lives.

ACT FOUR

Scene One

BERENICE (*alone*)

Phoenissa comes not. Unrelenting time
Moves for my rapid thoughts with leaden wings.
Nervous and restless, languishing, depressed,   955
Rest kills me and my strength abandons me.
Phoenissa comes not. How this endless wait
Affrights my heart with ominous presage.
Phoenissa will have no reply for me.
Titus, the ingrate, has rejected her.   960
He flees me. He evades my righteous wrath.

Scene Two

BERENICE, PHOENISSA

BERENICE

Phoenissa, did you see the emperor? Well,
What did he say? He'll come?

PHOENISSA

           I saw him and
Portrayed to him the anguish of your soul.
I saw tears flow he did not want to shed.   965

BERENICE

And he will come?

PHOENISSA

           Doubt it not. He will come.
But how can you receive him so distraught?

Compose yourself. Come to your senses, and
Let me arrange these veils in disarray
970 And this dishevelled hair that hides your eyes.
Let me repair the ravage of your tears.

BERENICE

No, leave it. He will see his handiwork.
And what care I for these vain ornaments?
If my fidelity, my tears, my groans,
975 Nay, not my tears, my certain ruin and
Impending death; if these can't bring him back,
Tell me what will your fruitless help avail,
Or these poor charms that do not touch him more?

PHOENISSA

Why do you make him this unjust reproach?
980 I hear a sound. The emperor is at hand.
Come, flee and go back in at once. You can
In your apartments talk to him alone.

Scene Three

TITUS, PAULINUS, RETINUE

TITUS

Paulinus, go and soothe the queen's unease.
I'll see her. But I need some solitude.

(*to the retinue*)

985 Leave me.

PAULINUS (*aside*)

Ah! How I fear this combat. God!
Let the king's honour and the State's prevail.
I'll to the queen.

Scene Four

TITUS (*alone*)
Well then, Titus, what now?
Berenice waits for you. What is your plan?
To take farewell? But have you weighed this well?
Is your heart steeled for cruelty enough?   990
For, after all, the combat facing you
Calls not for strength but barbarous savagery.
Shall I sustain her moving, languid eyes
That know so well the way into my heart?
When I behold these magic-laden eyes,   995
Hanging on mine, o'erwhelm me with their tears,
Shall I remember my inhuman task?
How can I say: 'I'll never see her more.'
I come to pierce a heart that worships me,
And why? Who bids me do so? I myself.   1000
For, after all, has Rome announced its will?
Does shouting echo round this palace? Can
The empire, on the edge of the abyss,
Now only by this sacrifice be saved.
All's still, and I, too easily alarmed,   1005
Bring on misfortunes that I can postpone.
And who knows if, touched by her qualities,
Rome would not as a Roman welcome her?
Rome can by *its* choice justify my own.
No, once again. No overhasty moves.   1010
Let Rome weigh in the balance with her laws
So many tears, such love, such steadfastness.
Rome will be *for* us. Titus, face the facts.
What is this air you breathe? Is not this Rome
Where hate of kings, imbibed with mother's milk,   1015
By fear or love can never be effaced.
Rome judged your queen when it condemned its kings.
Have you not from your childhood heard that voice?
And have you not heard honour's voice proclaim
Your duty to you even among the troops?   1020

Later, when Berenice arrived with you,
Did you not hear how Rome regarded it?
Must it be dinned into unwilling ears?
Coward, renounce the empire and make love.
1025 Haste to the borders of the universe
And thus make way for worthier hearts to reign.
Are these the plans for greatness and renown
Which would endear my memory to all?
For a whole week I've reigned, and up till now
1030 I have done nought for honour, all for love.
How can I justify this precious time?
Where are these happy times I ushered in?
What tears have I dispelled, what smiling eyes
Show me the joyous fruit of my good deeds?
1035 Have I transformed the empire's destinies?
How many days has heaven allotted me?
Of these few days, awaited for so long,
How many, wretch, have I already lost?
Let's do at once what honour bids, and break
1040 The only bond. . . .

Scene Five

BERENICE, TITUS

BERENICE (*coming out of her apartments*)
No, let me go, I say;
In vain your counsel tries to hold me back!
See him, I must. Ah! my lord, there you are.
So then it's true. Titus abandons me?
We part, and it is he who so commands.

TITUS

1045 Ah! lady, do not crush a wretched prince.
Let not our feelings carry us away.
My heart is racked with anguish fierce enough
Without more torture from a loved one's tears;

268

But summon up this spirit that so oft
Forced me to recognize my duty's voice.   1050
Now is the time. Silence your love for me,
And, in the light of reason and renown,
Dwell on my duty at its most austere.
Yourself against me fortify my heart.
Help me to quell my weakness if you can,   1055
To hold back tears welling up ceaselessly
Or, if we cannot bid our tears to stop,
At least let honour help us bear our woes.
And let the whole world plainly recognize
The tears wrung from an emperor and a queen.   1060
For, in a word, my princess, we must part.

BERENICE

Ah! cruel one. Is this the time to speak?
What have you done? I thought that I was loved.
Accustomed to the joy of seeing you,
I lived for you alone. You knew your laws   1065
The first time I confessed my heart to you.
To what excess of love you've led me on!
Why did you not adjure me: 'Wretched queen,
You are too far committed! Curb your hopes.
Give not a heart that cannot be received.'   1070
Did you accept it but to give it back
When its one wish was to depend on you?
The empire planned our downfall ceaselessly.
There still was time. You could have left me then.
Unnumbered grounds could have consoled me then. 1075
I could have blamed your father for my death,
People and senate, the whole empire, Rome,
The whole world, rather than so dear a hand.
Their hate, long since against me unconcealed,
Had long prepared me for catastrophe.   1080
I would not have received this cruel blow
When I was hoping for undying bliss,
When your auspicious love's all powerful,
When Rome is silent, when your father dies,

1085 When the whole empire bows the knee to you,
When I had nobody to fear but you.

TITUS

It's I alone who could destroy myself.
Then I could live lulled by illusions. Then
I took good care never to look ahead
1090 And seek out what could one day sever us.
I wanted love to be invincible.
Careless, I hoped for the impossible.
Who knows? I hoped to die before your eyes
And thus forestall this cruel last farewell.
1095 The obstacles seemed to renew my love.
Though the whole empire spoke to me, the voice
Of glory had not sounded in my heart
As when it trumpets to an emperor.
I know what torments are in store for me.
1100 I feel that without you I cannot live.
My heart is straining hard to leave my breast;
But living's not the question: I must reign.

BERENICE

Then revel in your glory, cruel one.
Reign. I give up. I'd not believe you till
1105 These very lips, after a thousand oaths
Of love that should unite us till we die,
These lips, admitting to their faithlessness,
Condemned me to eternal banishment.
I wished myself to listen to you, but
1110 I'll hear no more. For ever now, farewell.
For ever. Ah! my lord, reflect how harsh
These cruel words fall on a lover's ear.
How will we pine a month, a year, from now
When we're divided by a waste of seas,
1115 When the day dawns and when the day will end,
With Titus never seeing Berenice
And all day long my never seeing you?
But how deceived I am! What labour lost!

Consoled of my departure in advance,
Will you even deign to count the days I'm gone?   1120
These days, too long for me, you'll find too short.

TITUS

I shall not have to count so many days.
I hope that all too soon sad-voiced report
Will force you to confess that you were loved.
You'll see that Titus was unable to. . . .   1125

BERENICE

Ah! if that's true, my lord, why separate?
I talk not of a happy wedding now.
Has Rome condemned me not to see you more?
Why then begrudge me even the air you breathe?

TITUS

Alas! there's nothing that you cannot do.   1130
Stay. I'll resist no more. How weak I am!
I'll have to fight and fear you ceaselessly,
And ceaselessly keep guard upon my steps
Drawn to you every moment of the day.
My heart beside itself forgets all else,   1135
Remembering only that it worships you.

BERENICE

Well then, my lord, what if you do? Is Rome
Ready to rise against you in revolt?

TITUS

And who knows how they'll stomach this offence?
If they speak out, if murmurs swell to shouts,   1140
Must I then justify my choice with blood?
If they keep silent, and will sell their laws,
What risks do you expose me to? What price
Must I, perhaps, pay for their tolerance?
What will they not then dare to ask of me?   1145
Shall I maintain the laws I cannot keep?

BERENICE

You count for naught the tears of Berenice?

TITUS

Count them for nothing? How unjust you are!

BERENICE

Good god! for unjust laws that you can change
1150 You plunge yourself into eternal grief.
Rome has its rights, my lord. Have you not yours?
Are Roman interests holier than ours?
Speak out.

TITUS

Ah! how you rend my heart, my lord.

BERENICE

You are an emperor, and yet you weep.

TITUS

1155 Yes, lady, it is true. I weep. I sigh.
I shudder. But, when I accepted power,
Rome made me swear I would maintain its rights.
This must be done. Already more than once
Rome of my peers has tried the constancy.
1160 Ah! if you traced Rome to its origins,
You'd see them always subject to its laws –
One holding to his word, goes back to seek
Amidst the foe the death awaiting him;
The other dooms his own victorious son;

1162 refers to Regulus who was captured by the Carthaginians, allowed to
go back to Rome, where he argued against the enemy's peace proposals,
and then returned to Carthage, as he had promised, where he was put to
death.
1164 refers to Manlius Torquatus who condemned his son to death for
having engaged in single combat against his orders.

And one, with dry, almost indifferent eyes,   1165
Sees his two sons expire by his command.
Unhappy race. But fame and fatherland
Have always with the Romans won the day.
I know that wretched Titus, leaving you,
Eclipses all these men's austerity,   1170
Which cannot with this signal feat compare;
But, after all, think you I am unfit
To set the future an example which
Without great efforts none can emulate.

BERENICE

No, all is easy for your barbarous heart.   1175
I think you fit to rob me of my life.
My heart sees clear into your feelings now.
No more I ask to be allowed to stay.
Why should I stay, shame-ridden and despised,
And by a hostile mob be laughed to scorn?   1180
I wished to force you to reject me thus.
All's over. Soon you'll have no cause for fear.
Do not expect a volley of abuse
Or cries to heaven, that strikes the perjurer.
No. If my tears can still move heaven to wrath,   1185
Dying, I beg it to forget my pains.
If I will raise a prayer against your wrongs,
If, before dying, hapless Berenice
Would leave you some avenger of her death,
I seek him only, ingrate, in your heart.   1190
I know your love can never be effaced,
That present grief, past tenderness, my blood,
Which in this very palace I shall shed,
All these are enemies I leave to you.
And, unrepentant of my steadfastness,   1195
For my whole vengeance I rely on them.
Farewell!

1165 refers to Brutus who condemned his two sons to death for plotting
to restore Tarquinius.

Scene Six

TITUS, PAULINUS

PAULINUS

In what mind has she just gone out,
My lord? Is she at last disposed to leave?

TITUS

Paulinus, I am lost. I'll not survive.
1200 The queen intends to die. Go. Follow her.
Let's run to help.

PAULINUS

What! did not you yourself
Order just now that she be kept in sight?
Her women bustle round her constantly.
They'll steer her gently from such sombre thoughts.
1205 No, no. Fear naught. These are the hardest blows.
My lord, continue. Victory is yours.
I know you could not shut out pity as
You listened to her. Nor could I myself.
But look ahead. Think in this bitter hour
1210 What fame will follow from a moment's pain,
What plaudits all the world prepares for you,
What place in history.

TITUS

No. I'm barbarous.
I hate myself. Nero, so much abhorred,
Could never carry cruelty so far.
1215 I will not suffer Berenice to die.
Come. Rome may say whate'er it likes of me.

PAULINUS

What, my lord?

TITUS

Ah! I know not what I say.
Excess of sorrow overwhelms my heart.

PAULINUS

Do not impair your reputation. For
The news of your farewell is spread abroad.   1220
Rome that despaired, with reason triumphs now.
Open, the temples smoke to honour you;
The people praise your virtue to the skies,
Crowning your statue with a laurel wreath.

TITUS

Ah! Rome. Ah! Berenice. Ah! wretched prince!   1225
Why am I emperor? Why am I in love?

Scene Seven

TITUS, ANTIOCHUS, PAULINUS, ARSACES

ANTIOCHUS

What have you done, my lord? Sweet Berenice
Perhaps is dying in Phoenissa's arms.
Tears, counsel, reason, all are lost on her,
And sword and poison loudly she implores.   1230
You, you alone can vanquish this desire.
She hears your name. It brings her back to life.
Her eyes, towards your apartments always turned,
Seem to demand your presence instantly.
I cannot bear this sight. It tortures me.   1235
Why tarry? Go and show yourself to her.
Save so much virtue, beauty, grace, my lord,
Or drop all semblance of humanity.
Speak but one word.

TITUS

Alas! what can I say?
Myself, I hardly know if I'm alive.   1240

275

Scene Eight

TITUS, ANTIOCHUS, PAULINUS, ARSACES, RUTILUS

RUTILUS

My lord, the tribunes, consuls, senate, all
Have asked to see you on the State's behalf.
A vast throng follows which impatiently
In your apartments waits until you come.

TITUS

1245 I understand. You wish to reassure,
Great gods! a heart ready to go astray.

PAULINUS

Come, my lord, and receive the senate in
The neighbouring chamber.

ANTIOCHUS

Haste and see the queen.

PAULINUS

What, my lord, could you, by this shameful deed,
1250 Trample upon the empire's majesty.
Rome . . .

TITUS

Well, no more. We'll go and hear them. Come.

(to Antiochus)

I cannot, Prince, avoid this duty. Go
And see the queen. I hope on my return
That she'll no longer ever doubt my love.

ACT FIVE

Scene One

ARSACES (*alone*)

Where shall I find this overfaithful prince?   1255
Heaven guide my steps, favour my eagerness.
Grant me at once to bring to him the news
Of happiness for which he dare not hope.

Scene Two
ANTIOCHUS, ARSACES

ARSACES

What happy chance has sent you back, my lord?

ANTIOCHUS

If you have any joy of my return,   1260
Then my despair alone's to thank for it.

ARSACES

The queen is leaving.

ANTIOCHUS
Leaving?

ARSACES
                    Yes, tonight.
She's given her orders. She's offended at
Titus for having left her to her tears.
A noble grief succeeds to wild despair.   1265
Now she renounces Rome, the emperor, and
She even wants to leave before all Rome,

Seeing her prostrate, triumphs at her flight.
She'll write to him.

ANTIOCHUS
           Who would have thought it? Gone!
1270 And Titus?

ARSACES
         He has not appeared to her.
The people stop him, gather round, entranced,
Applaud the senate's titles to him, and
These titles, these respects, and this applause
Become for Titus solemn pledges which,
1275 Binding him with an honour-forgèd chain,
Despite his sighs and Berenice's tears,
Now fix in duty's path his wavering steps.
All's over. They may never meet again.

ANTIOCHUS
How many grounds for hope, Arsaces. Yes,
1280 But fortune mocks me with such cruel skill.
I've seen my plans so often set at naught.
Trembling I listen to your every word.
My heart gripped by a dark foreboding feels
That even its hope arouses fortune's spite.
1285 But look. What! Titus makes his way to us.
What can he want?

Scene Three

TITUS, ANTIOCHUS, ARSACES

TITUS (*as he enters, to his escort, who stays in the wings*)
           Stay there. Let no one in.
At last I come to keep my promise, Prince.
Berenice haunts and harrows me. I come,
My heart pierced by your tears and hers, to calm

Sufferings less cruel than my own. Come, Prince.   1290
Come here. I wanted you yourself to see
For the last time whether I love the queen.

(*Titus goes into the queen's apartments*)

Scene Four

ANTIOCHUS, ARSACES

ANTIOCHUS

Well then, this is the hope you gave me back.
You see the triumph that awaited me.
So Berenice was leaving Rome enraged!   1295
Titus had left her irrevocably!
What have I done, great gods! What ill-starred course
Have you assigned to my unhappy life?
Each moment is a never-ending surge
From fear to hope and back from hope to rage.   1300
And still I live?

(*sees them enter*)

Titus and Berenice!
Ah! cruel gods, you'll mock my tears no more.
(*exit*)

Scene Five

TITUS, BERENICE, PHOENISSA

BERENICE

No, I'll not listen to you. I'm resolved.
I mean to leave. Why should you reappear?
Why come and thus envenom my despair?   1305
Are you not pleased? We'll never meet again.

TITUS

I beg you, hear . . .

BERENICE

The time for that is past.

TITUS

One word.

BERENICE

No, no.

TITUS

How you lay waste my soul!
Princess, whence comes this sudden change of mind?

BERENICE

1310 The die is cast. You wanted me to leave.
I have resolved to leave immediately,
And I am leaving.

TITUS

Stay.

BERENICE

Ingrate, *I* stay!
And why? To suffer an injurious mob
To make these places echo with my fall?
1315 Do you not hear this cruel, gloating joy
While I alone must drown my grief in tears?
What crime of mine, what insult drives them on?
What have I done but give you too much love?

TITUS

Why listen, lady, to a senseless crowd?

BERENICE

1320 I see nought here which does not wound my eyes.
All this apartment you've prepared for me,
This place so long the witness of my love,

Which seemed to pledge me yours for ever, these
Festoons, in which our two names intertwined,
To my sad gaze are everywhere displayed,   1325
Are all impostors that I cannot bear.
Let's go. Phoenissa.

TITUS

How unjust you are!

BERENICE

Go back, go back to these grave senators,
Who come to laud you for your cruelty.
Well, did you listen to their words with joy?   1330
Is you concern for honour satisfied?
And did you promise to forget me? Nay,
It's not enough to expiate your love.
Did you now swear eternal hate to me?

TITUS

No, I have promised nothing. Hate you? I?   1335
I never could forget my Berenice!
God! what a time she chooses to inflict
This cruel, harsh suspicion on my heart.
Know me for what I am. These last five years,
Go over every moment, every day,   1340
In which by mounting ecstasies and sighs
I have unfolded all my heart's desires.
Today outdoes them all. Never, I vow,
Have you been loved with greater tenderness.
And never . . .   1345

BERENICE

What! you love me, you protest,
And yet I leave. It's you who orders me.
What! Do you find such charm in my despair?
Are you afraid my tears will be too few?
What does your heart's return avail me? Ah!
I beg you, cruel one, show me less love.   1350

Do not bring back too dear a memory.
Let me at least depart, persuaded that,
Already exiled from you in my heart,
I leave an ingrate glad to see me go.

(*Titus reads a letter*)

1355 You've snatched from me my freshly written note.
You'll see from it all my love wants of you.
Read on, ingrate, read on, and let me go.

TITUS

You shall not go. I'll not consent to it.
Your plan to leave, then, was a cruel trick.
1360 You seek to die, and so, of all my love,
There will remain only a memory.
Send for Antiochus. Bid him come here.

(*Berenice sinks into a chair*)

Scene Six
TITUS, BERENICE

TITUS

Lady, I must confess sincerely this.
When I affronted first the dreaded hour
1365 In which, constrained by a stern duty's law,
I had for ever to renounce your sight;
When I foresaw this sad farewell draw near,
My fears and combats, your reproachful tears,
I steeled myself for all the sufferings
1370 Which the most grim disasters could inflict.
But, despite all my fears, I must admit
I had foreseen only the smallest part.
I thought I was less ready to succumb
And I'm ashamed to see my will distraught.
1375 I've seen before me ranged the whole of Rome.
The senate spoke to me. Prostrate, I heard

Uncomprehending, with, as sole reward
For all these raptures, icy silence. Rome
Is still uncertain what your fate will be.
And I myself, I hardly can recall   1380
If I'm an emperor or a citizen.
I came to you without a fixed design.
My love swept me along. Perhaps I came
To find myself and recognize myself.
What do I find? Death painted in your eyes.   1385
I see you leaving Rome to seek it out.
This is too much. My sorrow, at this sight,
Has mounted to its final paroxysm.
I suffer every ill conceivable.
But there is one way out. Do not expect   1390
That, weary of such constant inward strife,
By smiling nuptials I shall dry your tears.
Whate'er the pass you've brought me to, renown,
Inexorable, haunts my every step.
Always it shows to my astounded soul   1395
The great gulf fixed between the throne and you,
And tells me that, after my public stand,
Now less than ever I should marry you.
Indeed, I'm even less disposed to say
That I'll renounce the empire's rule for you,   1400
And follow you with gladly shouldered chains
To the far corners of the universe.
Yourself would blush at such base conduct and
Be loath to see me follow in your wake,
An emperor with no empire and no court,   1405
A base example of love's weaknesses.
To cure the throes to which my soul's a prey
There is, I realize, a nobler way.
More than one Roman, many a hero too
Has shown me, lady, how to tread this path.   1410
When endless blows have sapped their steadfastness,
They've all regarded this relentlessness
Of fortune bent on persecuting them

    1409 *many a hero:* such as Cato and Seneca.

283

As a mute order to give up the fight.
1415 If any longer I must see your tears,
If I still see you are resolved to die,
If ceaselessly I tremble for your life,
If you refuse to let it run its course,
Lady, you must prepare for other tears.
1420 I'll stop at nothing in my present state
And in the end it may well be my hand
Will stain with blood our ill-starred last farewell.

BERENICE

Alas!

TITUS

No, there is nothing that I would not do.
Lady, henceforth my life is in your hands.
1425 Ponder this well, and, if I'm dear to you....

(enter Antiochus)

Scene Seven

TITUS, BERENICE, ANTIOCHUS

TITUS

Come, Prince, come hither. I had sent for you.
Be witness here of all my weakness. Say
Whether my love is lacking tenderness.
Judge me.

ANTIOCHUS

I'll believe all. I know you both.
1430 But in your turn know an ill-fated prince.
You've honoured me, my lord, with your esteem,
And I can swear to you with guiltless heart,
I've striven to be among your dearest friends
Even to the point of laying down my life.
1435 I've been, against my will, confidant of

Both loves – the queen's for you and yours for her.
The queen may disavow me if she will;
She's always seen me, ardent in your praise,
Respond by friendship to your confidence.
You think you have a debt of gratitude   1440
But in this fateful hour could you believe
You have a rival in so true a friend?

TITUS

A rival? You?

ANTIOCHUS

          It's time to speak the truth.
Yes, I have always worshipped Berenice.
I've tried and tried again to crush this love.   1445
In vain. At least I've kept it in my breast.
The fond, beguiling semblance of a change
Had given me back, this day, a gleam of hope,
But the queen's tears have now extinguished it.
Her weeping eyes implored you to her side.   1450
I came, my lord, to summon you myself.
You have come back. You love, and you are loved.
You have given in. I never doubted it.
For the last time I looked within my heart.
I brought my courage to the sticking point;   1455
I mustered up my reason's last reserves.
But never did I feel more deep in love.
More is required to break so many ties;
Only by dying can I sever them.
I haste towards death. This was my news for you.   1460
Yes, lady, I recalled his steps to you.
I was successful. I do not repent.
May the heavens shower on you, on all your years,
An endless sequence of prosperities.
Or, if it holds some blow in store for you,   1465
I'll bid it pour the vials of its wrath,
Designed for you, over my wretched life,
Which gladly I will sacrifice to you.

BERENICE

Ah! stop, too noble-hearted princes, stop!
1470 To what extreme do you reduce me both.
Whether I look at you or scan his face,
Everywhere looms the image of despair.
I see naught else but tears, hear only talk
Of anguish, horrors, blood about to flow.

(to Titus)

1475 You know my heart, and I can say, my lord,
That it has never coveted the throne.
Rome's royal grandeur and the Caesars' robes
Were never my ambition, as you know.
I loved, my lord, I wanted to be loved.
1480 This day, I will confess, I was alarmed.
I thought your love was coming to an end.
I realize I'm wrong. You love me still.
Your heart was ravaged, and I saw your tears.
Berenice is not worth so much concern,
1485 Nor should the world, unhappy at your love,
When Titus captures all its sympathies
And it enjoys your virtues' earliest fruits,
Now in a trice be robbed of its delight.
I think that from five years ago till now
1490 I have assured you of a love unfeigned.
But more than that. In this grim hour, I wish
To make a crowning effort. I shall live
And shall obey your orders absolute.
Farewell. Reign. We shall never meet again.

(to Antiochus)

1495 After this farewell, Prince, you may conceive
That I do not forsake the man I love
To listen to addresses far from Rome.
Live. Make a noble effort on yourself.
Model your acts on Titus and on me.
1500 I love but flee him. Titus worships me

286

But parts. Bear far away from me your sighs.
Farewell. Let us, all three, exemplify
The most devoted, tender, ill-starred love
Whose grievous history time will e'er record.
All's ready. I am waited for. I'll leave   1505
Alone.

　　　　　　　(to Titus)

　　For the last time, farewell.

　　　　　ANTIOCHUS
　　　　　　　　　Alas!